Three Strikes, You're Gone

Samantha Baca

Haven Brook Series

'Til Death Do Us Part

The Cradle Will Fall

The Ties That Bind

A Very Haven Christmas

Three Strikes, You're Gone

Contents

One	1
Two	3
Three	5
Four	13
Five	21
Six	31
Seven	43
Eight	47
Nine	51
Ten	55
Eleven	57
Twelve	67
Thirteen	75
Fourteen	83
Fifteen	87
Sixteen	93
Seventeen	95
Eighteen	97
Nineteen	99
Twenty	103
Twenty One	105
Twenty Two	107
Twenty Three	109
Twenty Four	115
Twenty Five	123

Contents

Twenty Six	129
Twenty Seven	137
Twenty Eight	143
Twenty Nine	147
Thirty	153
Thirty One	157
Thirty Two	167
Thirty Three	173
Thirty Four	177
Thirty Five	185
Thirty Six	189
Thirty Seven	195
Thirty Eight	199
Thirty Nine	203
Forty	207
Forty One	211
Forty Two	215
Forty Three	219
Forty Four	225
Forty Five	231
Forty Six	235
Epilogue	245
Other Books By Samantha	249
Acknowledgements	251
About the Author	253

One
Kayce

"I'll be right there," I called from under the car I was working on. I waited for a response from whoever it was that had come in but was met with silence. I slid out and pushed the creeper to the side so it was out of the way before wiping my hands on the worn-out towel that hung from my pocket.

As I was walking out of the garage, I spotted someone dart out of my office and run out the front door. The icy chill from outside sent a shiver through me as I raced down the hall to my office, wondering who had been there and what they were doing.

Everything looked normal, nothing was out of place. It was a small office to begin with, so there wasn't much in the way of valuables for someone to take. I pulled the chair out and sat down, feeling shaken up by the random visitor.

Just as I had convinced myself that it was nothing, I looked down on my desk and found a large white envelope with my name on it. My gut instinct said to leave it alone and call the police, but I quickly pushed that irrational fear to the side. What was I going to say? Someone came into my office and left an envelope for me? That wasn't exactly a crime and I would probably be the laughing stock of our tiny police department. It would likely be the highlight of their day on this dreary Monday morning.

I shook my hands in the air, trying to force my nerves to calm down before picking it up. It was silly to be this nervous about a damn envelope. I pulled the top out, noticing that it hadn't been sealed, just tucked inside. My fingers started shaking as I slid the contents out onto my desk.

There were a handful of pictures that were laying facedown. I picked the first one up and flipped it over, gasping when I saw what it was. Quickly, I turned the others over, my stomach souring over the sight in front of me. At the bottom of the pile of pictures was a note written on an old concert ticket in black marker.

Just in case you forgot...
Because I didn't.

THREE STRIKES, YOU'RE GONE

Two
Wyatt

The dark sky was a quick reminder that I only had a short window left to make it to Easterville and get checked into my hotel before I lost my reservation. Between stopping for gas more often than I had expected to and dealing with the check engine light, it was taking me a lot longer to get there than it should have. Needless to say, I hadn't gone into all of those details with my mom when she called and asked about the truck, and reminded me that my brother Chase had said that it needed to be looked at before I ended up stranded somewhere on the side of the road.

I looked down at the gauges on the truck and blew out another frustrated breath. There was no way that I was going to be able to make it the rest of the way without filling up. This thing was guzzling gas faster than a college kid in a beer-chugging contest. I saw a sign up ahead for a gas station and pulled off at the exit. I went inside the small convenience store to grab some snacks for the road since I was probably going to miss dinner at this point. I didn't know much about Easterville, but I assumed that since it was a smaller town than Haven Brook, most of the decent places to grab a bite to eat would be closing by the time I had a break to go eat.

I tossed the bag full of snacks and a few bottles of water into the passenger seat of the truck and shut the door. Gas was more expensive here than it had been at any of the other stops, but thankfully, I was getting reimbursed for it. I would go through the receipts and cut them in half, turning in the fair amount of gas that a normal person would use. It wasn't their fault that I had a truck that sucked down gas quicker than any other vehicle I'd ever seen.

The truck was having more issues than I was willing to admit right now, mainly because I hadn't had the time or energy to work on it. My fingers trembled from the frigid cold as they struggled to turn the key in the ignition. I groaned as the truck failed to start after several attempts. I gave it a little more gas as I tried again, feeling the frustration build as I saw the white smoke floating out of the exhaust once it started. *Fuck...*

The highway was empty when I got back on, most likely due to the heavy snow that had been falling the majority of the day. I was thankful that the exit I needed for Easterville was only an hour away. I was going to be pushing it, barely making it on time for my check-in, but I was trying to keep my faith that somehow luck would intervene and things would go my way. Just one little break to get me started on the right foot. That was all that I needed.

I felt like I was on pins and needles the entire way, not knowing when the truck was going to decide to give out and leave me stranded on the side of the road in this terrible weather. I let out a long, heavy breath when I saw the first exit sign for Easterville, knowing that my hotel would be at the next exit. Only a short way to go.

I gripped the steering wheel tighter, praying that I would make it to the next exit. In the rearview mirror, white smoke was billowing out from the exhaust. There was a loud pop as the truck backfired and the engine started to die. I swerved to the right at the last minute, barely making it onto the offramp. I continued to pull to the right and felt as if luck was mocking me as I slid right into the parking lot of an auto shop as the truck died.

Three
Kayce

I was just about to turn the lights off and leave for the night, when I saw a truck come sliding into the parking lot, a trail of white smoke clouding behind it. At first, I panicked when I thought about the stranger who had been in my office earlier, but then I remembered that Lacey's soon-to-be brother in law was supposed to be heading to town soon, and if I remembered right, this looked like the kind of truck he would be driving.

My cousin Lacey had been checking in with me nonstop for the last hour to see if I had heard anything about whether or not Wyatt had made it to town. She was worried about his old truck being on its last life. She was right about that. Just by looking at the amount of smoke that was still coming out, I had a list of things in my head on what was likely wrong with it. And unfortunately, none of them were quick or easy fixes.

I watched as he climbed out with a scowl on his face, and what I assumed were a string of curse words filling the crisp air around him. I had briefly caught a glimpse of him last year when I went to see Lacey after she was released from the hospital. Things had happened so quickly while I was there that I didn't remember much about him, other than he was recovering from being stabbed while trying to save Lacey's life.

Of course, there were the constant pokes and prods from her about how good-looking he was, and oh, did she mention that he was single too? *Wouldn't it be the cutest if we got together? Then her little cousin could fall in love and marry her fiancé's little brother…* She had been fantasizing about a relationship between us for as long as I could remember. I simply humored her, letting her believe that I was open to the idea of her setting me up with him the next time I went to Haven Brook, which might also be the same reason I hadn't gone back…

As he ran a hand down his face in frustration, I caught a glimpse of how muscular his body was. She wasn't lying when she said that he was in good shape, however, she forgot to mention that he had the body of the guys that women drooled over on the cover of dirty romance novels. He reached up and adjusted his baseball cap, the tight-fitted hoodie stretching across his broad shoulders and pulling up slightly at his waist. I felt my cheeks flush as I saw a sliver of skin before he lowered his arms and looked at me.

I had been staring for so long that I completely forgot that he might turn around and notice me. I offered an awkward smile and a little wave, feeling like a complete idiot as he headed my way. I stepped back and opened the door, inviting him inside. A blast of cold air came in with him, sending a shiver through me as I took in the dark chestnut eyes that were watching me with amusement.

"Sorry to barge in here," he said, rubbing his hands together. "My truck decided to die on me so it looks like I'm stranded for the time being. Is it okay if I leave it here for now? I can call a tow truck to come get it in the morning."

"A tow truck? Where do you plan to have them take it?" I asked, my brows pulled together as I tried to keep the smile off my face. It seemed as if I knew more about him than he did about me. From the looks of it, he had no idea who I was, which I was suddenly thankful for.

"A mechanic?"

"Like the one you're currently standing in?"

I watched a faint blush creep across his face as he looked down in embarrassment.

"I didn't want you to think that I just assumed that you would work on it. I know usually most shops have a waitlist and I really need to get my truck up and running."

"Well, I hate to break it to you," I sighed. "But I'm the only auto shop in Easterville. And, not to brag—but I'm the best." I winked.

"You're Kayce," he said with a smile and nod of his head.

"And you're Wyatt," I replied with a cheesy grin.

"I didn't see the sign outside, Lacey just told me that you worked at Wrenched, but she didn't mention that you were the only mechanic in Easterville. I guess I could have assumed that this was your place when you opened the door, but I just thought…" His thought trailed off, leaving the words unspoken.

"That I was the receptionist?" I offered.

A sheepish grin crossed his face as he nodded.

"Sorry," he said sincerely.

"Don't be." I waved him off. "Honestly, I get it all the time. Even though I've lived here all my life, there are still a handful of folks here who refuse to believe that the only mechanic in town is… wait for it… a *woman!*"

"Eh, it's their loss," he said as he leaned back against the wall and shoved his hands in his pockets.

"Why's that?"

"Because it's fucking hot to see a woman working on cars." He licked his lips and locked eyes with me, forcing a blush to creep up my neck. I remembered that Lacey had warned me that he was the town playboy back home, but honestly, I didn't expect to be on the receiving end of his charm within the first ten minutes of talking to him.

"No offense," he added, noticing my embarrassment.

"None taken, I appreciate the comment." I narrowed my eyes. "I think…"

He laughed, the corners of his lips curling up into the sexy dimples in his cheeks. No wonder he could get any woman he wanted. That smile alone had me wanting to strip my panties off and throw them at him.

"So, is it okay if I leave my truck here for the night?" He pointed his thumb over his shoulder to the parking lot. "I have to get to the hotel and see if they'll still let me check-in." He glanced down at his watch. "And I'm already almost an hour past the cutoff time they gave me."

"Which hotel are you staying at?" I asked, knowing he was out of luck.

"There's more than one hotel in this town?" He pulled his brows together in suspicion.

"Two, actually," I laughed.

"I'm staying at the Honey Lodge," he said, squinting his face as he looked upward, trying to pull the information out of his head. "Which, if I run over there, I might be able to get there in time."

"You're going to run two miles to the hotel?" I pulled my head back and looked at him like he was some sort of alien.

"I run five miles every morning," he assured me with a cocky smirk.

"For fun?" I scrunched my face and earned a burst of laughter from him. I should have known that he was a runner by how lean and sculpted his body was. He was also probably one of those health-nut freaks that only ate organic foods and avoided the greasy, good stuff. My stomach growled in response as I thought about the barbeque food that I was planning to stop for on my way home.

"Well, more for training. But I don't mind it." He shrugged his shoulders nonchalantly, the hoodie moving fluidly with his body as it gave me more assurance as to what I would find if I were to take it off of him right now. I knew that Lacey was head-over-heels in love with Grant, but now I understood why she was constantly going on and on about his little brother and how attractive he was. As he stayed leaning against the wall in his dark denim jeans and black work boots, I could easily see what her obsession was all about. Apparently, good genes just run in that family.

"I hate to tell you, but you're not staying there tonight." I shook my head and shifted my weight, trying to balance my bag on my hip as it started to get heavier. "And you'll have to get there first thing in the morning, with a candy bar, if you want to grab a room for tomorrow. I wouldn't run there though." I laughed, envisioning it in my head.

"Why won't I get a room tonight?"

"Because Mr. Ashby is a stickler for the rules. He's a cranky old man that hates late check-ins as much as he hates when people want to extend their stay. However, Mrs. Ashby will be working in the morning and she's a sucker for candy bars—Paydays, to be specific. A couple of those, combined with that sexy smile—and you'll have a room for tomorrow."

I felt his eyes widen at my words and realized my mistake as soon as I said it. I swallowed hard, hoping to force the embarrassment away before the blush stained my cheeks again.

"You think I have a sexy smile?" he asked, pushing off the wall and taking a step toward me. He was tall—way taller than me, forcing me to lift my head to look at him. His scent was intoxicating, cedarwood with hints of vanilla that made me want to lean in closer for a better whiff.

"It's nice, but I wouldn't go too far with thinking that it's overly sexy," I stammered nervously. "I mean, it will probably get you the hotel room tomorrow if that's what you're looking for…"

"Good to know." He pulled his bottom lip in between his teeth and let it pop free as he took a step back, allowing me some space to breathe. What the heck was that? It was like I couldn't think within such close proximity to him. My brain was foggy while his magical voodoo smile worked its wonders on me. I tried to force a smile, but it came out as some awkward movement of my face which made him turn and fake cough to keep from laughing.

"Well, I'm closing up here for the night," I blurted out, desperate to change the conversation. "You can leave your truck here, and I'll look at it in the morning."

"Sounds good, thanks," he said, turning to walk outside. I followed him out and pulled the door closed behind me after turning off the light switch. The cold air whipped past me, sending a chill through my body while my fingers trembled against the cold metal of the lock. A few minutes later, the door was locked and I shifted the bag up higher on my shoulder, knowing that I was going to pay for this in the morning. It was too much weight to try to carry for this long, but I hadn't been smart enough to set it down while I was talking to Wyatt.

He walked to his truck and yanked on the handle to get the rusty, old door to open. I thought he was just grabbing what he needed from the truck but was surprised when he pulled the door closed and sat there. I walked over and knocked on the window, feeling silly as he rolled it down to talk to me.

"What are you doing?" I asked, lifting my hand in the air beside me.

"I'm staying in my truck because it's freaking cold outside," he explained as if it should make sense. "I don't have a candy bar to offer the cougar at the hotel, so I'm waiting it out inside of my truck."

I rolled my eyes and brought my palm to my face.

"Boys are so stupid," I sighed playfully, rolling my eyes. "Get out of the truck, you're gonna come stay with me tonight."

I stepped back, allowing him room to open the door to get out.

"Kayce, thank you for the offer, but I can't put you out. I'll be fine in the truck, thank you though." I watched as a shiver ran through him, the cold air biting at his skin. The sucky thing about older trucks, like the one he was driving, was that they were all metal and that meant that nothing was going to keep the cold out of it tonight. The snow had finally stopped falling, but the temperature was supposed to plummet in a few hours with more snow on the way.

"Your brother is marrying my cousin which makes us practically family. Get out of the truck you big oaf, before we both freeze our asses off." I raised an eyebrow at him and folded my arms while I waited. He sat there for a moment, thinking about it before I added, "I'm not afraid to call Lacey and have her tell Grant what a stubborn ass you're being."

Now it was his turn to roll his eyes as he rolled up with the window and climbed out of the truck. He grabbed a duffle bag from the passenger seat and slung it across his shoulder before walking with me to my car. I watched as his eyebrows raised when he saw the 1998 Dodge Ram 2500 that was parked at the opposite end of the parking lot.

"That's your ride?" he asked, a hint of amusement in his tone.

"Yeah, why?" I replied, my eyes narrowed.

"Don't get me wrong—it's a dope ride," he said, putting his hands up in front of him. "I just didn't expect it to be your truck, that's all."

I couldn't blame him for his reaction. It was the same one that I had gotten from almost everyone who saw me driving it. With a 6 inch lift on it, I had mastered getting in and out without killing myself or causing a scene for people to gossip about. She was a beast, there was no doubt about that. I had put in hours of love, sweat, and tears to make the modifications that I wanted. It was the best damn truck in all of Colorado, and you could bet your ass that no one was talking shit about it when I was the only one in town that could pull vehicles out of the thick, muddy areas after a heavy snowstorm.

"I may be short, but trust me, I have no problem getting where I want to go," I replied sarcastically, knowing that it was an open-ended meaning.

"Her name is Oakley," I added when we got closer. I ran a hand down the side of the truck, touching the black pinstripes that were added to the crimson red color I had recently painted it.

"Oakley? As in…"

"Yup, Annie Oakley. Because she was a badass that made her own way in a male-dominated world. We're doing the same thing," I said proudly, patting the vehicle as if it was a dog that had just earned some praise.

"Very fitting, I like it."

I pressed the button to unlock the doors, praying that they weren't frozen shut. Relief washed over me when I heard the click and opened the door. Wyatt walked around to the other side and climbed in, shivering again as the cold followed us inside the cab. He set his stuff on the floorboard in front of him and buckled up.

I pushed the key inside of the ignition and turned it, hearing the beautiful purr she made every time I started her up. There was something about the sound of a 5.9 diesel engine coming to life that made my skin tingle with excitement. Once we were both situated, I put the truck in reverse and pulled out of the parking lot.

"Do you like barbeque?" I asked, glancing over at him before turning my attention back to the road.

"Is that a trick question?" he joked. "I think it's a sin not to like barbeque."

"So am I taking you to grab some, or do you need me to drop you off at a church for confession first?"

"Lacey was right about you," he laughed, turning to look out the window.

"What do you mean?" I asked, feeling partly amused and slightly worried.

"She told me you were a wild one, warned me about your sarcastic humor and wit." He winked as he turned slightly in his seat to look at me.

"If you only knew," I muttered with a low laugh before turning into the parking lot of the Tasty Pig.

THREE STRIKES, YOU'RE GONE

Four
Wyatt

"This is good," I mumbled before sinking my teeth into the last bite of meat left on the rib. Kayce wasn't lying when she said the Tasty Pig had the best barbeque she's ever had.

"I told you." She winked and popped a piece of fried okra into her mouth.

We got back to her apartment less than thirty minutes ago and she promised she would give me the official tour of it after we ate because she was starving. It was a nice place but small enough that I could see the majority of it without needing a tour. The living room and kitchen were combined in one area that was barely big enough to fit her couch and coffee table, which I found out served as her dining table as well. It was a simple piece of black, beat-up wood, but it lifted to make a table in front of the couch.

The TV was mounted on the wall, a small bookshelf underneath it that was overflowing with books that don't fit in the tiny space. She didn't strike me as a reader, but shit, she also didn't strike me as a mechanic either. Guess it was true what they said about not judging a book by its cover. Or in this case, don't assume the beautiful girl with dark purple hair isn't a successful businesswoman who is handling her own shit and isn't afraid to get her hands dirty.

"Do you guys not have a good barbeque place back home?" she asked, nibbling the side of the corn she held between her fingers. Her question pulled me back to reality and I stopped for a second to think about who had the best barbeque back home.

I shook my head and frowned.

"We don't really have a real barbeque place back home," I said with a shrug. "We have Slow-Mo's. They have some killer ribs and barbeque chicken, but other than that, I've always just grilled at home."

She tilted her head to the side and thought about what I had said, as if it seemed strange to her.

"What's that look for?" I laughed, wiping the barbeque sauce from my mouth with the napkin.

"Nothing," she snickered. "I guess I just can't imagine a world where there's no Tasty Pig."

"Well that's because you haven't tried my food yet—it would make you forget the Tasty Pig ever existed," I assured her with a smirk.

"How can you be so cocky about that?" She lowered the empty cob to her plate alongside her napkin and demolished ribs. "You don't even have a real barbeque place to compare yourself to."

"Trust me, I don't need anything other than a grill and some meat and I'll have your mouth watering."

My eyes followed the trail of crimson that flushed across her skin as she tucked her chin and looked away. Without giving it much thought, I licked my lips and wondered what she tasted like. The thought of Kayce reacting to me this way sent a direct message straight to my dick, making my jeans suddenly tighter than a few seconds ago. The problem was that I knew there was nothing that could happen between us. She was Lacey's cousin, and Grant had already threatened to break my neck if I even *looked* at her the wrong way.

"Well, I guess we'll just have to agree to disagree." She got up to throw her plate away and looked down at my empty plate, asking permission to take it as well.

I nodded and stood up, picking up my mess before reaching over to take hers.

"What are you doing?" she asked guardedly.

"Cleaning up." I walked around the table and wandered into the kitchen, looking for the trash can.

"It's under the sink, but you can just set it on the counter and I'll run it downstairs later with the other trash."

"I can run it down now, I don't mind."

I added the plates to the bag that contained the empty take-out containers and pushed them down, making sure they didn't leak.

"We can take it later." She scooted past me, her grin spread from ear to ear as she opened the freezer and pulled out a tub of vanilla ice cream.

She wiggled her eyebrows before opening another take-out box that was pushed off to the side of the counter, away from the empty boxes. The scent of peach cobbler filled the air and I found myself leaning closer to inhale the delicious aroma.

"Their barbeque is amazing, but this peach cobbler is downright divine. It's better than an orgasm," she whispered, her eyes barely meeting mine before she ducked her head and looked away.

"Sounds too good to be true," I teased. "Or maybe you just haven't found the right guy to give you better orgasms."

I watched the way her body reacted, the sharp intake of air that filled her lungs. In all fairness, I had tried to turn it off and not pursue her, but her orgasm comment screamed game on. I was pretty damn good at reading women, and she was giving me all of the signals that she was just as interested in whatever this was as I was.

"Maybe you just haven't had the best cobbler in the world?" she countered, pulling a spoon out of the drawer beside her before closing it. She dipped it into the container, scooping out a small piece of cobbler before turning to me and lifting it to my mouth.

I parted my lips, opening my mouth to allow her to put the spoon in so I could take a bite. As her golden-brown eyes watched me, I reached up and gently held her wrist, pulling her hand away as slowly as possible while my lips wrapped tightly around the spoon. Once it was out of my mouth, I allowed the cobbler to sit on my tongue for a second as I locked eyes with her. I moved it around, swallowing before licking my lips.

My hand was still holding her wrist, the tension between us getting thicker by the minute. Her chest rose and fell heavily, a look of desire flooding her face. She pulled her bottom lip in, releasing it when I moved my hand and took the spoon from her.

"My turn," I said softly, my voice deeper and hoarser than normal. I scooped out a piece of cobbler, making sure it wasn't too much for her to take. I scolded myself for the inappropriate thought before realizing that there was nothing appropriate about what we were doing. We had already started to cross a line, and there was no going back at this point. Hell, I wasn't sure that either of us would if we could.

"Open." I nodded subtly, lifting the spoon to her lips as she opened her mouth to accept the bite. Her breathing was heavy, her full breasts spilling over the top of the t-shirt that pulled tight against her body. The temperature was definitely rising in here, there was no doubt about that.

I watched her eyes close, a soft moan escaping her mouth as she pulled the cobbler from the spoon. I felt my erection get harder as I imagined what she would look like with something other than that spoon in her mouth. The way she slid her tongue along the bottom of it before it went in wasn't lost on me. She was teasing me as much as I was her.

"If your reaction to the cobbler right now is comparable to the best orgasm you've ever had, you might need to find a new boyfriend," I said dryly.

"I don't have a boyfriend," she replied matter-of-factly, opening her eyes and meeting the challenge in my stare.

"Good."

"Good?" she repeated, turning it into a question.

"Mmm-hmm," I murmured, scooping another bite of cobbler from the container. I held it in the air between us before adding, "because I'm about to show you what a real orgasm feels like." I popped the spoon into my mouth and smiled, watching the curiosity in her eyes as she watched me chew.

"Who said I was willing to have sex with you?" she asked, her hands moving to her hips.

"I never said anything about sex," I countered, scooping out more cobbler onto the spoon. "I simply said that I'm going to show you what a real orgasm feels like. You know, for comparison." I shrugged my shoulders and laughed when she reached over and pulled the spoon to her mouth, taking the bite before I could.

"You're full of shit," she scoffed, wiping the corners of her mouth with her finger before pulling it into her mouth and sucking it clean.

"Why's that?"

"Because there's not a guy alive that would just give a woman an orgasm without wanting something in return."

"Sure there is." I pulled my head back in disbelief that she would think that. Who the fuck had she been with that was so selfish and self-centered that they didn't take care of her without having their own agenda?

"Bullshit." She folded her arms over her chest and pursed her lips. Maybe it was the way she had her hair pulled up on top of her head, exposing her slender neck, or maybe it was the way her ass looked in the leggings she had put on when we got home—either way, she had my body reacting to every inch of her.

I stepped closer, setting the spoon down beside us. She was pinned in the corner where the counter joined the short island that jutted off into the living room, leaving her no way to escape as I took another small step toward her. I gently reached forward and put my hands on her hips, guiding her further back until there was nowhere left to go. She watched me closely, unsure of what I was doing as she braced herself against the counters with her hands.

I bit the inside of my cheek, trying to distract myself from leaning down to kiss her. Now wasn't the time for that, and I sure as hell couldn't let feelings get in the mix. I promised her the best orgasm of her life, and damn it, I was going to deliver. My eyes never left hers as my fingers slid across her waist and dipped below the waistband of her leggings before pushing them down her hips.

Her eyes widened as she felt them move down her legs and land in a pile on the floor at her feet. I chuckled softly, bringing my hands back up to her waist as I sat her on the counter. She looked surprised, but thankfully she didn't reach down to try to cover herself. Instead, she leaned back slightly on the palms of her hands and smiled. I licked my lips as I got down on my knees and reached forward, pulling her to the edge of the counter as my hands wrapped around her ass.

My tall frame aligned perfectly with the height of the counter, allowing me plenty of room to move around. She was wearing a pair of cotton boy short panties that looked fucking sexy on her. I debated on whether to push them to the side and get started or if it would be easier to just take them off. Being a selfish man, I decided to get rid of them so I could have a perfect, unobstructed view of her pussy.

"Lift your ass," I commanded, sliding her panties off her when she did. "Good girl," I murmured, trying not to sound condescending.

I looked over and found the container with the rest of the cobbler and handed it to her, along with the spoon.

"For comparison," I teased with a wink. She laughed as she took it, sliding the spoon into her mouth at the same moment I leaned forward and licked her slit. She gasped loudly, earning another chuckle from me.

I pushed her legs open, pinning them against the counter with my shoulders as I slowly licked her again, tracing a path across her lips. I heard the spoon scrape across the Styrofoam container as she got another bite of cobbler. Pushing myself closer to her, I parted her folds with my fingers and slid my tongue inside, feeling her body react to my touch. Her legs started to push back against me as she squirmed on the counter while my tongue slid in and out of her. I held them in place with my shoulders while I slid two fingers inside, bringing my mouth to her clit and sucking. I could hear her labored breathing as I sucked harder, my fingers pumping inside of her easily with how wet she was.

"That's right, come for me baby," I groaned against her pussy. "Come on my face." I sucked harder, knowing that it would send her over the edge by the way her body was responding. The sound of metal clinking to the floor confirmed that I had won this battle against the cobbler as her hands dug into my hair, pulling it as she arched her back and moaned.

I fingered her faster, rotating my hand so I could rub her g-spot as I sucked her clit harder. She panted as her legs trembled against my shoulders.

"Fuck!" she screamed as her pussy spasmed around my fingers, her orgasm ripping through her. I kept going, waiting until I knew she couldn't take anymore before I pulled them out and stood up. I stayed close to make sure she didn't fall given how close she was sitting on the edge. Her eyes fluttered open, the rush of blood flushing her cheeks.

I glanced down and laughed when I saw the rest of the cobbler on the floor in a mess.

"I'm gonna venture to guess that I won that round," I said with a smirk, nodding to the floor.

"I can't even answer that until the blood makes its way back to my brain," she laughed and shook her head.

"Do you need help down?" I offered, extending my hand to her.

"I'm not that short," she balked, taking my hand anyway. "But thank you." She hopped down and grabbed her leggings and panties from the floor.

I turned to give her some privacy so she could get dressed but felt her hand reach out and grab my arm. As soon as I was facing her, her hands snaked up around my neck as she pulled me close to her and planted her lips on mine.

I leaned down and kissed her deeper, her mouth parting as my tongue slid inside. I could feel the energy between us and knew that I needed to stop, if I wanted to keep things from going further between us. But the way she kissed me—I knew there was no going back now. I slid my hands down and lifted her, her legs wrapped around my waist while her bare pussy hovered above my throbbing dick. I wanted to be inside of her, to fuck her senseless, but I needed to make sure this was what she wanted.

"Are you sure you want to—"

"Fuck you?" she interrupted. "Yeah, I'm sure," she panted, moving her lips down the side of my neck as I moaned. I walked her into the living room, not sure where she wanted to do this. It wasn't my apartment so it wasn't like I had any idea about where she was okay with having sex. Fuck, if it was my apartment, I would fuck her on every surface until we claimed the entire fucking space.

"Where?" I asked in between kisses, her fingers clawing my back.

"I don't care. Pick a spot and get naked," she moaned as she slid down me and planted her feet on the floor. We stood in front of the couch, staring at each other for a half of a second before she lunged forward and starting pulling my hoodie off. Within seconds, I was down to my boxer briefs. I reached over and lifted the shirt over her head, desperate to bury my head in her cleavage. Things had slowed down slightly for us, a quick moment to breathe—or stop and think. I worried that she might come to her senses and reconsider, but instead she reached over and pulled my underwear off before leading me to the couch.

I bent down and grabbed a condom out of my wallet before sitting down beside her. My dick was hard, desperate for relief when she reached over and stroked me a few times. Her hand was soft, but her grip firm as she pumped up and down, watching as precum dotted the tip. She licked her lips and leaned back against the couch, spreading her legs. As quickly as I could, I ripped open the package and covered myself before I climbed over and slid inside of her. Her legs were wide open as she took me in, scratching my back as I pushed myself in deeper.

We fucked in this awkward position for a few minutes before I grabbed her and rolled her on top of me, pulling her down on my dick as she started grinding her hips against me. I leaned back and ran my hands up her thighs, over her hips, and along her sides before I reached up and caressed her breasts. The fabric of her bra was thin, her nipples pebbled from my touch. I wanted more. Needed more.

I reached back and unclasped her bra, freeing her tits before tossing the fabric across the room. She rode me harder, grinding down on me as I leaned forward and pulled a nipple into my mouth. I sucked hard, feeling her pussy clench around me in response. The harder she fucked me, the more her perfect breasts bounced in my face. I shifted to the other, pulling that nipple into my mouth and sucking as she arched her back and came hard on my dick. I pulled back and dug my fingers into her hips as I felt my orgasm rip through me moments later.

When I opened my eyes, she was looking at me with a devious smile on her face as she bit the tip of her finger.

"You're right," she said playfully. "That was better than cobbler."

Five
Kayce

Awkward. That's how I would describe the feeling between Wyatt and me after our little—whatever the hell that was. Fun? It was definitely fun. And good. But now that it had happened, I had no idea what I was supposed to do next. It's not like we were together, so it felt weird to act like we were. But, he also just ate me out on my kitchen counter like I was better than the barbeque he had just devoured a few minutes before. And then, we fucked. On my couch. Where I've sat to have tea with my grandma when she came over to visit.

When I offered him to stay with me tonight, it was because it was the right thing to do. I knew that he had already blown his chance at getting a late check-in with Mr. Ashby so I did what anyone would do to help family. Keyword—FAMILY. Because that's what we would be once his brother married my cousin. We're not blood-related, but it still felt a little like maybe it was a line we shouldn't be crossing. So yeah, things were awkward.

I had no idea what I was supposed to do next. Do I allow him to give me the best orgasms of my life, and then ask him to sleep on the couch because it would be too intimate to share my bed with him? I leaned against the wall in the bathroom and closed my eyes. I had come in here to freshen up ten minutes ago, and if I didn't go back out there, he might think something was wrong with me. I mean, technically he wouldn't be wrong. Something had to be wrong with me with what I just did.

My phone vibrated on the counter, startling me. I picked it up and groaned when I saw Lacey's name on the caller ID. There was no way to avoid talking to her so I sighed and slid my finger across the screen to answer the call.

"Hey," I said as cheerfully as I could muster.

"Hey, what's wrong?" she asked immediately. I could picture the frown she was wearing and knew that she had already sensed that something was off from the tone I used with the one measly word I had said.

"Nothing's wrong, I'm just tired." I leaned forward and looked in the mirror, making sure there were no random hickeys that he had given me that I hadn't seen yet. I kept my voice low, struggling to find the right level to keep Wyatt from hearing me in the other room and to avoid having Lacey guess why I was muffled. The bad thing about living in an apartment this tiny was that you could hear *everything* easily through the thin walls.

"Bullshit," Lacey snorted. "Something is off, I can hear it in your voice…"

"Really, I'm just feeling a little worn out."

"Alright," she said suspiciously. "If that's what you're sticking with then I guess I'll just have to wait for you to give in and spill the beans when you're ready."

I ran a hand through my hair to fix it, even though I wasn't going anywhere other than to bed. The thought of Wyatt seeing me like this made me feel self-conscious.

"What do you mean Wyatt didn't answer his phone?" Lacey asked away from the phone. I could hear Grant talking in the background and my stomach started swarming with butterflies.

"Maybe Kayce can go look for him? See if maybe he got stuck somewhere and needs her help?" Lacey continued her conversation with him as if I wasn't there on the other line. I wanted to tell her that Wyatt did get stuck somewhere and that's why he missed his brother's call. He was stuck in between my legs, and I enjoyed every second of it.

"Wyatt's here with me," I blurted out. I closed my eyes and waited for it. Three. Two. One.

"He's there with you?" Lacey asked, bringing her attention back to me. "How long has he been there? Grant's been trying to call him for over—"

"Kayce!" she hissed out loudly. "You didn't!"

I closed my eyes and lowered my face to my hand, immediately feeling ashamed of what I had done. Not that she was trying to shame me. It was more likely that she would start planning our wedding by the end of the phone call. I was the one who was getting ready to slap a scarlet letter across my chest.

"What did she do?" Grant asked in the background, loud enough that I could hear him clear as day. I groaned again, sitting down on the closed lid of the toilet.

"Nothing, I'll tell you about it later," Lacey whispered, either not noticing that she said it loud enough for me to hear, or not caring.

"Really Lace? You're going to talk to your fiancé about what I just did with his little brother?"

"I knew it," she giggled. "I knew you two would get together. I just didn't think it would happen so fast."

I shook my head in frustration. *You're telling me.*

I heard a phone ring through the door and wondered if Grant was calling Wyatt. It would be weird and uncomfortable, but I wouldn't doubt it. Lacey was going on with how she just knew this would happen, but I wasn't listening to a word that she said as I got up and moved closer to the door to listen.

"What's up, man?" Wyatt said, answering his phone. In the background of my call, I could hear Grant asking how Wyatt's drive was and if he had any problems with the truck. The conversation seemed to be steering clear of our little fuck fest, so I moved away from the door and sat down on the toilet, trying to catch up with whatever Lacey was rambling on about.

"And I think white lilies would be the perfect accent," she cooed.

"What are you talking about?" I asked confused.

"I knew you weren't listening," she laughed. "I guess you've got it bad. Can't say that I blame you."

"I don't have *anything* other than some feelings of guilt and embarrassment," I assured her, lifting my butt off of the seat to pull out a brush that I had been sitting on. "And maybe a little pain in my butt," I muttered, reaching back to rub the sore spot.

"Really? I didn't know you were into that, but okay," she giggled and I knew she was enjoying every second of this.

"No, not really. I sat on a brush, you pervert."

"I wasn't going to judge if you were into it."

"We're not having this conversation about your future brother-in-law," I assured her. "It's just gross."

The line went quiet for a minute so I pulled the phone away to make sure I hadn't lost the call. Nope, she was still there.

"Lace?"

"I'm still here. But you're right—that is gross. Thanks for ruining the fun I was having."

"Sorry, but at least you still have an attractive fiancé to have fun with when we hang up."

"Ugh, probably not," she grumbled.

"Why not?" I stood up and listened at the door again to see if Wyatt was still on the phone. I couldn't stay in the bathroom forever, and it felt weird hiding in here to talk to Lacey about him.

"Because Grant doesn't want to have sex or do anything until I'm at least twelve weeks. He thinks it's bad luck and doesn't want to risk hurting the babies."

"Well, you are having twins, so I'm sure that makes things a little more difficult than just one. You can't blame him for wanting to be careful, he just loves you and the babies."

"I know," she breathed out heavily. "Thankfully, I'll be ten weeks on Wednesday so he won't be able to use that as an excuse for much longer. I'm literally counting down the *days*."

"I think you might have a problem," I laughed.

"How do you think I got in this position to begin with? Even with Liam and Annie running around the house, I find myself trying to find reasons to send them over to his mom's house so I can jump on him. My doctor assured me that it's just the hormones, but I swear, he's never looked so good as he does right now."

"Right now, right now?" I quirked an eyebrow, wondering if she had finally lost her damn mind. It was a Monday night and he worked as a PE coach at the kids' school. I couldn't picture anything about that being sexy.

"Yes!" she hissed, pulling the phone closer to her mouth. "He's wearing a snug white t-shirt with gray sweatpants!"

"NO!" I gasped dramatically, playing along. "Not GRAY sweatpants!"

"Laugh now, but when you see a sexy man wearing them, you'll know what I'm talking about."

"I don't know, I don't tend to see many men parading around in sweats. I guess married life is just too much for me. Maybe it's a good thing I've vowed to stay single?"

"Just wait and see," she laughed harder. "Well, Grant is talking to Wyatt now so my reason for calling is taken care of. I'll let you go so you can get back to *whatever* it was you were doing."

"I'm getting ready for bed and calling it a day. And was your reason for calling was to find out whether I had sex with Wyatt?"

"No, I called to make sure he had gotten there okay. I just happened to be pleasantly surprised to hear that things had happened between you guys after all."

I rolled my eyes and shook my head. Ever since we were little girls, Lacey and I have always shared everything with each other so it was no surprise that she would find out about me and Wyatt right away. I felt bad for not telling her about the incident at work today with the random envelope and pictures, but until I knew who had left them and what they wanted, I didn't want to scare her. Hell, I didn't want to scare myself either, but I found that I had been cautiously looking over my shoulder all day after that.

"Alright, get those cute kids of yours to bed, and I'll talk to you soon," I said, suddenly missing Liam and Annie. Maybe it wouldn't be bad to make a trip down there soon to visit them. Both of their birthdays were coming up soon, which would be a good excuse to get down there. Not like I was hoping to see Wyatt again while I was there… even if he was Liam's uncle and would likely be there for his birthday as well. All purely innocent motives, if you asked me.

"Keep me posted on how things are going?"

"Lacey, I'm not going to keep you updated on my sex life with Wyatt," I snapped with a little more frustration than was necessary.

"So there's a sex life? You made it sound like it was a one-time thing when I first called," she said smugly.

"It was a one-time thing. A stupid, not thought through, one-time thing. That's it."

"Why are you fighting this so hard? You don't have to put a label on what happened, but Kayce, you're a single woman, and he's a single man. There's nothing to be embarrassed about if you both wanted it."

"I know, but Lace, he wasn't even around me TWENTY-FOUR hours before we had sex. That has to be some sort of new record for me," I admitted with embarrassment.

"Maybe because you guys—"

"Don't you dare say *are meant to be*," I groaned.

"No. Maybe because you guys have an insane amount of chemistry. Sometimes it's impossible to pull away from someone that you feel such a strong pull with. I know that things were hard for Grant and me given our pasts. Neither of us wanted to jump right in, but we also couldn't walk away if we tried. Sometimes, it's just better to give in to the attraction."

I knew what she was saying, and it made sense, but it didn't make me feel any better about what had happened. That wasn't the impression that I wanted to make on Wyatt. I also didn't want him to think that I was some tramp that just threw herself at any man that walked in her path.

"Alright, I gotta go," Lacey said, interrupting my thoughts. "But try not to overthink this. You're both grown-ups who had a good time. Leave it at that if you have to."

"Talk to you later," I replied, ignoring the rest of what she said.

I hung up the phone and gave myself a quick glance in the mirror before I opened the door and walked into the living room. Wyatt was sitting on the couch wearing the same hoodie he had on earlier and a pair of sweatpants. Not just any sweatpants. GRAY fucking sweatpants.

"Sorry, Lacey called while I was getting cleaned up," I said nervously, pointing over my shoulder to the bathroom.

"No worries, I just got off the phone with Grant."

"Everything okay?" I asked, my voice rising an octave as I worried about whether Grant knew what had happened between us.

"Yeah," he breathed, rubbing his hands together. "He promised to come down here and break my neck if I put my hands on you again."

I felt my heart skip a beat as I walked closer to him and sat on the opposite arm of the couch.

"What did you say?" I felt nervous asking him but it seemed like one way or another, we were going to address the elephant in the room.

"I told him that it wasn't my hands he needed to worry about… it was my tongue."

I felt the heat prickle my skin as the blush crept up my neck and across my cheeks.

"You didn't?!" I gasped, bringing my hands up to cover my face.

I felt him scoot over on the couch before he reached up and pulled my hands down.

"No, Kayce, I didn't. I don't talk about my sex life with my brother. You don't have to worry about that. But if you want to talk about where my tongue might be going, I'm always open for that conversation." He winked, the sexy dimple in his cheek making another appearance.

His words stunned me for a moment, turning me on as I thought about what had happened less than thirty minutes ago.

"Still thinking about that peach cobbler?" he asked as if reading my mind.

"Shit!" I exclaimed, jumping up and running into the kitchen. I looked at the carton of ice cream that was still sitting out on the counter that we had never gotten around to eating, along with the cobbler that was now in a puddle on the floor. I felt Wyatt walk up behind me and chuckle when he saw the mess that we had made. The ice cream had already melted and left a puddle in the middle of the black countertop.

"Sorry about the cobbler," he said quietly, with a hint of humor in his voice.

"Don't be," I sighed. "I was willing to part with it in exchange for that orgasm." I kept my back to him, afraid to turn around and look him in the eye.

"Here, let me help clean this up, then I'll run the trash out for you." He gently ran his fingers up the side of my arm, leaving goosebumps in its trail.

He stepped past me and grabbed the pile of napkins that came with the barbeque. With ease, he bent down and scooped up the cobbler, tossing it into the already full take-out bag that was now serving as a trash bag. I grabbed the mop from the closet by the front door and waited until he had picked up the last few pieces before we swapped places. He grabbed the carton of ice cream from the counter and added it to the stuff he was taking to the trash.

"I'll wipe the counter down," I said when he looked around for something he could use to clean up the melted ice cream.

"Okay, I can help when I get back. Where is the dumpster?"

"Downstairs, on the left, just past the giant, overgrown tree."

He nodded and carried everything gracefully out the door, careful not to spill anything on his way out. I quickly wiped down the counter and tossed the rag back in the sink to rinse it later before squirting some of the cleaning solution into the bin of my Swiffer mop. I loved this thing more than I loved any of my other cleaning appliances. Just a couple of sprays and my floor would be spotless and smell like pine.

I had just finished mopping the floor when I heard the door open and Wyatt walked in. I took off the cleaning pad and tossed it in the sink next to the dishrag while I drained the rest of the cleaning solution and rinsed it out. Everything else could wait until tomorrow, the essential stuff was done for now. I heard the door to the bathroom close and took the opportunity to get situated on the couch. I had turned on the tv and was flipping through the channels to find something to watch when he came out.

Wyatt joined me on the couch, given there was nowhere else to sit. We sat in awkward silence for a few minutes, both pretending to be interested in the infomercial. I knew it was still early, but I couldn't handle any more of the tension between us. I pretended to yawn while bringing my arms up over my head, trying to sell it that I was tired.

"Well, I think I'm going to call it a night," I said as groggily as I could. "Do you need anything?"

"I'm good," he said as he shook his head. "Thanks again for letting me stay here, I appreciate it."

"No problem." I smiled and got up. I was walking away, feeling confident that I had dodged a bullet when he spoke.

"Hey, Kayce?"

I stopped in my tracks, frozen and afraid to turn around to look at him.

"About tonight—I don't think any less of you and I hope you don't think any less of me. I'm sure you've heard that I have a reputation back home, but I wasn't going for a quick score with you. As much as I wanted to back off and *not* touch you, I couldn't. There's this electricity between us, and I couldn't walk away if I tried. For what it's worth, I'm sorry if I've overstepped or made you uncomfortable. I don't mind if you'd rather that I leave."

I slowly turned to look at him and tried to swallow past the lump in my throat as I listened to his words. He was being honest, I could see it in his eyes.

"Want to sleep next to me?" I asked nervously. As weird as everything had felt earlier, it now felt even stranger to not let him sleep with me in my bed. We did have sex after all, so nothing should be awkward or uncomfortable at this point—even though it was for me. Plus, I knew that my couch sucked to sleep on. I had done it a handful of times after having a few too many drinks and regretted it more than the hangover that usually came the next day.

"Is that what you want?" His face was stoic, his body tense as he waited.

I nodded and turned on my heel, walking to my bedroom before I could overthink it and change my mind. I heard his footsteps behind me and forced out the breath that I had been holding.

I stood next to the queen-sized bed and pulled back the comforter and sheet. I reached down to take my leggings off when it suddenly hit me. My face froze in panic as my cheeks reddened.

"What's wrong?" he asked from the other side of the bed, setting his phone down on the nightstand.

"Nothing," I lied in a whisper.

"Kayce…" He dropped his head slightly and pinned me with a look.

"Fine—I sleep naked. Okay?" I muttered in frustration.

"Okay… so why is that a problem?"

"It's not, I just—I can't just strip down and climb into bed knowing that you'll be lying next to me."

"Why not? Are you worried that you won't be able to keep your hands to yourself?" He arched a brow.

The temperature in the room increased tenfold as my palms started to sweat. As discreetly as possible, I ran them down the front of my pants.

"No, that's not it at all. It's just weird and awkward…"

"Because I would see you naked?" He paused for a minute, processing the information. "Again."

"It was different earlier," I whined. "That was for sex. There was an end goal. This is for sleep."

He turned to the side and pretended to cough to stifle his laugh. His dark brown hair caught in the light by the bed, casting a warm glow through it. He coughed again, clearing his throat before he turned back to look at me with a straight face.

"Okay, I have a solution to the problem," he assured me with a nod. It was my turn to arch a brow at him as I waited.

He reached down and pulled his hoodie up and over his head, revealing a ridiculously perfect body underneath. His abs were on point and his chest was more solid than an engine block. I let my eyes travel leisurely down his body, taking in every beautiful inch as his fingers hooked into the waistband of his sweats and he pulled them down.

While part of me was relieved that he had underwear on underneath, the dirty girl inside of me was hoping for another view of his rock-hard dick. My eyes lingered there for a second too long when I felt his eyes watching me, noticing what I was staring at.

"Problem solved," he said, stretching his arms out at his sides. "Now it's your turn."

I laughed and bit the inside of my cheek to keep from saying something stupid. Instead, I pulled my shirt over my head and tossed it to the floor before slipping out of my pants. I was still wearing my bra and panties but this was easier than trying to sleep in full clothes.

"I thought you slept naked?" he teased with a smirk, not bothering to hide that he was blatantly checking me out. "Did you need help with the rest?" He wiggled his brows.

"I'm not going to strip down naked in front of you," I said sarcastically. "This will be fine."

"Alright, suit yourself." He shrugged and reached down, pulling his underwear down and kicking them to the side with the pile of his other clothes. He looked overly confident standing there naked, not an ounce of fat anywhere on his perfectly fuckable body. I fought the urge to look at the one-eyed monster as it started to rise in greeting.

I turned my back to him and reached behind me, unclasping my bra and sliding it down my arms before I let it fall to the floor. I tucked my fingers into the top of my panties and slid them off, tossing them in with the other pile of clothes before I lifted the covers and slipped into bed. I felt childish and immature, but something about the way he was looking at me made me so nervous and aroused that I didn't care. Maybe it wouldn't be that bad to share my bed with him tonight after all…

<u>Six</u>
Wyatt

His eyes looked like they were bulging out of his head as he held a hand to his chest and looked around, panicked.

"Dad!" I screamed, trying to force him to snap out of it.

I watched as he leaned against the truck, his body slowly slumping to the cold cement floor of the garage, the wrench falling out of his other hand. I kneeled down beside him, trying to help, but not knowing what to do.

"Dad, what's wrong? What can I do?" I begged, watching as different emotions flashed through his eyes. The most obvious one—fear. I jumped up and looked around, hoping that one of our neighbors would hear me. No one else was home so it was pointless to call Grant or Chase.

"HELP!!! PLEASE, SOMEONE!! HELP MY DAD!!" I screamed into the silent air around us.

I turned back around and found my dad lying beside the truck. Our eyes locked onto each other's one last time before he let out his final breath.

I leaped forward in the bed, gasping for air the way I always did when I had this dream. Only this wasn't a dream. It was a fucking nightmare that I couldn't stop no matter how hard I tried. I felt the bed shift beside me, glancing over to make sure I hadn't woken Kayce. Her purple hair was fanned out across her back as she laid on her stomach, face buried deep in the pillow. The contrast of the blue sheets to her bright colored hair made her look like some sort of beautiful mermaid.

I forced a deep breath out, then slowly pulled one in. My heart was racing, and I knew that there was no way that I was going to be able to go back to sleep after that. The week had already started out rough but I had prayed that today would be a better day. It was still early enough to try to turn it around.

As quietly as possible, I climbed out of bed and slipped my sweatpants on. There was a chill in the air so I threw my hoodie on as well. Glancing down at my phone, I found it was barely four-thirty in the morning which meant that I had a lot of time to kill before I could head over to the hotel to get things situated. I also needed to find a rental car for the time being while I had Kayce look at the truck. There was plenty on my plate, and nothing that I had planned to have to deal with when I first came out here.

My first meeting with the possible recruit wasn't until Wednesday morning, but I came down early to see what the town was all about. This was my first recruiting job, and I knew from personal experience that if I was going to try to convince this kid to leave his hometown, I'd better have a good argument on what he would be gaining by moving to Haven Brook. If I could lay low for the first few days without him knowing I was here, I would get a good idea of who he really was and that meant that I would have an advantage with getting him to commit.

I grabbed my duffel bag and went to the living room to work for a bit. I considered making coffee, but given that I didn't know where she kept anything, I didn't want to risk waking her up by looking for stuff. I decided to just wait until she was up and see if there was a coffee shop close by. I had already had sex with her but had no idea if she drank coffee. Yeah, I was off to a good start.

I rolled my eyes and shook my head, trying to force the sarcastic thoughts away. Grant had been quick to lecture me about what happened, reminding me that she wasn't just some girl in a new town that I would never see again. Nope, she was the cousin of his fiancé and at this point, I believed him when he said he would cut my dick off and beat me with it if I did anything to hurt her.

Thankfully, I was able to divert the conversation to the truck which held Grant's attention long enough to forget about everything else. It was a hot topic in our family whenever it came up, but I appreciated that Grant held a little more sentimental attachment to the truck like I did. Chase didn't understand why we were still messing around with it, but Grant knew why I couldn't just walk away from it. I would go to my grave with that truck by my side because it was the last memory I had with my dad. I owed it to him to take care of it and keep it in our family for as long as I could.

I opened my bag and pulled out my laptop, hoping that I had enough battery to get through a couple of hours' worth of work. I had made sure it was fully charged before I left, but given how everything else was going so far, I wouldn't be surprised if it died in five minutes. It would be just my luck.

THREE STRIKES, YOU'RE GONE

I leaned back against the cushion on the couch, propping my feet up in front of me as I set the computer on my lap. I was so focused on waiting for it to start up that I hadn't heard Kayce come out of the room. The screen lit up as the icons started popping up and a picture of me and my mom displayed as the wallpaper.

"Oh my gosh, that is the cutest picture," Kayce said over my shoulder. I felt myself jump as she startled me, turning to look at her while making sure I didn't drop the laptop.

"Sorry, I didn't mean to scare you," she laughed, resting her hand on my shoulder.

"You're fine," I laughed with her, enjoying her touch. "I just didn't hear you come out. You're like some early morning sly ninja."

"Hmmm." She pursed her lips and tapped her finger to her chin. "You're right. I think I'll add that to my resume." She shot me a playful smile over her shoulder as she turned and walked into the kitchen. "Do you want some coffee?" she asked, bending over to get something out of the cabinet.

"Sure, if you're making some for yourself, I'd love a cup. If not, please don't go through the trouble for me."

"It's not a problem at all," she said breathlessly as she pulled a blender out from under the sink and set it on the counter.

I raised an eyebrow, wondering what she was doing.

"Where exactly do you put that filter thingy?" She raised on her tiptoes and lifted the lid, looking inside before looking over at me. Her face was utterly adorable, but I worried that she might be serious.

"You're going to make coffee in *that*?" I asked, setting my laptop down on the coffee table.

"Uhhh… yeah." She tilted her head to the side and looked at me like I was the crazy one. "Why, are you too good for my coffee? Do you need some sort of hipster coffee drink with organic beans and cream whipped by a leprechaun?"

I walked over to the counter, resting my hands as I lowered my head to look her in the eyes.

"You do know that this isn't a coffee maker. Right?"

Her face fell as she lifted her hand to her mouth. The golden brown color of her eyes had flecks of green in them as the corners of her lips turned up and she burst into laughter.

"Yes, Wyatt, I know that this isn't a coffee maker," she laughed hysterically. "But man, you should have seen your face." She pointed a finger and kept laughing before she bent down and pulled the coffee pot out from under the same cabinet.

"You're rotten." I shook my head playfully, walking around to the other side of the counter. She was wearing a pair of black leggings with a loose t-shirt that was probably two sizes too big for her. While it would probably make other women look frumpy, she looked incredibly cute in it with her hair pulled up into a messy knot on the top of her head.

"Do you need help?" I offered, noticing the hoarseness in my voice again.

"Nah, I got it. Thank you."

"I take it you don't make coffee much?" I nodded to the blender that she had to pull out to get to the coffee maker, which also made me wonder if she even had coffee if she didn't make it often.

"Coffee runs through my veins," she said as she plugged it in. "But, Saturday was girl's night which meant frozen margaritas. Priorities." She gave me a quick wink before she scooted over and opened the cabinet, pulling out a bag of coffee grounds and a filter.

"How do you like your coffee?" Her hand froze in the air while she waited for my answer before filling the filter with coffee.

"Strong, but I'll drink it however you want yours."

"Good. I like it strong too."

I watched as she packed the filter with as much coffee as it could take before she plopped it into the maker and added the water. A few minutes later the room was filled with the delicious aroma of coffee brewing.

"Why are you up so early?" She asked as she busied herself around the kitchen, pulling down coffee mugs and grabbing the creamer from the fridge. She set everything between us, then stopped and gave me her full attention while she waited for me to speak.

I didn't want to talk about the dream or how the nightmares of the day my dad died still haunted me, so I just blew it off with a shrug.

"I had work to get done. Nothing major. I couldn't sleep so I figured I would start looking into the fabulous town of Easterville."

"What did you find?" She turned her back to me to grab a spoon out of the drawer. Flashbacks of eating her out on the counter last night came flashing through my mind, making my dick twitch at the thought.

"Not much, someone scared the shit out of me before I could look," I laughed. "Why are you up so early?"

"I'm naturally an early bird. Always have been, which is odd because I'm also a night owl. I like to stay up late and get up early which has never made sense. I guess I'm just one of those people who doesn't need a lot of sleep." She held her hands out to the side. The coffee trickled to a stop before she pulled the carafe out and poured each of us a cup.

She held hers with two hands and lifted it to her lips. Before taking a sip, she closed her eyes and took a deep breath, inhaling the aroma of the steaming mug of coffee first. Her lips parted while her eyes stayed closed, the hot liquid forcing its way inside. Everything about what she was doing was so fucking arousing that I was worried I was going to break the mug I was holding in my hand just to keep from coming from the image in front of me.

Slowly, her eyes opened after taking a drink, embarrassment washing over her when she saw the way I was looking at her. There was no hiding what I was thinking, but I was thankful that I had moved back to the other side of the counter so she couldn't see the erection that was trying to force its way out of my sweatpants.

"Well, if you're up for it, I'll take you to breakfast this morning," she offered, setting her mug down in front of her. "That way you can get the best breakfast burrito in all of Easterville since you're looking at what we have to offer." She raised her eyebrows with faux excitement.

"Are you telling me that the best thing Easterville has to offer is a breakfast burrito?" I asked wearily, lifting my mug to take a drink.

"No, not the best *thing*. Just the best breakfast option. Trust me, it's delicious and you'll never want another breakfast burrito again after you try this one."

"Alright, fine," I sighed dramatically. "If you insist that it's the best, then I guess we'll have to go try it. But there is one condition…"

"What's that?"

"I'm paying," I said flatly, making sure she heard the tone to know that I wasn't playing.

"Don't be such a caveman," she replied, rolling her eyes as she grabbed her mug off the counter. "I can and I *will* buy you breakfast.

I just need fifteen minutes to shower real quick, then you can jump in while I get ready," she called over her shoulder as she walked away and closed the bathroom door behind her.

I took my coffee to the couch and sat down, still shaking my head at the thought of her paying for my food. It was bad enough that I had crashed at her place last night, but my only other choice was to freeze my ass off in the truck since I didn't get in early enough to secure my hotel room. I set the mug down and opened my laptop, trying to think about what could possibly be the most interesting thing in Easterville.

While most people would google things like *places to eat, things to do,* I found myself googling 'Wrenched'. A few seconds passed by before the screen changed and a general search of the auto shop popped up. There were a handful of pictures linked to it with comments about how hot the mechanic was, but there wasn't an actual website for Wrenched. I looked through a few of the photos before I clicked on one of her and some guy.

I leaned forward and read the caption underneath.

Jolted lead singer Brent Fallows with girlfriend Kayce Fields

Girlfriend? I clenched my fist, wondering if she was still with this douchebag-looking prick who was caught on camera checking out another woman's ass as she stood next to him. In a way, I hoped she was, only so I could make her scream my name while he listened, knowing he would never be able to please her the way I had.

I scrolled through more pictures of them together. Aside from her hair changing colors, they all looked the same. He was constantly focused on every other woman around them, while she stood there, looking unimpressed and bored.

A squeak from the bathroom drifted under the door as the shower turned off. I closed out the browser window I had opened and shut down the computer. The door opened a few minutes later as I was sliding the laptop back into my duffle bag. As I looked up, I found Kayce walking out with her hair wrapped up in a towel on her head, her cup of coffee in one hand, and her other hand holding the corner of the towel against her body.

My eyes took their time, slowly scanning her body as the blush crept across her skin. I licked my lips, fighting the urge to walk over and strip her of the fluffy material that was covering her sexy fucking body.

"I saved you some hot water," she whispered as she stood in the living room. She didn't look like she wanted to walk away from this either, but one of us had to force ourselves to think straight. I grabbed my bag from the floor and stood up, pulling it over my shoulder.

"Thanks, I think a cold one is in store for me at this point," I muttered as I walked past her and closed the door.

She was gorgeous, there was no doubt about that. But it was like there was some secret language that our bodies were speaking to each other and neither of us knew what it was. Our heads were able to rationalize that we were doing something stupid, but our bodies were the ones who weren't getting the message.

I turned the handle and didn't bother waiting for the water to warm up before I stripped down and climbed inside. Maybe the burst of cold water would convince my dick to stand down before we got ourselves in over our head.

I hadn't thought to pull my toiletries out of my bag beforehand so I was stuck using whatever she had in the shower. I was thankful to find that she wasn't one of those girls who used expensive products or things that were heavily scented. I reached for the bottle of shampoo and squirted some in my hand, wondering if it would be helpful to deal with the other situation while I was here.

The subtle vanilla scent filled the shower, making me think of her naked body under the hot water a few minutes ago. I groaned as I added more shampoo to my hand before reaching down and gliding it over my cock. I pictured Kayce's mouth as it wrapped tightly around my dick, sucking hard as she worked me over with her tongue. I stroked faster, the smooth glide from the liquid coating me as I imagined being inside of her slick, wet pussy. I held my hand against the wall to brace myself while I jerked hard and fast, my dick growing harder as my balls started to ache. My breathing grew more rapid as I imagined her riding me, her thighs clenching around my body as she threw her head back and came on my dick. The way her mouth parted and her nipples perked when she was about to come had me jerking harder until I shot ropes of cum across the shower.

I cleaned up and finished washing my body before I got out and felt the cold chill of the tile floor beneath me. Suddenly, I was regretting not taking a hot shower after all. I pulled the towel around my waist and dug through my bag, grabbing a fresh pair of jeans and a clean t-shirt. I had left my suitcase in the truck but knew better than to not pack at least one clean outfit in my duffle bag, which had worked in my favor this morning.

By the time I had brushed my teeth and got dressed, Kayce was already in the kitchen when I came out.

"I hung my towel on the hook behind the door, I hope that's okay," I said as I walked out and pulled the door closed behind me.

"That's perfect, thank you."

She looked sexy with her hair pulled up into a high, messy bun that sat on top of her head. The front was puffed up like the retro girls I used to see in the calendars my dad would buy me every year. He would tell my mom that he got them for me because of my love for classic cars but then would wink when she wasn't looking to let me know that he only bought them for me because of the girls. I could totally picture Kayce as a pin-up model next to an old muscle car.

"You ready to get going?" she asked, breaking me free from my thoughts of her climbing up the hood of a hotrod, her ass in booty shorts on full display with her lips parted open.

"Yeah, sorry." I shook my head and smiled.

She reached down and picked up the same bag I had seen her with last night. It looked heavier than it did last night and I wasn't sure how she was even able to carry it. I rushed over and grabbed it before she could slide it up onto her shoulder.

"Here, let me help you with that," I said softly, our fingers brushing against each other as I took it from her.

"It's okay, I got it. It's heavy," she countered, not bothering to move her hand from mine.

"Which is all the more reason why I should help you with it."

She paused and narrowed her eyes at me.

"Are you insinuating that because I'm a woman, I'm not strong enough to carry it myself?"

I met the glare she was giving me and smiled. A genuine smile. Not some dickish smile that she was probably expecting.

"Not at all. I think it's fucking amazing that you carry this to begin with, and I have no doubt that you are strong. However, I was raised to be a gentleman, which means that if a woman is carrying something— I'm going to offer to carry it for her. Not because you can't do it yourself, but because my momma raised me better than that."

Her features softened a bit but her grip on the strap of the bag remained firm.

"Can I please be a gentleman and carry your bag?"

She paused for a moment to think, making it obvious that she was messing with me.

"Fine," she sighed. "But I get to buy breakfast."

I rolled my eyes as I took the bag from her and lifted it onto my shoulder. I shifted the duffle bag around my shoulders to balance the weight, then followed her downstairs to her truck. I handed her the bag before she got in, then walked around and climbed in. I wasn't going to be nosey and ask what she had in that damn thing, but part of me wondered if it was the body of the fucking loser wanna-be rock star she was dating. If it was, I would gladly help her bury that shit in some abandoned field where no one would ever find it.

The roads were empty, and I didn't know if it was because it was barely six in the morning or if this was just the normal for Easterville. We passed by Wrenched, and I was relieved to see the truck still sitting where I had left it, all in one piece. It had been hard to walk away last night, not knowing if it would still be there this morning. A wave of calm hit me and reminded me why that truck meant so much to me.

Ten minutes later, we were parked in an empty parking lot and walking into a building that looked like it belonged in the 1970s. A bell chimed as we opened the door, with a nauseating wave of orange shag carpet greeting us as we walked inside. There was wood paneling along the walls and off in the corner were a few animal heads that had been mounted. I pulled my lips together, forcing myself to stay quiet so I didn't say anything rude while we waited for someone to come seat us.

Kayce peered up at me, a smug smile on her face as she studied me. I knew she could tell how uncomfortable I was and that I was definitely judging the town by this so-called treasure. Haven Brook wasn't known for much in the way of food, but at least our breakfast burritos had surpassed the time capsule that we were currently trapped in.

I looked around for a sign so I could text Grant and let him know where to send the coroner to come to collect my body. Time of death: six-fifteen. Location: Jumping Joe's.

Just as I was taking stock of the things around me, a woman in her twenties came flying around the corner, screeching to a stop right in front of us.

"Howdy! Dine-in or to-go?" she asked, tucking a strand of curly blond hair back behind her ear.

"Dine-in," Kayce confirmed.

"Right this way," the woman said cheerfully before grabbing a few menus and making her way over to the table. She stopped and waited for us to sit down before she walked off.

"So, this is the best of Easterville," I said carefully, picking up the menu to look it over. It was a long piece of laminated paper that looked promising until I saw that there were only two options listed on the menu. Kayce's eyes danced wildly as she watched me examine the menu, flipping it over to see if there was more on the back. I raised an eyebrow and looked past the menu at her.

"The only options are burrito or," I paused and looked back at the menu for dramatic effect. "Or burrito."

"Well, things here are simple." She shrugged, smiling as the waitress came back with two glasses of water.

"Alright, what can I get you?"

"You mean there's more than burritos?" I asked dryly, setting the menu down in front of me. I placed my hands on the table and looked up at her.

"Well, duh," she snorted, laughing with Kayce as if I just said the funniest thing.

"Humor me," I prodded. "What else is there to get here?"

"Trust me, sugar, you don't want anything else. This is *the place* to go for breakfast burritos in all of Colorado. Don't you go messing that up by trying to order something different."

I clicked my tongue against the roof of my mouth and looked at Kayce. Her smile was still stretched across her face as if she was enjoying every second of this.

"I'll have the bacon burrito," she said, turning her attention away from me and back to the waitress.

"I'll do the same," I replied, pushing my menu to the edge of the table. She nodded and scooped the menus up before walking off to the back, yelling *two bacon!* on her way into the kitchen.

"So… what do you think?" Kayce asked, trying to stifle her laugh.

"I think you might be someone to keep an eye on. Lacey insisted that I could trust you, but I'm starting to wonder if her pregnancy brain is impacting her judgment," I teased, squinting my eyes at her.

"Trust me, it looks totally like something you'd find in an outdated horror movie, but their burritos are the best."

"I guess we shall see."

I looked around the small room, noticing a few of the other tables starting to fill up with customers. The clock on my phone said it was almost six-thirty, so maybe this was the time the town started their days. It would be good to get a feel for how things worked here so I could compare them to how things would be in Haven Brook.

"So, Lacey mentioned that you were here for work. What do you do?" Kayce asked, pushing the paper off of her straw and crumbling it into a small ball in her hands.

"I'm a Recruiting Coordinator for Haven Brook University."

"What does that mean? Sorry, don't hate me, I've never been much into sports." She squinted her eyes and scrunched up her face.

"Basically, it means that I find talented players and essentially stalk them until they commit to our university," I laughed, knowing there were many levels of truth in that statement.

"High school kids?"

"Yeah, mostly juniors. Some seniors. It just depends. Right now, I'm here to meet with a senior at Easterville High. He has a lot of talent and the potential to do two years with Haven Brook before moving up."

"What's his name?" she asked, leaning back as the waitress returned and set our plates down in front of us. The burritos were massive and took up the entire plate. The smell of bacon made my stomach growl as my fingers itched to pick it up and dig in, though I wasn't sure that I could even pick the beast up.

"You might want to give it a few minutes," she warned, watching my fingers as they started to reach for the burrito. "They crisp the burrito which is what makes it so delicious, but it takes a few minutes before it's edible without scalding your mouth."

I nodded and pushed the plate away to keep the temptation at bay.

"Junior Soto," I said, ignoring the loud growl from my stomach. Maybe there was some truth to these being the best breakfast burritos after all?

"He's definitely one of the best that we have," she agreed, cutting into her burrito with a knife to let some of the steam out.

"Well, that makes my job harder," I joked.

"Why is that?"

"Because I have to convince him that Haven Brook is *the place* to be so he'll commit to our school." I paused to cut into my burrito like Kayce had. I took a bite and closed my eyes as I chewed. This was beyond delicious. "And unfortunately, we don't have breakfast burritos like this in Haven Brook."

Kayce covered her mouth as she laughed, the sound almost as wonderful as the food in front of me.

<u>Seven</u>
Kayce

I was pleasantly surprised by how much Wyatt had enjoyed breakfast, even though I knew he would be crazy not to. We finished breakfast and when he wasn't looking, I slipped some cash to Naomi, the waitress, for our meals. We climbed back into the truck and made a pit stop at the gas station before heading to the hotel. I advised him to grab at least three Paydays and couldn't help but laugh when I saw him come out with a bag filled with them. I'm not sure how much bribing he thought he was going to have to do, but this should cover him.

A few minutes later, we were parked in front of the Honey Lodge, patiently waiting inside at the front desk for someone to come greet us. I had assumed that Trudy would be working but almost burst into another fit of laughter when I saw Fred round the corner, his eyes narrowed at us behind the thick lenses of his bifocals.

"Can I help you?" he grumbled, sitting down on the padded chair behind the desk. He glanced over at the bag of candy bars that Wyatt was trying to discreetly pull to the side, out of his view.

"Um, hi, I'm Wyatt Walker. I had a reservation yesterday but wasn't able to make it in time due to some car trouble," he said, forcing a smile as Fred glowered at him. "I apologize for the late notice, sir—"

"Mr. Ashby," he corrected.

"Mr. Ashby," Wyatt repeated. "However, I wanted to see if I might be able to get a room for the rest of this week. I'm here on business."

Fred looked between us, studying me then Wyatt. I had known him long enough to know that he was as harmless as a butterfly, even though he liked to act like he was tough.

"Where's Trudy?" I asked, interrupting his thoughts as he glared at Wyatt again.

"She's home, sick, probably from all of the candy that the good-looking out-of-town kids bring her to bribe her to give them a room," he said sarcastically, looking back at Wyatt who was now pushing the bag further away. "She has diabetes, you know?"

I turned my head to the side and coughed, trying to hide the laughter that was threatening to come out.

"We hope she feels better soon," I said sincerely. "What do you say, do you have a room that this good-looking out of towner can have?" I tilted my head to the side and gave him my best smile.

"No."

He picked up the newspaper that was lying on the desk, shaking it open. I gently reached over and pushed it down, making sure he could see me.

"I'll give you a free oil change…" I offered.

He lowered the newspaper to his lap and thought about it.

"Two. Trudy needs one too, even though Lord knows she never goes anywhere other than to Bingo to blab about Tracy Miller." He shook his head as if this was a heated topic for him.

"Deal," I said, interrupting him before he could go on. I stuck my hand out, smiling when he reached over and shook it.

Ten daunting long minutes later, Fred was handing Wyatt two key cards to his hotel room and confirmed that he would need to call down daily for the Wi-Fi password if he wanted to use it. He grumbled about how the kids around town try to use it for free, and he had to put a stop to that. I laughed, knowing how true and funny it was, even though his scowl confirmed that he didn't see any humor in it.

"Thank you again for the room, sir, I appreciate it," Wyatt said, grabbing the bag of candy from the desk.

"Leave the candy," Mr. Ashby said with a sheepish grin. "Trudy's not the only one around here who likes a sweet bribe." He wiggled his eyebrows and smiled for the first time.

"Fred!" I gasped and brought my hand to my chest. "You just got two free oil changes from me, AND a bag full of candy out of him." I shook my head and tsked at him. "If Trudy knew…"

"Who do you think she learned it from?" He shrugged and laughed hysterically as we walked out and left him to his stash of sugary treats.

The air was bitterly cold as we walked outside, the wind sending a chill right through us. We jumped in the truck, and I turned the heater on to help warm us up.

"So, did you want me to drive you around back to your room?" I asked, not sure what his plans were for the day. I needed to get to the shop before long, but since I didn't have any clients waiting on me, I wasn't in a rush.

"Sure, that would be great. Thank you," he said, looking down at his phone. "Do you remember him giving me the Wi-Fi password?" he asked, his brows pulled together as his fingers swiped across the screen.

"He did, I think it was NOCANDY, all capital letters," I laughed.

"I put that in, but it's showing spotty service. Maybe it will be better in my room."

I looked around at the mountain that the hotel was butted up against and knew that he wasn't going to have any better luck in his room. The internet service here was crap because of the lack of towers nearby and the thick forest that surrounded the hotel on three out of four sides.

"It's not going to be any better in your room," I said, shaking my head as I pulled around to the row of rooms by the back parking lot. "Why don't you go get yourself settled inside and then bring whatever you need for work, and I'll take you to my shop. I have great service there and you can work out of my office."

"I don't want to be in the way," he insisted with his hands up.

"You won't. Besides, I might have questions about your truck, and it'll be helpful if you're right there to answer them." I smiled but didn't miss the look that flashed across his face. The sadness mixed with pain when I mentioned working on the truck. "Unless you don't want me to look at it?"

"No, it's not that. Sorry, I'm just out of it today. I'll go drop off my stuff real quick," he said before climbing out and shutting the door.

I leaned back against the seat, taking in the warmth of the heater as I tried to relax. There was negative energy in the air, and I couldn't put my finger on what it was. I closed my eyes and focused on my breathing. In. Out. In. Out. It was weird, when Wyatt was around, I felt fine, safe even. But once he got out of the truck and went into his room, I had this terrible anxiety that crept up on me. I hadn't quite shaken this feeling since yesterday in my office, but for whatever reason, I felt better when he was around.

THREE STRIKES, YOU'RE GONE

Eight
Wyatt

It was almost one o'clock, and Kayce had spent most of the morning helping one of the locals with their work truck that had broken down over the weekend. She promised to look at my truck when she was done, but I reminded her that I wasn't in a hurry. Now that I knew how small the town was, I was confident that I could easily get around where I needed to without my truck. As long as it was up and running by the end of the week so I could head back home, that was all that I needed.

I had been working on my laptop, going over the paperwork that had been sent over for Junior. There were plenty of other students that we could have been recruiting, but he was listed as the top priority and based on his stats, I could see why. This kid was the wet dream of baseball. My phone vibrated across Kayce's desk, showing the head coach's name on the caller ID.

"Hey, Chuck," I answered.

"How's the great town of Easterville treating you?" he snickered sarcastically.

"Well, I finally got a room at the luxury Honey Lodge after bribing the owner with a bag full of candy bars, and I had the best breakfast burrito in all of my life," I said with a laugh.

"So, you've been to Jumping Joe's. It's definitely a must while you're there."

"Yeah, I think that's all that's really a *must*," I countered. "Other than The Tasty Pig. That was pretty good too." I thought back to the cobbler incident last night and felt my dick twitch in response.

"Are you ready for your meeting with Junior Soto tomorrow?" he asked, interrupting my dirty thoughts.

"Yeah, I have all of the paperwork printed and I've gone over his stats sheet. This should be quick and easy unless there's another school that he decides to commit to instead."

"Don't go putting that karma out in the universe, kid," he warned playfully, even though we both knew that it was a possibility. The only good thing about him being from such a small town was that it was more likely for him to be under the radar of the larger D1 division schools that would try to snatch him up as well.

"Don't worry, I'll make sure I don't leave here without his commitment," I assured him. This was my first recruit, and I was determined not to screw it up. I remembered how excited I was when I committed to Haven Brook University and how huge it felt when I was picked up by a pro team before my injury. I tried to push the thoughts away of what could have been as I hung up with Chuck. My life had done a complete 180, and even though I wouldn't change anything about saving Lacey's life, I hated that it cost me everything I had worked hard for since I was a kid.

I still went to my follow-up doctor appointments as part of my agreement with the Colorado Cougars and humored them by continuing the physical therapy even though I knew it wasn't helping. Numerous doctors had told me that the likelihood of pitching again was slim. Being a left-handed pitcher who had to have three separate heart surgeries to repair the damage from being stabbed was pretty much a death sentence to my career as a professional ballplayer.

I heard the door open up front as Kayce came back inside from dealing with another customer. She had made it seem like she wasn't usually that busy, but today seemed to be slammed for her. I felt bad about taking up her office and keeping her from getting work done. I logged out of my email and shut down my computer before unplugging it and stuffing it back into the backpack that I had brought with me.

"Hey, how's it going?" she asked as she came in and picked up the bottle of water that was sitting on the edge of her desk. She twisted the top off and took a drink.

"It's good," I said, standing up to move out of her way. "I'm all done with what I needed to do, so you can have your office back."

"Oh, no worries," she said and waved it off. "I'll do all of my paperwork tomorrow. But I'm done with the other cars, did you want to go show me what's been going on with your truck?"

I felt the lump in my throat as I tried to push my words out.

"Sure," was all that I was able to get out. I set my backpack down on the couch against the wall and followed her out to the parking lot where it was still sitting. The snow was beginning to fall again which didn't feel promising that I would make it back to Haven Brook this weekend after all. Thankfully, it wasn't as cold as it had been which was keeping the snow from sticking.

"Lacey mentioned that you were having some problems with it backfiring recently," she stated as she walked to the back of the truck and squatted to look at the tailpipe.

"Yeah, it's been guzzling gas and I've seen clouds of white smoke as well. My guess is that it's the carburetor."

"When was the last time that you had any work done on it?" she asked as she walked around to the front and waited for me to pop the hood. I closed the door and went to help her lift it when she gave me a glance that told me she didn't need my help.

"It's been a while," I shrugged, not wanting to get into the details. "I've done basic maintenance on it, but it hasn't needed much other than that until now."

"It's a 1969?"

I was impressed. She definitely knew vehicles, and I could tell by the way she was treating mine that she also respected them.

"Yeah." I felt my hands starting to sweat, the memories of my dad trying to push their way to the surface.

"Do you know if there was ever any major work done to it before you bought it?" she asked as she turned away from the truck and looked at me.

I shook my head, partly trying to answer her questions but also trying to force the thoughts of that day out of my head. My dad and I were getting ready to start a big project on the truck before he died, but we never got around to it. I had always hated that I didn't know much about what work it still needed because I always spent my time with him rambling on about baseball.

"It's okay if you don't know," she assured me, stepping closer. "I can get in there and find out what's going on. I agree, I think it's the carburetor as well, but I'm worried you might have a bad head gasket. I'll poke around some more and see what I can find."

His eyes looked like they were bulging out of his head as he held a hand to his chest and looked around, panicked.

"Dad!" I screamed, trying to force him to snap out of it.

I watched as he leaned against the truck, his body slowly slumping to the cold cement floor of the garage, the wrench falling out of his other hand. I kneeled down beside him, trying to help, but not knowing what to do.

"Dad, what's wrong? What can I do?" I begged, watching as different emotions flashed through his eyes. The most obvious one—fear. I jumped up and looked around, hoping that one of our neighbors would hear me. No one else was home so it was pointless to call Grant or Chase.

"HELP!!! PLEASE, SOMEONE!! HELP MY DAD!!" I screamed into the silent air around us.

I turned back around and found my dad lying beside the truck. Our eyes locked onto each other's one last time before he let out his final breath.

I gasped as I felt her hands on my arm, pulling me out of the nightmare that had been trying to consume for almost eleven years now.

"Hey," she said softly. "It's okay, we'll figure it out."

While her words were meant to be a comfort, there was one big problem with them. No matter how hard I tried, I would never be able to figure it out. My dad's death was the one thing that continued to haunt me, no matter what I did to try to stop it.

<u>Nine</u>
Kayce

After a slew of curse words, Wyatt was able to get the truck to start and pulled into the garage bay. It wasn't a big garage, especially with my project car off in the back of it that I hadn't had a chance to work on in a while.

I took note of several things that helped solidify my suspicions about what was wrong with it. He put it in park and turned off the engine, while I went back to my office to grab the bag I needed. I carried it into the garage and set it down on the work table, hearing the loud sound it made from the weight of it. There was something strangely satisfying about that sound.

I opened it up and started pulling some tools out, deciding what I needed first.

"Oh, thank God," Wyatt said. "It's just tools…" A cheeky smile spread across his face.

"What did you think it was?" I asked, laughing as I stopped what I was doing to wait for his answer.

"A dead body."

My eyes bugged out as I stared at him, the grin on my face pulling tighter as I tried to cover it behind my hand.

"Why on earth would you think that I have a dead body in here?"

"I don't know… it's super heavy and I guess I just thought it might be Brent Fallows—boyfriend and the lead singer of Jolted." He shrugged his shoulders but the grin didn't fade.

"You Googled me?" I asked. I tilted my head to the side and rested my hand on my hip.

"Maybe."

My eyebrows slowly inched higher up my face as I waited for him to come clean.

"Alright. Fine. I Googled you this morning."

I shook my head and pretended to be offended by this blatant invasion of privacy, but secretly I felt excited and giddy that he had been interested enough to do it in the first place.

"So, did you find what you were looking for?" I kept my head down, while I rifled through the bag, looking for my favorite wrench. Once I had the tools I needed lined up, I straightened and looked at him, wondering why he hadn't answered me.

" I found lots of articles about your boyfriend, Brent," he said cautiously.

"He's not my boyfriend. We broke up," I clarified a little too sharply.

He nodded as if that was the answer he was hoping for.

"Now that we've settled that, is there a girl back in Haven Brook that's going to threaten to come kick my ass for sleeping with you?"

"Probably more than I can count," he mumbled and turned his head away.

I grabbed the tools from the table and debated whether or not to bother responding. Lacey had told me plenty of times how Wyatt had a different girl every day of the week, so why did this bother me so much all of a sudden?

"Let's take a look at the truck, shall we?" I said through gritted teeth, hating the jealousy that was running through me at the thought of Wyatt with another woman.

He gave me a devilish smile as if he was enjoying the fact that I was flustered by what he said. From that point on, we didn't talk. He stood off to the side, while I did my thing. I pulled out the creeper and slid under the truck, making sure that I checked everything before reporting back to him on what I thought was wrong with the truck. Plus, I just wanted to be able to hide for a few moments and not feel the pull of his body so close to mine.

When I couldn't delay any longer, I scooted out from under the truck and got up. I set the tools down next to the bag and brushed my hands on the front of my pants.

"It's your carburetor," I said as I stood at the table and looked at him. "Usually you'll find that the vehicle is acting more sluggish, so you give it more gas. Well, that extra fuel that you're going through is forcing it to stall out and is also creating the backfire. I also noticed that the head gasket is bad, which is what's creating all of the smoke that's coming out of the exhaust. I can fix both, but I'll have to order some parts."

"How long do you think before it's up and running?"

"Honestly, I don't know." I shook my head. "It'll be at least a few days for the order and with the storm that's supposed to hit this week, I don't know if that will delay things further. Also, I won't know if there's anything else going on until I get in there to fix those items. If I find additional problems, then that will add on to the time it takes me to get it running again."

He closed his eyes and let his head fall backward, rotating it along his neck.

"I'm sorry it's not better news," I added gently.

"It's not your fault, I just have terrible luck this week," he replied with frustration. "I should have been more focused on taking care of it to keep it from getting to this point, to begin with."

"Why haven't you?" I asked politely. One thing that I'd learned in this business was that those who had older vehicles tend to take good care of them. If you're not interested in the maintenance and upkeep of an older vehicle, you get a new one with a warranty and let the dealership handle things that come up. But when you have a 1969 Chevy C10, you'd better be taking care of that beautiful piece of art.

"My dad and I were working on the truck when he died," he said quietly.

He looked at the floor and avoided me as my soul crumbled at the heartbreak in the words he'd just spoken.

"I'm so sorry, Wyatt, I didn't know," I apologized.

"Not many people do. It's not something that I like to talk about."

"I get that," I said quietly, stepping closer, reaching out to touch his arm.

"No, you don't," he bit out, pulling away from me. "I don't avoid talking about it, because I'm sad that he died. I avoid talking about it because I'm the one who killed him."

He gave me an icy cold glare before turning and walking away. I saw him grab his backpack out of my office before he walked out the door and let it slam shut behind him. I stood there in the quiet, wondering what in the world had just happened.

Ten
Wyatt

I felt like a dick. A big, hairy, unattractive dick that no one in their right mind would ever want. Not even the crackhead that was offering to blow me for a pack of cigarettes outside of The Tasty Pig when I stopped to grab dinner before heading back to my hotel room.

While I hadn't run like I had told Kayce I would yesterday, I did walk all the way from her shop to my hotel room as I burned off the anger and frustration that was still pulsing through me. It had been a long time since I had talked to anyone about my dad and the words burned as I said them out loud. The worst part was the pity on her face that I didn't deserve.

I knew that it was wrong to storm out of there the way that I did, but I couldn't risk staying any longer and saying something that I would regret. Besides, what was she going to think of me now, anyway? I wasn't Grant's cute little brother to her anymore. No, now I was the monster who was responsible for killing my dad, and then letting his truck waste away because I refused to take care of it the way that my dad would have.

The TV blared in the small room as the local news channel started reporting new road closures due to the storm that was barreling in. *Fucking lovely*. As if I needed any more delays to keep me here any longer.

I flipped through the channels until I found something with sports and finished the last few bites in my to-go box. I had debated grabbing a side of the peach cobbler because it was indeed *delicious*, but decided against it when I thought about how eating Kayce on her counter was much more fulfilling.

After my last bite, I tossed the plastic fork in the box with my used napkin and closed the lid. I was too lazy to run outside to find a dumpster to put the trash in so instead I piled it neatly on the counter by the bathroom and sat down on the bed. It was still early, barely almost seven o'clock, but my body felt tired and drained from the past few days.

I was just about to pull off my hoodie and get ready to lay down when I heard my phone vibrate. Hoping it was Kayce, I picked it up and slid my finger across the screen to unlock it. The disappointment of not hearing from her since I stormed out of her shop was beginning to irritate me and put me in an even worse mood. Not recognizing the phone number, I ignored the call and set the phone down.

It was already dark outside and the snow was still falling which ruled out any physical options for relieving some of the tension. Instead, I settled for a quick workout in my room that consisted of the basics— jumping jacks, sit-ups, and some squats to keep my ass nice and firm. Thankfully, I was on the ground floor and at the end of the building so it wasn't likely that my work out would bother anyone. Hell, I wasn't sure if there were any other guests at this damn hotel in the first place. For all I knew, I was the only guest.

When I was done, I debated on calling Kayce to apologize for my behavior earlier but decided that my mood was still too sour to risk ruining her night. I settled on taking a hot shower instead. Hopefully, the water would pull some of the tension out of my body and let me relax enough to get a good night's sleep. Tomorrow morning was my meeting with Junior at his school, and I needed to make sure that I was at my absolute best so I didn't fuck anything else up this week.

Eleven
Kayce

Today had gone a lot differently than I would've thought. I had no idea what to do after Wyatt stormed out of the shop. It was apparent that he was still harboring some heavy guilt over what happened to his dad, but it wasn't like I could chase after him and convince him that it wasn't his fault. In all honesty, I had no clue. He didn't seem like the kind of guy who would kill someone, but then again, that's been said about plenty of murderers. *He seemed like such a nice guy… everyone just loved him… surely he didn't mean to kill all of those people.*

I rolled my eyes at the thought, knowing how completely ridiculous and absurd it was. I didn't have to know Wyatt to know that he wasn't capable of anything violent. For heaven's sake, he saved Lacey from her father when he showed up at Grant's house to kill her. He sacrificed his life to save hers—without even knowing her, so yeah, I was pretty confident he wasn't some sort of monster in disguise.

I held the phone between my ear and my shoulder while I leaned back in the chair at my desk, tossing the small Nerf ball between my hands. The sound of elevator music played while I waited for someone to come back on the line. After Wyatt left, I was able to clear my head and focus on the truck without being distracted by his presence. It wasn't even just his cologne that triggered me. It was his voice when he spoke and the way he ran his hand through his short hair that made me want to volunteer to have his babies. There was something about him that made me crazy, and I felt like I was walking around in a fog every time he was in my presence.

After some poking around, I was able to find a few other things that needed to be fixed as well. The head gasket was pretty much blown, so I went ahead and called to order a new one from the shop in Glenview. They were the closest automotive repair shop that had a full inventory of parts, and I had been going to them for years.

Leroy let out a low whistle when I rattled off the things that I needed and asked if maybe I should just toss in the towel on this one and buy a new car. All joking aside, he meant well. I had known him since I was a little girl and my grandpa would take me there to pick up the parts he had ordered. Leroy knew my abilities as a mechanic, and while he didn't doubt my ability, he knew how big this job was going to be. Especially when I added a few things to the list that weren't needed right now. It wasn't my fault that I had such a strong, emotional pull to that truck. Someone needed to take care of it, even if it was me.

As I was getting ready to close up the shop, I heard a noise outside in the parking lot. My stomach dropped, panic rushing through me as I worried that it was the same person who had been in my office yesterday. I had my bag hung on my shoulder, the weight of my tools comforting on my hip. I reached down and patted the bag, making sure that I could easily get into it quickly if needed.

I walked slowly down the hallway, keeping my steps as light as possible as I approached the window in the front lobby. The lights in the garage bay were off which sent a chill through me since I knew that I had purposely left them on. I always waited to turn them off until I was locking the front door because I hated the idea of someone hiding in the shadows when I wasn't looking.

My chest heaved as I struggled to control my breathing, the fear mounting with each passing second. I slowly walked forward, keeping my eyes focused for any sort of movement around me as I crept along the wall. The front door was still closed but the door to the garage was open. I didn't want to deal with any of this, I just wanted to get the hell out of there and hide under my bed until it was safe.

A few more steps and then I would be at the end of the hallway, forced to choose a door. The one outside that led to darkness and the unknown. Or the one to the garage bay that also led to darkness and the unknown.

I took a deep breath and tried to steady my hand as I reached into my purse and pulled out the first tool that I could find. I gripped the wrench tightly and kept my back against the solid wall as I took the few steps I needed toward the garage. With shaky fingers, I reached in and flipped on the light switch, allowing my eyes a few minutes to adjust to the bright lights as they flickered over Wyatt's truck.

I quickly scanned the room, looking for an intruder. My heart was racing, the blood rushing in my ears. I stepped inside, glancing over my shoulder to make sure no one had snuck up behind me, turning my attention to the envelope that was placed on the windshield of Wyatt's truck.

Slowly, I walked toward it, still unsure of whether it was safe. A quick look around the room confirmed that no one else was in it with me. It was a small area with a bay big enough for two cars but wide open with plenty of space to work. While it was ideal for working on vehicles, it was lacking as a place to hide given everything was out in the open.

I pulled the envelope out from under the wiper blade and read the words written on it in red marker this time.

Ready or not—Here I come.

I looked around, hoping to find something that would give me a clue as to what these secret messages meant and who was leaving them. Deciding that I had enough, I tucked the envelope into my bag and adjusted it on my hip before making my way to the front door. With one hand gripping the wrench, I used my free hand to lock the door which was freaking difficult to do when your fingers won't stop shaking. I walked quickly through the parking lot, constantly checking my surroundings while making sure I didn't slip and fall on the patches of ice that were starting to form from the snow that had fallen earlier.

My phone rang, vibrating against my thigh as I hopped up into my truck and locked the doors. I set my bag down on the passenger seat, making sure it was within reach if I needed it while putting the wrench in the cup holder next to me. My grandpa always joked that they were tools, not weapons. Little did he know that they came in handy a time or two when I needed them. I lifted my butt and slid my phone out of my pocket, seeing a missed call from Lacey.

Looking around one last time, I made sure everything was safe before unlocking my phone and calling her back. I put it on speakerphone and set it in the other cup holder as I put the truck in reverse and started backing up.

"Hey," Lacey said sweetly, and for a second, I wondered if she was talking to me.

"Hey—son of a bitch!" I screamed, slamming on the brakes. My heart pounded against my chest as I looked in the rearview mirror and found a deer standing behind me. Where in the hell did that asshole come from?!

"What's wrong?" Lacey asked, her voice laced with concern.

"Nothing," I said shakily, my heart feeling like it was beating in my throat. "A damn deer jumped out behind my truck and scared the shit out of me."

I watched it in the rearview mirror, waiting to see if it was going to move on its own or if I was going to have to go around it. After a quick stare down, it gave me one last look before turning and walking back to the empty field across the street. *Stupid deer.*

"Are you okay?"

"Yeah." I felt my shoulders fall as I exhaled heavily, checking my surroundings one more time before pulling out of the parking lot. I was desperate to get the hell out of there and get home where I felt safe. Suddenly, I missed the calm that I had been feeling every time Wyatt was around.

It was already late. I was exhausted, and my stomach was growling. I listened to Lacey tell a quick story about the deer that had decided to live at Grant's mom's house last summer and laughed when she rattled off the string of curse words Connie had used when it started eating her petunias. I still wasn't ready to tell her about the mysterious envelopes, so I tried to force myself to relax as I focused on the false sense of security I found with the number of other people who were out on Main Street tonight.

"I think Connie and I would be great friends," I joked, hoping she didn't pick up that it was fake or that I hadn't been listening as much as I should have.

"Well, if you come down here for the wedding next month, you can spend some time with her," Lacey suggested.

"You know I wouldn't miss it," I assured her as I pulled into the parking lot and circled around to the drive-thru, ignoring the loud growls that were coming from my stomach. I inched forward and stopped at the speaker to place my order. It wasn't a fancy dinner but it was what I could afford right now, and let's be honest—it was delicious.

"Are you at Taco Bell?" Lacey asked with a laugh.

"What? It's Taco Tuesday!"

"Every day is Taco Tuesday with you." She laughed harder, and I joined in, knowing she was right.

"Hey, don't judge. Their food is delicious and cheap. You can't get that anywhere other than Taco Bell. Besides, plenty of people do Taco Tuesday, it's a real thing," I added as I pulled forward and handed the cashier my debit card.

"Yeah, but does it still count as Taco Tuesday if you don't eat tacos?"

"Well, I guess I can challenge them to have a chalupa day. But I really feel like every day should be chalupa day."

I smiled at the woman who handed me my bag of food at the next window and set it down on the seat beside me, behind the bag of tools. Not only were they also weapons when needed, but they also made a handy seat belt for my precious food. I pulled out onto Main Street and went to my apartment. I could hear Annie and Liam in the background talking about starting a chalupa movement at their school in my honor. I smiled and remembered how silly Lacey and I had been when we were their age and the fun we used to have before we hit those teen years and had to worry about stupid stuff—like boys.

"How's she doing?" I asked as I hopped out of my truck and walked around to the passenger side to grab my things. I stayed alert, making sure I watched for any sudden movement around me before rushing up to my apartment.

"She's good. They go back to school next week. They were supposed to start back this week, but we keep getting hit with these snowstorms that have been shutting everything down. I swear, I haven't seen a winter like this in Colorado in all of the years I've lived here."

"Yeah, we're supposed to have a bad one move in by this weekend, but I heard it might come earlier. We're just barely starting to thaw out from the last one." I said as I stood at my door, making sure not to drop my food as I fumbled with the key.

Finally, the door opened and the warmth of the room helped push away some of the icy chill that had clung to my skin. There was no doubt that the next storm was going to be a bad one. I locked the door and slid the deadbolt into place before I set the keys down on the counter next to my bag. I set the food down as well and did a quick sweep of my apartment, making sure everything was okay before I got comfortable. After the weird and creepy things that had been happening at work, I didn't want to assume that my apartment was safe, even though I knew it was a lot harder to get into it than my office was.

Feeling content, I grabbed the bag of food and made my way over to the couch.

"How's Wyatt's truck? Grant said that you're going to help him fix something on it?" Lacey asked as I opened the bag and dug out a chalupa. The heavenly aroma of chicken floated through the air around me as I pulled it out of the wrapper. I closed my eyes and took a bite, savoring it while forgetting that I was still on the phone. A soft moan escaped my lips before I took another bite.

"Is that noise what I think it is?" I heard Grant ask in the background. I started coughing as I almost choked on a piece of chicken, realizing that she must have had me on speakerphone, and he heard me.

"Yeah, it's exactly what you think it is," Lacey confirmed.

"I knew it was a mistake for them to meet…" Grant mumbled in the background.

"Lacey!" I exclaimed, feeling the heat pinch my cheeks. "Stop it! Grant, it's not what you think—"

"Yes, it is," Lacey interrupted. "And stop judging her for her love of chalupas. Let the girl enjoy whatever she wants to. It's not like I don't have stories to tell about you and brownies."

"I don't even want to know," I muttered, taking another bite while reminding myself not to make any embarrassing noises. It was bad enough that he knew that I had sex with his brother. I didn't need him to have any inklings of what I might sound like during climax.

"I thought Bunny was there." Grant's voice was louder as he got closer to the phone.

"Bunny?" I asked around a mouthful of chicken.

"He's talking about Wyatt," Lacey giggled.

"Okay, why do you call him Bunny?" I hoped that maybe it was some sort of cute nickname from when he was little.

"Let's just say his reputation around town earned him that nickname from all of the women who claim he can go as long as the Energizer—"

"Okay, I get it!" I blurted out, desperate for him to stop so I didn't have to hear about Wyatt with other women.

"Is he there? I mean, I get that you're just molesting the damn chalupa, but is he there with you?" Grant asked seriously.

"No," I responded, wiping my mouth with the back of my hand as I pushed the food to the side with my tongue so I could talk. "He had been with me at the shop for a while but then he got upset and left. I haven't talked to him since."

I wished he would have stayed. Maybe if he had, whoever it was that had been in my garage wouldn't have had a chance to get in there to begin with. I knew that they had to have gone in there while I was in my office on the phone, but I hated the thought of someone creeping around in the building without me knowing. I shivered as I thought about it.

"Why did he get upset? What happened?" Lacey asked, pulling me back to the conversation.

I crumpled up the empty wrapper and tossed it in the bag after pulling another chalupa out. I took a smaller, more manageable bite before answering.

"We were talking about the truck and the lack of maintenance on it over the years. I asked him why he hadn't had any work done and when his dad came up, he got upset and stormed out."

"Shit," Grant whispered loudly.

"I'm sorry, I didn't know," I explained, setting my food down in my lap. "I was just trying to figure out why he hadn't done any maintenance on it."

I bit my tongue after I said, realizing how rude it sounded.

"You know, we've told him for years that he should look into selling it and get something else. Something newer that doesn't need the upkeep. But Wyatt," he sighed. "He won't listen. He's been driving that truck since the day he got his license. I think it's just too hard for him to let go of it because he thinks that by doing so, he's also letting go of our dad."

"Did they work on it a lot when he was growing up?" I asked, eager to know more about him.

"Nope," he laughed. "Wyatt was always into baseball. That's where his heart has always been. My dad was the one who was into cars and I think part of him always hoped that at least one of his sons would share that same passion with him. By the time Wyatt was old enough to learn, my dad really gave it his all, hoping that maybe he could get him to fall in love with that old truck."

"So, did it work? Did Wyatt finally fall in love with the truck?" It seemed like a possibility given the way he reacted to it and how protective he was over it.

"Wyatt fell in love with the time he got to spend with my dad. They had an agreement that every night after dinner, they would work on the truck for an hour. During that time, my dad would show him things as they went, and Wyatt would talk to my dad about baseball. It was this perfect mix of combining the two things they both loved while spending time together. My dad loved that Wyatt was into baseball. He even coached his little league team. But there was this special bond between the two of them when they were working on the truck that none of us ever had with him."

My heart fluttered at the thought of Wyatt as a kid, excitedly telling his dad about baseball. I could imagine the twinkle in his eyes as his whole face lit up.

"When my dad died, Wyatt was the only one home with him at the time. They were outside, working on the truck when he had a heart attack. Wyatt called for help, but it was too late. Ever since, no one has been able to touch that truck. Wyatt's heart shattered that day. My dad was his best friend, and he lost him in the blink of an eye. That's why he'll never give it up, and more importantly, why he hasn't been able to work on it. The truck is the last piece of my dad that he has."

I felt the tears fall down my face, my heart breaking for him. Everything made so much sense now, and I felt like an ass for pushing him earlier. If I had known, I never would have said the things that I did.

"I feel terrible," I admitted sadly.

"Don't, you didn't know. I wasn't trying to make you feel bad, I just wanted to let you know why he is the way he is with the truck. I'll call and check on him in a few."

I didn't bother telling them that I had ordered the parts to fix the other stuff that he would need sooner than later. It was bad enough that I had already overstepped by insinuating that he hadn't bothered to take care of the truck. I wasn't ready to admit that I had also been out of line with taking it upon myself to fix stuff that he may not want fixed. Maybe he was planning to do some of the maintenance himself later? Who knew, but it wasn't my place to decide for him. If anything, I could always give him the parts I ordered, and he could decide if and when to do it.

I talked to Lacey for another hour after Grant went upstairs to help the kids get ready for bed. They were probably one of the cutest couples I had ever seen, and they seemed to mesh so well together that being a blended family had been an easy transition for everyone. I had to laugh at the irritation in her voice when she told me that he was limiting how many times she was able to go up and down the stairs during the first trimester of her pregnancy. Luckily for her, she only had a few more weeks.

"Alright, I better get going," she said with a yawn. "Grant said the kids are in bed and waiting for me to come say goodnight. I'm going straight to bed after that."

"Sounds good. I'll talk to you later this week," I confirmed and hung up.

My mind was busy as I thought about what Grant had told me about Wyatt and his dad. I still felt terrible and reached for my phone, deciding whether or not to give him a quick call to apologize. It was after eight-thirty so I assumed he was still awake, but I didn't know him well enough to know for sure.

As I swiped my phone to unlock it, I found a text message from an unknown number.

Unknown: Did you remember to lock your door?

THREE STRIKES, YOU'RE GONE

Twelve
Wyatt

"I'm not a big fan of *no news is good news*," my mom scolded on the other end of the phone. I had forgotten to call her yesterday with the update from the doctor that I had seen last week.

"It's the same news that it always is. *You're making progress, slowly but surely. Your body has been through a lot. You're lucky to be alive, focus on what else will make you happy other than baseball*," I said each word in a whiney, high-pitched tone to make sure she understood my level of irritation.

"Well, I'm sorry that it wasn't better news. I know how frustrated you are, and I'm not trying to dismiss that. I just wanted to know what they said because I care," she explained softly.

"I know, Ma. I know."

"So, how is the new job going?" she asked cheerfully, changing the subject.

I laid back against the padded headboard and closed my eyes. My head was killing me this morning from sleeping like shit last night. Between the guilt that was still eating away at me for how I treated Kayce and the bed being hard as a rock, I couldn't fall asleep.

"The job is fine," I said lazily, rubbing my temple with my fingers. "There have been a few delays, but I'm hoping to be home this weekend."

"What about the storm that's supposed to hit? Please tell me that you're not considering driving through that…"

"I don't think it really matters right now, ma. My truck is stuck in Lacey's cousin's garage while she tries to fix it. At this point, I'm not going anywhere."

"Do you need some money to extend your stay at the hotel?" she asked.

I hadn't even thought about that until now. Not that I needed her money—that wasn't the problem. I was more worried about Mr. Ashby being a stickler and not letting me extend my stay. Who knew how booked they were? I couldn't imagine that they were so busy that he couldn't tack on another week, if needed. I made a quick note to go down and see him before I went looking for breakfast.

"Thanks, Ma, but I've got it covered."

"Okay, if you're sure…"

"I promise," I laughed, knowing that I could be forty and she would still mother me like I was her baby boy who needed her help.

"Alright. Well, I better let you go. Buck and I are going shopping to get some stuff for Lacey and Grant's wedding. I can't believe that it's right around the corner, there's so much to do," she said light-heartedly.

"We'll get it done, don't worry. I can help you when I'm back in town, but just make sure you leave all of the manly stuff for me. I don't want to come back to pressing flowers and folding napkins into swans," I teased, remembering the last time I got roped into helping her with setting up for a party.

"That was one time, and if memory serves me correctly, you were very proud of those swans and showed all of the girls at the Country Club." She paused for a minute. "Maybe that's where I went wrong with you. I gave you the greatest weapon that those poor girls never saw coming—a sensitive guy who helped his mama."

"Hey, none of them have complained since then, have they?" I clicked my tongue against the roof of my mouth.

"Oooh, honey, you don't want to hear half of the things I've heard," she laughed.

I was just about to ask her what exactly she had been hearing when I heard Buck in the background.

"Gotta go, sweetie, I'll talk to you later. Love you!"

"Love you too. Tell Buck hi for me."

I heard him holler hello in the background before she hung up. It still felt a little odd to see my mom's relationship out in the open now given that I had known about it for so long when she thought she was still being sneaky. I was glad that she had finally found someone to spend her life with who truly made her happy. She spent the last eleven years by herself, raising us boys after my dad died. She deserved to have fun and live life for herself for once.

It was still early in the morning, not even eight o'clock yet. I took a quick shower to help wake me up before wandering down to the front desk to ask about extending my stay. If only some miracle would appear out of thin air; Junior would commit to Haven Brook University, and Kayce would have my truck fixed before the weekend. Then I wouldn't need the room longer than my original reservation. But I doubted that luck was going to find me any time soon. Well, *good* luck anyway.

I stood at the front desk, waiting patiently as I heard the toilet flush down the hallway. A few minutes later, an older woman came walking toward me. Her salt and pepper hair frizzed out around the ponytail she had it in. I smiled as she got closer, watching the way her pale blue eyes lit up when she saw me.

"You must be Wyatt Walker," she said, her voice a tad bit gruff.

"And you must be Mrs. Ashby," I replied warmly, turning my body to face her as she walked behind the desk and sat down.

"Please," she waved her hand. "Call me Trudy."

I nodded in agreement and offered her another smile, hoping it would work in my favor since I had forgotten to bring a candy bar.

"What can I do for you?" she asked, pushing her reading glasses up her nose before moving the mouse around to wake the computer screen up.

"I was hoping that I might be able to extend my stay." I rocked back on my heels. "I know it's last minute, and I apologize, but with my truck breaking down and the storm that's coming…"

"Oh dear," she chuckled and winked at me. "Let me see what I can do."

She took a few minutes looking at the computer and part of me wondered if she was really checking for availability, or if she was just messing with me.

"NO!" A man's voice boomed down the hallway. I looked up to see Fred heading our way, a scowl plastered on his face.

"Oh Fred, stop being so cranky," she scolded as he walked around the counter to stand behind her, giving me a cold glare on his way.

"The answer is no, Trudy."

"But, Fred, he's stuck—"

"No."

She turned in her seat to look at him and folded her arms over her chest. He mimicked her as he looked down at her. Neither of them budged for a solid three minutes, and I started to feel awkward and uncomfortable just standing there.

"Fred, we're giving this boy a room and extending his stay, and that's the last of that." Her tone was curt, but I could swear I heard a tad bit of playfulness behind it.

"He brought candy to bribe you with… A LOT of candy," Fred said disgustedly, looking up at me before returning his attention to his wife.

"Yeah, and WE ate the candy… remember? That night, in bed, while we were watching that movie with the really steamy love scene." She lowered her voice but not enough to shield me from the details she was giving him.

I groaned and looked away, not caring if they heard me. She burst into laughter as he whispered something in her ear, the scowl he was wearing a few minutes ago replaced by a grin that split his cheeks.

"Okay, fine," he sighed, looking up at me. "He can extend his stay."

I forced a smile even though I was still struggling to keep any images of them messing around with the bag of candy bars I brought out of my head.

"But—" Fred said sharply, pointing a finger at me as the scowl returned. "It will cost you more candy bars."

"You got it," I said quickly, slapping my hand on the top of the desk. "An extra week stay for me and twice as many candy bars coming your way!"

I heard Trudy squeal with delight as I waved and walked out, ready to be away from their weird little love fest. The snow that had fallen last night had turned into ice this morning, making it a difficult walk to find food. I hated not having my truck and being stuck in this tiny little town. If I was back home, I could call one of my brothers or Noah, and they'd come get me then we'd all be on our way again. But no. I was stuck here, pretending to be some sort of ice skater just to find decent food to silence the grumbling in my stomach.

What felt like hours later, I had finally made my way onto Main Street. I was walking toward Jumping Joe's when I saw Kayce's truck drive past me. I lowered my head, hoping that she hadn't seen me while also praying that she was going somewhere *other than* where I was going. When she turned into the parking lot and waited at the back of her truck, I knew I hadn't been lucky on either wish.

I quickened my pace, making sure not to slip on a patch of ice on my way. She was smiling as she waited for me, shivering every few minutes as the wind blew a gust of cold air in her face.

"Good morning," she said, her teeth chattering.

"Morning," I forced out. The cold had settled into my bones, and I wasn't sure that I was thawed out enough to get more words out if I wanted to.

"Let's go inside where it's warm," she suggested, turning to walk to the front door.

I followed behind her, shivering as another gust of wind whipped past us. The bell chimed as we went inside, the heater blowing full force through the small space.

"What in the world are you doing walking in this weather?" she asked, looking around to find the hostess.

"I was hungry." I half shrugged, unsure of what else to say without sounding like a dick again.

"Why didn't you call me? I would have come and picked you up."

"I didn't want to bother you," I answered, as the same girl that waited on us yesterday walked up to the front and smiled.

"Back for another one?" she asked happily, clutching the menus to her chest. "Do you need a menu, or have you had enough to know what's good?"

"I'll have the same as yesterday," I laughed. "And coffee. Lots of coffee."

She smiled and pointed to the selection of tables that we could choose from while she went to the back to put our order in. Kayce and I slid into a booth toward the back and waited as she brought a pot of coffee and two cups with her. She set them down, then rushed off to help another customer who had come in for a to-go order.

We sat quietly, drinking our coffee as we waited for the other to talk. I knew I owed her an apology, I was just struggling with how to start it since I also owed her an explanation for what had happened. Talking about my dad had never been an easy thing to do, and I didn't want Kayce to pity me the way everyone else had.

"About yesterday," I said quietly, setting my cup on the table. "I'm sorry for the way I acted. I was being a jerk, and I didn't mean to take it out on you."

"It's okay," she held her hands up. "Really, don't worry about it. You don't owe me an apology. If anything, I owe you one. I was completely out of line with asking you the way I did."

I could see the empathy on her face, the sadness in her eyes as she looked at me. I lowered my head and gently spun my coffee cup around on the table, avoiding looking at her.

"Who told you? Grant or Lacey?" I asked softly.

"Grant." She waited for the waitress to set our food on the table before she spoke again.

The smell was intoxicating, and I now knew why she was obsessed with coming here. Hell, I would probably be here every morning too if I lived here.

"He didn't tell me on his own," she said quietly, as she cut into her burrito to let some of the steam out. It was too massive to hold it to eat. "I mentioned that you weren't with me when they called and that you had been upset earlier. I told them what happened, and Grant filled me in on everything else. I'm sorry if you didn't want me to know."

I looked up at her, our eyes locking.

"It's okay that you know," I assured her. "It's not that I try to hide it, I just don't like talking about it. But, I owed you an explanation for my behavior yesterday, and I'm glad that you got it."

Things felt weird and awkward between us, and I hated it. It wasn't like we had spent that much time together since I had only been in town for a few days. However, the time we had spent together before this was easier and there was less tension than right now. It was like the opposite of what you would expect to happen—we had sex without really knowing each other, and it was fine, not much had changed, but then we have a personal conversation about real life, and it was as awkward as having your first kiss as a horny teenager.

"I went ahead and ordered the parts for your truck," she said, interrupting my thoughts as she took a bite of her burrito.

"Thank you, I appreciate you getting that done. How much do I owe you for them?"

She took another bite and shook her head.

"Don't worry about it, I've got it covered. I order from a store in the next town over, and they put everything on my account and I pay when I pick it up."

"Well just let me know how much it is. I'll give you cash, or I can go with you and pay for it."

I had no idea if she wanted the company, but I hated the idea of her paying for my stuff on her own. It was beyond me if that was something that mechanics typically did, but she wasn't *just a mechanic.* I didn't like the thought of her spending her money on me, even if I was going to pay her for it later.

"About that…" she said wearily. "I'm hoping the order will be ready before the storm hits, but if not…"

"Then I'm stuck for a while longer," I finished for her before taking a bite of my burrito.

"Sorry, I know it's not the news you were hoping for," she apologized.

"Don't worry about it, it's fine," I said, meaning it for once.

It was weird but sitting across from Kayce made everything feel right again. The tension and stress that I had been feeling all night last night and this morning seemed to evaporate the moment I saw her. Suddenly, I didn't feel as concerned about whether I was going to get back home anytime soon and that should have scared me more than it did.

THREE STRIKES, YOU'RE GONE

Thirteen
Kayce

I rubbed my hands together to stay warm while I waited for Wyatt in my truck. He insisted that I didn't need to wait for him while he was in his meeting with Junior, but I assured him that I would be here when he got out. It seemed like waiting for him was just the polite thing to do since he didn't have a ride, and it was almost a blizzard outside, but deep down, it was really because I didn't want to go to the shop by myself.

The text from the unknown number last night had left me feeling rattled and uneasy as I read it over and over while obsessively checking all of the locks in my apartment. It was a small space, so I didn't have to worry about anyone hiding where I couldn't see them, but it didn't take away from the unnerving feeling of someone watching me. I tried to convince myself that it was all in my head and that I needed to shake it off and move on. The only problem was that I couldn't ignore the pictures that were still sitting in the envelope, tucked into the bag behind me.

I smiled when I saw Wyatt rushing back to my truck, jogging carefully so that he didn't slip on the snow or ice beneath him. He opened the door and jumped in, letting a gush of cold air in with him in the process.

"How did it go?" I asked, feeling the excitement that was reflected on his face. He buckled up and turned to look at me, the dimples in his cheeks prominent as his grin stretched tightly across his face.

"I got his commitment!" he said happily.

"That's awesome!"

"Thank you, I was a little worried at first," he admitted sheepishly.

I put the truck in reverse and pulled out of the parking spot.

"Why's that?" I asked, glancing over my shoulder to check for other cars before pulling onto Main Street.

"Just nerves, I guess. He's my first recruit, and I know how talented he is. I wouldn't be surprised if other schools weren't swooping in to grab him first."

"Benefits of living in a small town," I joked. "People barely know that Easterville exists, let alone that we have an amazing ballplayer at our high school."

"Ain't that the truth," he agreed, pulling his cell phone out of his pocket as it rang. "Sorry, I gotta take this," he apologized with a smile as he pushed the button to answer it.

I turned my attention to the road, trying to give him as much privacy as I could even though we both knew that I would be able to hear everything in the small space we were stuck in. The drive back to my shop was quick, and then he would have the opportunity to take his call wherever he wanted.

"Hey, Chuck," he answered. "I got his commitment, and he's very excited to join our program."

I loved hearing how proud he was when he talked about it. The way he lit up every time he talked about baseball reminded me of what Grant said about Wyatt as a child and how much he loved it. It warmed my heart to know how passionate he was and wondered if I would ever find something that I was *that* obsessive over. Yeah, I loved being a mechanic, but it didn't feel like I had the same spark with it that he had with baseball.

"I'm not sure when I'll be back to town, but I can keep you posted. My truck is currently out of commission, and we're waiting for the parts to come in. On top of that, there's a blizzard rolling through that is going to make travel difficult," he explained as we pulled up to the shop.

I put the truck in park and climbed out, grabbing my bag of tools from the backseat. I heard Wyatt's door close but was distracted by the giant hole in the window of the shop. My heart started racing as I hoisted the bag up onto my shoulder and rushed over, staring at the shattered glass that covered the freshly fallen snow.

"Chuck, I gotta go. I'll let you know when I'll be back as soon as I have an update," he said distractedly before he hung up. He was standing next to me, looking at the mess.

"What in the hell happened?" he asked, his voice barely a whisper.

"I have no idea," I murmured as I unlocked the door and walked inside.

Laying on the floor was the rock that had been thrown through the window. I bent down to pick it up, finding another concert ticket with a note written in black marker wrapped around it. My fingers trembled as I pulled it out from under the rubber band that was holding it in place.

The note was simple, just like the others.

Payback is a bitch.

My stomach dropped, and I felt the tension sitting heavy on my shoulders again. The pictures from the envelope on Monday were enough to shake me given that very few people had ever known about what had happened that night. I couldn't remember anyone that would have taken pictures. It would've been a sick and demented thing to do. But then again, whoever was breaking into my shop to leave me threats didn't seem like they were really sane either.

"Hey, are you okay?" Wyatt asked, gently touching my arm. I looked up at him as he looked down and read the note in my hand. He jerked his head toward it, his brows knitted together. "What's that?"

"I wish I knew," I exhaled, feeling defeated by the constant mystery.

"We should call the police."

He turned to walk away, pulling his phone out of his pocket.

"No!" I cried out, rushing over to stop him. I placed my hand over his. "We can't call them yet," I tried to explain, though I couldn't tell him why. The last thing that I needed was for the police to show up and start asking questions, especially since I couldn't tell them about the photos. There was no way that I could tell anyone about them. They needed to be burned in a fire so that they would never be seen again, but the problem was that I had no idea who had taken them to begin with. Most likely, they would just keep making copies until they got whatever they wanted.

"Kayce, someone threw a *rock* through your window and shattered it. And on top of that, they left you a threatening note that said—*payback is a bitch*. I don't see why you wouldn't want to notify the police…"

I held my breath for a second and puffed up my cheeks, trying to figure out what to say. Slowly, I released it and tried to get my courage up to talk to him.

"I can't go to the police because this isn't the first note they've left me. If I tell them about the others, then I have to show them what they've left, and I can't do that."

I kept my voice as steady and even as possible even though I was shaking from the inside out.

"What do you mean this isn't the first? How many have you received?"

"A few?" I wanted to be vague enough to keep from having to tell him everything without being too vague that he still pressed to call the police.

"Since when? When did they start, Kayce?"

I avoided him for a moment, trying to stall, when I felt him step closer to me. He lifted my chin with his finger, forcing my head up as his eyes locked onto mine.

"When?"

"Monday," I said wearily. "Right before you got here."

He ran a hand through his hair, shaking his head in frustration.

"Why didn't you tell me?" he asked.

"I barely knew you," I scoffed. "You came flying into my parking lot, like a bat out of hell, so I was a little bit distracted."

It wasn't a lie, I had been distracted from the moment that I saw him. Partly because of the way he showed up but more so by his devilish good looks and the way my knees felt slightly wobbly every time that he was around.

"How many notes have you gotten? Where? I want all of the details," he pushed assertively as he stood next to me, legs slightly parted with his arms folded over the Haven Brook University logo that wrapped across his chest.

"I can't give you all of the details, so please don't push me on this."

"Why not? Someone is obviously threatening you…"

"So?" I snorted. It wasn't the most mature response, but I had nothing to say to that. Someone was threatening me, and it scared the living shit out of me, but I wasn't about to admit that to him. I had been taking care of myself long enough to not need some knight in shining armor to come rescue me from a weirdo who had a grudge against me.

"So? That's your response—so?" He arched a brow as he pinned me with a look. I could feel the intensity as I squirmed beneath it.

"Yeah, that's my answer. Whatever this is—I'll handle it." I shifted the bag on my shoulder and walked down the hallway to my office, holding the rock and concert ticket in one hand. I could hear his footsteps right behind me, which didn't surprise me given how he had yet to give up.

His phone rang again. I silently prayed that he would answer it and forget about all of this. He looked down, rolled his eyes, and slid his finger across the screen.

"Hey, Grant," he answered sharply. "No, I'm fine, just dealing with something."

He gave me a look and continued to stare at me as he talked.

"Yeah, I got his commitment, which is great news, but I'm not sure when I'll be home."

I swallowed hard, listening to his conversation, hoping that he didn't say anything about this. The last thing that I needed was for Lacey to get wind of it and freak out. Her pregnant ass would be here in a heartbeat, blizzard or not.

"We're waiting for parts to come in for the truck, and then there's another storm that's supposed to hit soon so I'm sure I'll be here for another week or so." He paused and held my gaze so I couldn't look away. "Maybe longer."

They talked for a few more minutes, the conversation fading as I heard someone up front and went to see who it was.

"Leroy!" I exclaimed as I walked down the hallway and saw him standing by the front door, looking down at the mess of glass and snow that was blowing through.

"My goodness, what happened here? Did the storm do this?" he asked, handing me the box that he was holding as he looked back at the floor.

"I don't know, I just got in a few minutes ago, but it looks like maybe that old window was no match for this blizzard," I joked, trying to force a smile as I situated the box against my side.

"You didn't have to come drop these off," I said softly. "I would have gladly come to pick them up from you, Leroy. That storm is bad. You shouldn't be driving in it."

"Nah, don't worry about it," he replied, still focused on the broken window. "My son was coming into town anyway, so I just hitched a ride with him. You know, safety in numbers or something like that… that's what my Judy used to say."

I smiled warmly, remembering his sweet wife from the handful of times she had been at the shop when I went to pick things up. She had recently passed and the sadness in my eyes when he talked about her never seemed to fade.

"Did you come with Greg?" I asked, turning to set the box down on the empty chairs by the front desk.

"Yeah, he has that big truck that can handle anything," he laughed, nodding to the vehicle outside. "Kind of like your beast out there."

I waved to Greg, not sure if he could see me or not. Wyatt walked down the hallway, not noticing that someone was there. He stopped short and looked between us, before turning to go back to the office.

"Wyatt," I called, getting his attention. "This is Leroy, and he was kind enough to brave this blizzard to drop off the parts for your truck."

He beamed as he walked our way and extended his hand to Leroy.

"Thank you, sir, that was very nice of you," he said as they shook. "But you didn't need to come out in this storm to get them to us."

"Like I was telling Kayce, I caught a ride with my son, so it was no skin off my back."

We stood there in silence for a few seconds before he turned back to the window.

"Do you want me to help you fix this?" he asked with a shudder. The building was freezing cold, despite the heater blowing at full force. The hole in the window was definitely a problem, just one that I wasn't in the mood to deal with right now. But then again, neither was the massive gas bill that I was going to get from running it all day at the level I needed to keep us somewhat comfortable.

"That's okay but thank you. I'll get it taken care of soon," I assured him, feeling Wyatt's eyes on me. "Do you want to send me a bill for the parts since I didn't go down there to pick them up?" I asked, hoping to change the subject.

"Nah, we'll settle it the next time you come in."

"I'm happy to offer you some cash while you're here, at least for your time bringing it down here," Wyatt offered, glancing at me for guidance.

"I'm good, really," he laughed. "But unless you need help with that window, I should get going. Greg gets grumpy when he has to wait too long." He rolled his eyes and pointed over his shoulder to where the truck was parked.

"We've got the window, thank you." I walked over and hugged him before he made his way outside in the frigid cold.

I felt the wind whip past me, blowing a cloud of snow in my face as I pulled the door closed and looked at the window.

"Do you have any wood that I could use, and I'll get the window taken care of?" Wyatt asked, reading my mind.

"I think I have some scraps in the garage," I said, leading the way.

I flicked on the light, getting a flashback of the fear that I had last night as I made my way through the dark, not knowing what would be waiting for me. I pushed the thoughts aside and walked to the back of the shop where I kept the random crates and pieces of wood that I used when I needed to create a makeshift workstation.

There were a few decent-sized pieces that would likely cover the majority of the window but not the whole thing. We would have to bust out the rest of the glass that was left in the frame because it was too splintered to try to work around. That meant that I would have to get creative to fill the spots that the wood didn't cover.

I handed Wyatt the pieces that I had and kept looking for anything else that I could use while he took them up front and started cleaning the floor. I never knew that watching a man sweep the floor could be so sexy until I found myself practically drooling as I stared.

"Did you find more wood or were you too busy watching me?" he called over his shoulder with a chuckle.

Shit! I had been caught and there was no way to deny it.

"I'm still looking," I called back stupidly.

"I hate to break it to you, but I don't think the *wood* that I have will help your window at all."

His voice was louder this time as he made sure there was no way that I had missed what he said. I felt my body warm up at the thought of what he was saying, getting distracted all over again.

"It would be a lucky window if so…" I muttered under my breath as I pushed stuff to the side and found a few more scrap pieces of wood.

I carried them over to where Wyatt was finishing up sweeping and added them to the pile.

"Hopefully that will be enough," I said with my hands on my hips.

"Yeah, but I don't know that it will be enough to withstand the storm. Is there a place in town that you can call for a replacement?"

"No one that will come out today," I sighed.

"Well then, we'll have to make do with what we have and pray that my erection isn't needed," he laughed, gently bumping my shoulder as he walked around me to get a piece of wood.

I bit down on my tongue to keep from telling him that it wasn't the window that was suddenly in need… It was me.

Fourteen
Wyatt

I took a step back and looked at my work. It wasn't half bad given that all that I had to work with were scraps of wood that weren't the right size to cover the full window. I did the best that I could with what I had, but I still hated the idea that she wasn't going to be able to get anyone out here to replace it for her before the worst part of the storm hit.

I grabbed the tools that I had used and took them back to Kayce's desk, smiling when I passed by the garage and saw her bouncing her head to the sound of Pantera floating out of the room. Her mood seemed to have shifted some from earlier, and it was nice to see her enjoying herself. I was still frustrated that she wouldn't tell me what was going on or who the note was from, but I didn't know her well enough to push her. I could be a jerk and tell Grant, knowing that he would tell Lacey and she would find out for me, however, that was a one-way ticket to her hating me and shutting down even further.

I leaned against the doorframe and watched her for a few minutes before she looked up and noticed me.

"You scared the shit out of me," she gasped, laughing embarrassedly.

"Sorry, I didn't mean to. I just finished up with the window and thought I'd come check to see how you were doing."

"So far, so good," she said, looking at the truck. "But then again, I haven't gotten to the hard part yet."

"I see," I laughed, walking over to where she was standing. "Anything that I can help with?"

"Not that I can think of, but you can keep me company while I work if you want to."

I pulled out the rolling stool that was pushed under the table and sat on it, trying to stay out of her way as she climbed onto the creeper and slid under the truck. As much as I should have looked away, I couldn't. The sight of her on her back, legs slightly parted as she moved around was sending every inappropriate thought through my head quicker than a four-seam fastball.

"Can you hand me the wrench on the table?" she asked, reaching her hand out toward me.

I looked around, not seeing a wrench anywhere on the table. I moved a few other things around and still couldn't find one.

"I don't see one," I replied. "Is there somewhere else it could be?"

"It's probably in my bag," she sighed as she started to push herself out.

"I can look if you want me to," I offered.

"Thanks, it should be right next to the table, on the floor."

I looked down beside me and saw the bag that she was talking about, the same one that I was convinced held the dead body of that musician she had been dating. I pulled it over to me, knocking it over in the process. On the top of the bag was an envelope with Kayce's name on it. I set it down on the table, then went back to looking for the wrench. Finally finding one, I turned to ask her if it was the right one and bumped the envelope, knocking it to the floor.

A handful of pictures fell out of it and scattered across the floor. I bent down and picked them up so I could put them back in the envelope for her when one caught my eye. It was a picture of Kayce in the back of a limousine with her arm wrapped around the shoulders of another girl who looked like she was so strung out that she had passed out. Kayce's hair was bright pink and matched the tube top that she was wearing with the mini skirt that barely covered her. Her tongue was out as she posed for the camera.

No one else was in the picture other than her and some drunk chick. I gathered the rest of the pictures and fought the urge to look through them when I heard Kayce's feet shuffle as she moved around.

"Did you find it?" she asked.

"Yeah, sorry," I mumbled as I set the pictures back in the envelope and handed her the wrench.

She worked in silence for a few minutes while I sat at the table, staring at the photo of her with that girl. Something about the photo just didn't sit right with me and gave me the creeps. Maybe it was the visible track marks on that girl's arm or the way her mouth slightly hung open, just like my dad's looked after he was… dead.

I glanced over my shoulder, making sure Kayce was still busy under the truck before I turned around and picked up the pile of pictures. It was a total invasion of her privacy, but I couldn't stop myself. I moved the picture to the back of the others and stared at the next one. My stomach clenched when my fear was confirmed—she was dead and Kayce was the one holding the baseball bat that was covered in blood as the girl's body slumped down the wall beside her.

THREE STRIKES, YOU'RE GONE

Fifteen
Kayce

After calling his name from under the truck twice, I figured he had left since he didn't answer me. It wasn't until I scooted out from under the truck and found him sitting at the table, staring at something with such an intensity that he was oblivious to the world around him. I wiped my hands on the rag and tucked it back into my pocket before walking over to see what he was so focused on.

I walked up behind him, gasping when I saw the photos spread out on the table in front of him. His forehead wrinkled as the harsh expressions set in. I knew what he must be thinking when he saw them. It was the reason why I couldn't go to the police. All they needed was one look at the pictures, and they wouldn't believe a word I said after that.

"What the hell are you doing?" I snapped, stepping around him and snatching the photos from him. I clutched them to my chest as if that would somehow protect me from the harsh judgment in his eyes when he looked up at me.

"I'm sorry," he started, running a hand down his face as if that would erase what he had just seen. "I wasn't trying to invade your privacy."

"But you did anyway," I scoffed.

"You're right, I did. And again, I'm sorry for that. But, Kayce…"

"Don't." I held up my hand to stop him. It was a mistake to cross the line with him the other night when we had sex. I knew better. I should have left things as casual as possible. Now things were complicated with him sharing my deep, dark secret. The one that no one was ever supposed to find out about. Including Lacey.

"You know that I can't just look the other way and pretend like I didn't see those," he said softly, pushing the stool away from the table as he stood up. "And I'm not going to forget about what happened with the window either."

I swallowed hard, clutching the pictures tighter against my body as I wished this would all just go away.

"Please, Kayce, just tell me what's going on and let me help you."

His face was soft, the hardened features from a few minutes ago vanished.

"I can't," I stuttered, my voice cracking under the pressure. I wanted to tell him, to confide in someone and admit what I had done, to allow myself a moment of weakness to succumb to the grief that I had been trying to swallow down since last summer. Just one quick break, then I could lock it all up again and live with the consequences of the stupid decision that I had made one night after one too many shots of tequila.

"Kayce," he whispered my name as he stood in front of me and put his hands out for me to take. "You can trust me. Whatever this is—I will help you. Just please, let me in. Talk to me…"

A tear slid down my cheek, escaping the prison it had been confined to for the last six months. He reached out and grabbed me, pulling me into him. The warmth of his body as his arms wrapped around me felt heavenly.

"It's not what it looks like," I said against his chest.

"Okay," he said reassuringly, rubbing my back softly. "Do you want to go talk about it in your office? That way you have some privacy in case someone comes in?"

"Trust me, no one comes in unless they're sneaking around to leave me these stupid notes," I mumbled as I pulled away and looked up at him. Surprise flashed across his face before it was replaced with anger.

"I want the details, Kayce. All of them."

He pulled me by the hand and led me out of the garage and down the hall to my office. Once we were inside, he closed the door and stood against it, as if making sure that I wasn't going to try to make a run for it.

"I don't know where to start," I admitted as I sat down at my desk.

"Let's start with the pictures," he offered, nodding to where I had set them down beside my computer.

"Like I said, it's not what it looks like. I didn't kill her."

I pulled my shoulders back and tried to take a slow, deep breath to calm my nerves.

"Brent and I had been broken up for a while and I hadn't talked to him for months. Last summer he reached out to me because they were going to be passing through Colorado, and he wanted to get together. I agreed to meet him in Denver and ended up going to their concert. He always gives me a backstage pass, so I was hanging out, waiting for them to finish their set when I met this girl—the one in the pictures— who said she was dating Dray, their drummer. We talked for a bit, and she seemed like a nice girl."

I wiped a stray tear away from my face as I thought back to that night. The light that had been in her eyes when she talked, how full of life she was.

"We went to an after-party with the band and everyone was only drinking, except Dray and Stella. They were going a little harder than everyone else, and by the time we got to the party, they were both pretty high. The picture of her and me in the limo was taken before we got to the party. After that, everything just got out of hand. The night was a blur, but long story short—Dray has a short temper, and it's even worse when he's on drugs. They got into a fight, and he started hitting her. Brent didn't want the bad publicity, so he packed the band up, and we all left.

"We were driving on some deserted back road, in the middle of nowhere, when Dray just lost his shit and started hitting her again. Brent had enough. He told the driver to pull over, and he kicked Dray out of the limo. Well, Stella being high and in *love,* decided to go with him. The second they were out of the car, he started attacking her again. So, Brent got out, and the other guys tried to help him pull Dray off of her, but nothing worked."

A shiver ran through me as the memories came back. No matter how hard I had tried to forget, nothing would ever erase this night or the scars it left behind. I swallowed hard and forced the emotions back down to where they belonged.

"I saw a baseball bat on the floor when I had gotten in earlier, so I grabbed it and tried to help. I swung it a few times, aiming for Dray's head. That's whose blood was on the bat in the picture. It was enough to knock him out but not kill him," I paused and forced out the breath that I had been holding. "But it wasn't enough to save Stella. He had beaten her to death."

"Fucking asshole," Wyatt grunted from his position in front of the door. His arms were still folded across his chest.

"We were in the middle of nowhere with a dead girl and a passed-out drummer who was high on cocaine. It wasn't like we could just call the police. Brent had just booked their first international tour and if this went public, they would be done. His career would be over. So, they drug her body into the woods, out behind an abandoned barn. They dug a hole as deep as they could without any shovels, and made me bury her."

I remembered the anxiety I had felt that night, the hole in my stomach that filled with acid as I gently rolled her body into the shallow grave and used my hands to push the dirt around to make sure it covered her.

"They made you?" he asked, anger laced in his tone as his eyebrows nearly shot off his head.

"Brent said that the only way to guarantee that none of us ever talked about what happened, was if we all had something at stake. If one of us talked, it would take everyone down. I would be just as guilty for hiding a dead body and not reporting it."

"So, how did someone get these pictures? And why are they sending them to you?"

"I wish I knew," I sighed heavily. "I really do. I have no idea. The only people that were there that night were the band members, myself, and their manager—"

The words stopped abruptly when I finally put it together.

"Oh my God," I whispered, bringing my hand to my mouth. "He didn't get out of the car that night, he stayed inside. None of us had even thought about it because he had just as much to lose if anyone got wind of what happened. Without the band and their international tour, he wouldn't have a paycheck. So, if anything, he had even more to risk than the rest of them. Jolted was his only client and that meant a lot was at stake for him."

"Which would mean that he took pictures of what happened—in case he needed them later."

"I guess so, but that meant that he would have had to have gotten out of the car and found us because we were far from where the car was pulled over and it was pitch black out. And why now? Why would he be sending them to me with these vague notes? I had nothing to do with him—we barely knew each other. What could he gain from harassing me? " I asked, knowing that Wyatt wouldn't know any better than I would.

"Maybe I should call Brent and see if he's had anything strange happen to him?" I pondered out loud.

"I wouldn't," Wyatt said, pushing away from the door. "Until you know for sure that it was their manager, I wouldn't talk about it. You never know who you can trust in these types of situations. Best to keep this one quiet for now." Something in his tone changed that sent a shiver through me.

"That's a good point," I said cautiously, as I watched Wyatt pull out his phone and press it to his ear. He was the one convincing me that I could trust him, yet now he was saying that I should be careful of who I trusted. There was this nagging feeling in my gut that told me that maybe I should be worried about what he said.

"Hey, I need a favor," he said into the phone as he reached down and locked the office door behind him, keeping his eyes on me.

THREE STRIKES, YOU'RE GONE

Sixteen
Wyatt

I watched the reflections in the mirror above Kayce's head while I waited for Buck to grab a pen and piece of paper. She looked guarded as she watched me, her eyes following my every move as I reached down and locked the door.

"Get under your desk," I whispered, covering the phone with my hand. "Now."

I could hear footsteps approaching and knew whoever it was, they were headed our way. I pushed myself against the wall, trying to make sure I could see them without risking them seeing me through the blinds of her small window. Unless they were smart enough to look for someone in the reflection of the mirror, like I had, I should be safe.

She looked at me like I was crazy, then did as she was told and crawled under her desk a few seconds before there was a loud thud on the door. I whispered to Buck, telling him to hold on, while I waited to see what they were going to do.

I could hear muffled voices from the other side but couldn't make out what they were saying. My fist clenched at my side, ready for them to kick in the door and come for Kayce. Instead, a piece of paper was slipped under the door, and the voices faded as they walked down the hallway and left. Or at least I hoped they had left, there was no way to make sure without walking out there to check.

I waited a few minutes to make sure the coast was clear before I bent down and picked up the piece of paper.

"It's okay, you can come out now," I said to Kayce, rolling my eyes as I stared at the piece of paper in my hands.

She climbed out from under the desk and looked around, panic evident on her face as she tried to locate the threat. I extended the paper to her and pulled my lips into a thin line as she took it, her brows furrowing when she read what it was.

"You made me hide from Johnnie? The loyal customer who came in to pay on his account?" She held the paper out in front of her with her other hand planted firmly on her hip.

"I'm sorry, I didn't know. I just assumed because you said that no one ever *just shows up*, that maybe it might be the person leaving you notes," I explained quietly as I heard Buck come back on the line.

"Alright, what do you need?" he asked kindly.

"I hate to ask for this kind of a favor, but can you look into someone for me?"

Kayce raised a brow and glared at me. It seemed that I had some sort of knack for pissing her off, and I was getting better at it by the minute.

"What's the manager's name?" I asked her, praying that she would tell me.

"Mike Sullivan," she replied through gritted teeth.

I turned away from her, mainly to escape the look she was giving me, and finished my call with Buck. He promised to get back to me within a few hours with whatever information he was able to get. I knew that I should have talked to her about it before I asked him, but I was worried that she would refuse to let me help her. I trusted Buck and knew that he would help however he could without pushing me for details on why I needed it.

I slid my phone back into my pocket and unlocked the door. It seemed silly to be so paranoid but after what she had told me, I was feeling on edge, and I could see that she was too. I turned the knob and opened the door, blindsided by the baseball bat that came flying at my head before I hit the ground and everything faded to black.

Seventeen
Kayce

"You don't have to do this," I begged as Mike grabbed hold of my hair and dragged me down the hallway. I looked down at Wyatt's body that was slump on the floor, a small puddle of blood forming under his head.

"Shut up!" he yelled, his voice bellowing through the narrow corridor as his grip on me tightened. I glanced outside, thankful that it was still light outside, and prayed that someone—anyone, might be around to see what was happening. A gust of wind pushed a blanket of snow up against the door, the sound whooshing in through the small gaps between the wood, confirming that no one in their right mind would be out in this.

We had plenty of snowstorms living in Colorado, but I couldn't remember ever seeing one this bad in all of my life. The locals had been busy prepping after the news anchors asked everyone to find shelter and to avoid going out if they didn't have to. I started to panic, knowing that unless Wyatt regained consciousness soon, I was on my own against Mike.

I hadn't seen him since that night last summer, but a lot had changed. He wasn't the tall, skinny guy that I had remembered. Now, he was in shape and muscular, someone who had taken control of his fitness and appeared to be going to the gym regularly. Being in his early thirties without a wife or children probably meant that he had the spare time to go when the band wasn't on tour—which if memory served me right, they had just finished one.

I looked around for anything that I could use as a weapon as he dragged me to the front door. The wind was howling and the wood on the windows rattled. If I had enough time, I could pry off a piece of wood and use that, but I wasn't that quick, and apparently, Wyatt had done a damn good job of making sure each piece was well secured.

He fidgeted with the lock on the door for a few minutes, grumbling when it wouldn't turn to open. I was thankful that the damn thing was acting up again when he let go of my hair for a second to use both hands to get it to open. Knowing that this was the only chance that I would have, I carefully planned my next step. The lock clicked as he finally got it to turn and the door flew open with the wind. I ducked down and grabbed the brick that I use to hold the door open in the summer. I pulled my arm back and slammed it against the side of his face, cringing at the sound it made before dropping it and running outside. I didn't have a second to spare to watch his reaction as his head whipped to the side.

I darted out the door and into the thick snow that made it impossible to see more than a few inches in front of you. I heard him yell out a cuss word followed by another one as I ran as fast as I could, slipping on the ice as I went in the direction of the forest that sat behind the shop. My heart was about to beat out of my chest as I kept running, thankful that I knew the area better than he did. I felt terrible for leaving Wyatt behind, but there was no other choice. I was what he was there for, and I knew that he would stop at nothing until he got what he wanted.

Eighteen
Wyatt

My head was pounding as I sat up and leaned against the wall, trying to remember what had happened. I was desperate to get up and find Kayce, but every time I tried to pull myself up off of the floor, I felt lightheaded and had to sit back down. I looked around the office for any sign of her and felt my stomach knot when I knew that she wasn't there. Whoever had been there had found her the second they knocked me out with the bat. There was no way that they didn't.

I patted my pocket, trying to find my phone. My fingers felt around, desperate to locate it so I could call for help.

"Looking for something?" A man asked, walking down the hall, holding my cell phone in his hand.

I had no idea what Mike looked like, but my guess was that this was him. I had pictured the typical older guy with a beer belly and balding head, not a tall guy with muscles for days and a tattoo of a skull on his hand.

He squatted down in front of me and held it out. When I refused to take it, he shook his head and chuckled as if it somehow amused him.

"You know, when I came here to find Kayce, I didn't expect to find you," he admitted, standing up.

I wanted desperately to stand up and show him that I wasn't intimidated by him, but my body refused.

"Not that I need to know who you are—it doesn't matter at this point," he gave a half shrug. "But, I am curious to know who Lieutenant Dickson is and what information he has on me."

His brown eyes darkened as his hand gripped my phone tighter. I bit the inside of my cheek in frustration, hating that I had reached out to Buck in the first place. And honestly, I was surprised that he had tried to get back to me so quickly. It had barely been a few minutes since I had called him. Hadn't it? I didn't know how much time had passed from when I had called him to when I woke up from getting clobbered in the head with a baseball bat. My mind was still focused on Kayce and whether she was okay. If Mike was here, talking to me, where was she?

"I don't know who that is," I lied, raising my eyebrow to match the look he was giving me. He scoffed and shook his head.

"I was able to see the text message even though your phone was locked," he continued to explain. "You might want to change that setting in your phone. You never know who might read your messages without you knowing."

"Where's Kayce?" I asked, forcing the words out as my body fought the urge to sleep. I had been hit by a bat more times in my life than I cared to admit, but I had never felt this out of it afterward. After having several surgeries from the stabbing incident, doctors had warned me that I needed to be careful if I was still considering a career in baseball. One hit to my head of any kind and it could have a devastating outcome.

"Well, that's where you come in," he replied through clenched teeth. "It seems she's decided to play a game of hide and seek, and I'm going to use you as bait for her to come find us."

"She won't do it," I laughed, deliriously hoping that she would go find help and not try to be some sort of hero. "She barely knows me— there's nothing for her to come back for. If she left, then it's for good."

"See, that's where you're wrong." He tsked his tongue on the roof of his mouth. "I've known Kayce long enough to know that there are certain things that she's willing to fight for. And the way that she looked at you when I dragged her out of the room—that told me everything that I needed to know. Women in love do stupid shit all the time."

My head lifted as I looked him over, waiting for him to tell me that he was just bluffing to see if it would get a rise out of me. When his features locked in, I knew that he was telling the truth and that could only mean one thing—Kayce was in even more danger than she knew. We both were.

Nineteen
Kayce

I shivered in the cold, listening for any signs of footsteps approaching as I tried to make sure that I didn't get too far from the area that I knew. The forest was thick behind me, and it would be easy to get lost in if I made one wrong move. The blinding snow that was decreasing my visibility by the second. Soon, I would be in over my head, succumbing to the elements around me.

It was stupid to run off into the woods during the middle of a fucking blizzard without a jacket or a cell phone, but it wasn't like I had much of a choice. If I didn't run, then I would likely be dead by now anyway. I had no idea what Mike wanted, but I could tell from the look in his eyes that I wasn't going to live to find out either.

In an act of desperation, I patted my pockets one more time, praying that somehow the keys to my truck would magically appear. If I could get to my truck, I could go find help. Not that anyone in town would be able to do much, or even believe me, but now Wyatt's life was at risk. I needed to do something to save him.

I grumbled in frustration when my pockets came up empty. I was stuck in the woods, during the worst snowstorm that we have had in over fifty years, and someone was trying to kill me. Things couldn't possibly get any worse unless some wild animal suddenly decided to come hunt me for dinner. At this point, it would have been a welcoming invite.

I found a spot in front of a tree that sat off to the side of my shop and leaned against it. It was far enough away from the building that no one would easily spot me but close enough that I would be able to hear if someone left—if the wind wasn't whipping past me. I had thought about running out to Main Street and trying to find someone to come help, but I knew that would be a waste of time and energy. Most of the shops had already closed and everyone was hunkered down at home, waiting out the storm.

That is, everyone except Mike who was still in the shop doing God knows what to Wyatt. I pinched my eyes closed and said a quick prayer that he would be alright. He was strong—there was no doubt about that, but the impact to his head from the bat was enough to knock anyone out, including him. I tried to shake away the image of his body lying limp on the floor as Mike dragged me past it, completely helpless.

My body temperature was dropping as the cold dug its sharp claws into me, and I knew that I wouldn't be able to stay out here much longer without risking severe hypothermia or worse—death. If I could somehow sneak back into my shop, I could get out of the cold and save Wyatt. I pushed away from the tree and took a few steps, balancing myself with each one to keep from falling. The frigid cold had already turned everything to ice beneath me, making each move more treacherous.

I slowly took a few more steps, inching my way closer to the shop. The snow had started to slow down, allowing a small amount of visibility around me. I felt relieved that I hadn't gotten turned around in the woods. Just a few more feet, I would be on the side of the building and could sneak around to the back where the garage was. There was a spare key that I kept back there, just in case I needed it.

As I was about to take another step, I heard a man's voice and stopped. I froze in my tracks, straining to hear it through the wind that was muffling it.

"What the fuck do you mean *you lost her?*"

"I mean she fucking clocked me in the face with a brick and took off running," Mike said, his voice closer and clearer than the other one.

"And you didn't think to run after her?"

"In this weather? Are you fucking kidding me?" Mike scoffed. "Besides, there was another situation that I had to deal with."

I leaned closer, desperate to hear the other person without risking that they would see me. I needed to know who he was talking to, who was with him.

"This just gets better by the second," the other voice said sarcastically. "What's the other problem?"

"She wasn't alone. And whoever this guy is—he's been talking to a cop."

"Well then, I guess we better go shut him up before he says anything more than he already has."

"What about Kayce?" Mike asked.

"She'll either die in the woods or she'll pop up when she's ready to try to save the day. Either way, she'll be dead soon enough."

I peeked my head slightly around the tree that I was hiding behind and focused on the parking lot as I watched Mike walk back to the shop with the other guy. He looked familiar, but I couldn't figure out why. As they got to the door, Mike walked in first while the other guy held it open. When he turned his head to scan the area, I noticed the scar on his face and felt my stomach drop when I realized who it was.

THREE STRIKES, YOU'RE GONE

<u>Twenty</u>
Wyatt

I sat tied to Kayce's office chair, pulling at the knots in the rope that held me in place. Mike had gone outside to talk to someone. I knew that I didn't have long to try to get out of this mess, but I still had to try. The rope somehow felt looser than it had a few minutes ago. Either that or my hands were getting too numb to actually feel any movement around them. I heard voices coming down the hallway and stopped moving.

Mike walked into the office first and sat down on the chair across from me, resting his ankle on his other knee. When the other person walked in, I felt a hysterical laugh bubble out of me, unable to believe the irony of the situation. The amusement on Mateo's face matched mine as if neither of us could believe this was happening.

"Wyatt fucking Walker," he snorted and stood in the doorway, arms folded over his chest. "I didn't think I would get the opportunity to beat your ass again so soon."

Mike looked between us in confusion.

"You two know each other?" he asked.

"Oh yeah, Wyatt and I go *way* back."

I felt his icy stare on mine and knew that he was remembering the bar fight from last year.

"How's Mandy?" I asked with a cocky grin. I might have been tied to the chair with no way to defend myself, but that didn't stop me. "Is she still wearing those tight little miniskirts?"

His jaw clenched as he pushed off from the doorway.

"Looks like you don't know when the fuck to shut up and walk away," Mateo said.

"Just here getting my truck fixed so I can get back on the road," I said nonchalantly. It wasn't a total lie, but they both saw right through it.

"Is that so?" Mateo asked, stepping closer to me. "And you just happened to get stuck in *my* town?"

"I was here for work."

"And what work is that?" Mike asked from the chair he was still sitting in.

"None of your damn business," I said, keeping my eyes locked onto Mateo's. I discreetly tried to loosen the ropes behind me as Mateo took another step forward.

"Everything that happens in this town is *my* business," Mateo snarled as he stood in front of me. "Maybe next time you'll think twice before you come to Easterville. We're not too fond of *outsiders*."

I watched as Mateo's eyes landed on the duffle bag on the floor behind Kayce's desk. The Colorado Cougars logo was displayed front and center with my name underneath it. I hated that I wasn't an active player anymore, yet I still carried the bag with me proudly as if I was part of the team.

"Three strikes, you're gone, motherfucker," he taunted as he looked at me.

I held my breath as I watched his fist fly toward my face, clocking me straight in the temple.

Twenty One
Kayce

I waited a few minutes to see if I could hear anything inside before I turned the key and unlocked the back door that went to the garage. It was risky to be in the open with nowhere to hide, but my only other option was to die in the cold. My feet were already numb and my socks were soaked from the snow that I had to walk through to get back here. The back of the shop was nothing but forest and had a good four feet of snow that had been piled up from the wind.

I slowly closed the door, keeping it from slamming shut as I heard the latch click. Quickly, I scanned the room to make sure no one else was around, before I rushed over to the table and squatted down behind it. Thankfully, it gave me enough space to hide. My bag full of tools on the floor allowed me easy access to a weapon if I needed it. Granted, I had no idea what kind of weapons Mike and Mateo had on them, but I was sure they were packing something stronger than a wrench.

The muffled sound of voices floated in under the door, which meant they were either in my office or in the hallway since I couldn't see them. I worked quickly to pull a couple of things out of the bag and tucked them into my pockets. If I could get to my office, I could grab my gun and get Wyatt away from them. He wasn't the one that they were after and I knew that they would get rid of him the same way that they did Stella—as if he didn't matter. But, he did, and I would go to my grave making sure that everyone knew that.

I heard a vibrating noise and looked up. Carefully, I reached up from under the table and felt around until I found my cell phone. I felt a sudden rush of relief wash over me as I grabbed it and pulled it under the table. I could call for help, but honestly, who would I call? Our local police department was as tiny as my pinky and didn't have the manpower to stop Mike or Mateo. I could call Lacey and have her get help, but that would mean that she would send Grant in this deadly snowstorm, and I couldn't risk having something bad happen to him, not with a family of his own and twin babies on the way.

I swiped my finger across the screen to find a text message from an unknown number again.

Unknown: So, you like to play games? How about we'll hide your boyfriend, and you can see if you can find him. We'll even leave clues along the way to help you.

My fingers trembled as I held the phone, watching the dots bounce as another message was being typed.

Unknown: Just look for the random body parts and trail of blood.

I heard footsteps heading down the hallway and held my breath, as I froze beneath the table. A few seconds later, the front door opened and then slammed shut. I couldn't tell if someone had really left or if they were just doing it to try to freak me out. It was unlikely that they knew that I was in the garage, but not impossible. The door wasn't open long enough for all three of them to leave, which made me wonder where they were and if they had split up.

I knew that I had to make a decision quickly. I couldn't hide under the table forever—sooner or later they were going to find me. For once, being tiny and petite would come in handy, as I brainstormed a plan to hide in the shadows and make my way back to my office. I had to be fast, which meant that there was no time to second guess myself or be afraid. It was now or never.

I quickly moved out from under the table and was about to run when I looked in front of me and stopped in my tracks.

"Found you," he growled.

Twenty Two
Wyatt

I was pretty sure that the doctors would be banging their heads against the wall if they knew that I'd had two severe hits to my head in one day. My eyes fluttered open, and I looked around, unsure of where I was. It wasn't Kayce's office—that was for sure. Everything was dark and somewhat blurry as I blinked my eyes and tried to get them to focus.

My hands were still bound together with rope, but this time, instead of being tied to a chair, I was sitting in the back of a van. I felt my body jerk to the side as it went over a bump and wondered where they were going and why the hell they were driving so reckless in this weather. Not that they gave a rat's ass about whether I lived or died, but I figured that they at least wanted something from Kayce or all of this would be for nothing.

There were no windows and the only light that came in was from under the cracks of the doors at the back of the van. My back was leaning against something solid, but I couldn't tell what. Whatever it was, they had apparently braced me against it, while I was unconscious. I looked around, desperately trying to find anything that I could use as a weapon.

Suddenly, the van came to an abrupt stop, and I felt myself slide forward. I tried to pull my hands free from the rope, knowing it was my last chance. The doors opened and a gust of snow blew in, whipping me in the face. I held my breath for a second until the next gust passed before catching my breath. Mike was standing at the door, looking off to the side as he nodded and turned to look behind him. It seemed like he was looking for someone which meant that I needed to act fast.

I scooted forward as quickly as I could without him noticing. When he turned to face me, I leaned back and brought my legs up, kicking him square in the chest with everything I had. His body immediately

107

tumbled backward as he fell into the snow, struggling to catch his breath.

I slid the rest of the way out of the van and jumped down, thankful that my hands were tied in front of me, instead of behind my back. It was stupid on their part, but they didn't seem like the smartest kidnappers in the world. My guess was that this wasn't something that they did often. I looked around, hoping to find somewhere to go for help and felt my stomach sink when I realized where he had taken me.

We were in the middle of nowhere and off to the side of the road was the abandoned shed from the pictures. I could hear Mike groaning and cussing as he fought to get up and out of the snow. The force of the kick to his chest seemed to have done the amount of damage that I had hoped it would.

I could run, but there was nowhere to go and no one to ask for help. That left only one option, and it was the one thing that I really didn't want to do…

<u>Twenty Three</u>
Kayce

His fingers wrapped tightly around my throat, cutting off my air supply as my feet dangled in the air like some limp rag doll. I watched his eyes darken as he enjoyed seeing me squirm, my fingers digging into his skin as I struggled to breathe.

"You've always been such a feisty little thing, haven't you?" he teased, tilting his head to the side to look at me.

I could feel myself getting lightheaded. It wouldn't be too much longer before I passed out. Maybe that would be best? At least I wouldn't feel anything and wouldn't have to know what had happened.

He finally let me go to fall onto the concrete floor of the garage, as if somehow, I bored him and he had lost interest in the game.

I gasped loudly, pulling in as much air as I could, my lungs burning with each breath. I scooted away from him quickly, trying to put distance between us.

"You know, things didn't have to be like this," he said lazily as he slowly started stalking over to me. "We could have done this the easy way—but no, you wanted to make it harder than it needed to be."

I looked around, still trying to catch my breath. I could read the look on his face and knew that he was enjoying this. He turned to the side when something upfront caught his attention for a split second, most likely the wind rattling against the boards in the window. The fluorescent lights overhead caught the scar on the side of his face, reminding me of who I was and what I was capable of. I had protected myself from him before, and I would do it again.

When he turned back to face me, I locked eyes with him and pulled my shoulders back. I didn't make an effort to get up from the floor which seemed to amuse him as he chuckled and took another step closer. I crawled backward, slowly and deliberately, to where I needed him to follow me.

Off in the corner of the garage, in the other bay was the project car that I had been working on for over a year now. It was completely stripped and lifted onto a jack while I fussed around with it when I had time. When I took it off the hands of its owner, it was the same as it was now: tireless and needing more work than money could buy. Right now, it was the biggest weapon that I had.

I relied on my memory to guide me as I kept crawling backward like a crab trying to escape a starving seagull. One quick glance over my shoulder confirmed that I was right where I wanted to be. I turned back and smiled at him, before I flipped over and dashed under the car. I knew that it was easy enough for me to maneuver underneath it since I was already familiar with being down here—and my petite size was an added bonus compared to his husky build.

He laughed maniacally, the sound vibrating off of the walls of the garage, coating the room in its evil.

"That's your grand plan?" he snorted as he bent down to look at me. "You're going to hide under this piece of shit?"

I pulled my lips into a thin line and waited. I could tell that I was already getting under his skin, and if I pushed him enough, he would come after me.

"What? I thought you liked a challenge?" I replied snarkily, making sure that I was moving far enough to the back of the car while also keeping an eye on where he was at all times. Timing and position were everything right now- one small miscalculation and this could end badly for me.

"Since when has anything with *you* been a challenge? Your legs are open more often than the twenty-four-hour convenience store on Main Street."

I bit the inside of my cheek, trying to remember that the goal was to lure him in, not hit him with my best comebacks. I let the anger that was boiling inside of me fuel me for what I was about to do. There was no time to rethink this or second guess myself. If I wanted to live, I *had* to do this.

"Well then, what are you so afraid of? A teeny, tiny, little girl?" I mocked, tilting my head to the side as I challenged him.

"You asked for it," he growled as he climbed down onto the floor and started crawling toward me.

I rushed to the back as quickly as I could and got out from under the car in time to kick the jack out. I stepped back and gasped when I saw the car crash to the ground. The sound of metal hitting the concrete boomed through the garage, echoing off the walls. Bright red blood started spilling out in every direction as I took a step back and covered my mouth with my hand.

I fought the urge to scream and freak out; there wasn't time for that. I needed to find out where Mike and Wyatt were before it was too late.

It looked like a scene from some terrible, low-budget horror film. His legs were sprawled out in front of the car with his torso pinned beneath it. It looked as though he tried to turn at the last minute to escape, which resulted in his head getting caught as well. I looked away from his face, unable to handle the image as his brains pushed through the holes of his cracked skull.

There was no doubt that he was dead, yet I still approached his body with caution. I forced the bile down as it started to rise up at the metallic smell of blood permeating the air. I tried to breathe through my mouth to avoid throwing up, but it wasn't helping. The image alone was enough to trigger a vomit reaction. My breaths were more labored and intense as I struggled to keep it together. My sanity was hanging by a string, and that string was the lifeline that Wyatt was holding onto. One wrong move and it would break, costing him his life.

I slowly kneeled down, my fingers shaking as I fumbled around in his front pocket, trying to find his cell phone. I had to block out the thought of touching his *dead* body from my mind to get through it. If I stopped to think about what I was doing, I wouldn't be able to do it. I had to keep reminding myself that there was still work to do. Wyatt was counting on me right now and I couldn't let him down. If Mateo really had been working with Mike, then I assumed he would be calling to check in with Mateo soon, which meant that I needed to find his phone.

I groaned when I came up empty and knew that I was going to have to go around and check the other pocket. I sucked in a deep breath through my mouth, trying again, to avoid the smell of the blood around me. I stepped carefully as I walked around to the other side, making sure to avoid walking in the mess if I could.

My fingers were still shaking as I reached into his pocket and pulled out his cell phone. I held it in the air in front of me, praying for some sort of miracle that it wouldn't be locked. I was almost relieved when it vibrated with a new text message. I tried to open it, but his phone was locked. I let out a string of curse words until I looked down and found that he hadn't set it up to unlock with a password. It required his thumbprint. There was no turning back now, so I bent down and picked up his limp hand, pressing his thumb against the screen.

The phone vibrated and the screen bounced as it confirmed that it wasn't the right fingerprint. I tried again, reangling the finger to see if maybe it just hadn't read it right the first time. It did the same thing, confirming that it was still wrong. I only had a few more tries before I would be locked out. I stopped for a moment and studied my hand, thinking about which finger would be my go-to finger if I used a fingerprint sensor to unlock my phone. I was right-handed and it just felt natural that I would use my right thumb. I looked down at his body, remembering that his left was my right and vice versa. I rolled my eyes and tried again, this time with the other thumb. The screen lit up as it unlocked and I felt relief spread through me quicker than a wildfire.

I quickly went to the settings and changed the password, using his thumb one more time to gain access. After changing it from fingerprint to the code that I had created, I didn't have to worry about getting locked out again—not that I would need it for long once I found what I was looking for.

The text message was from Mike, confirming that he was there. It was vague, and I knew why. They weren't going to give those kinds of details in a text message that could be traced or used as evidence against them for what they were planning to do. I needed to know where *there* was, but I knew that I couldn't text him and ask because that wasn't something that Mateo would do. I had to be smarter and think like a criminal.

I decided to call him instead. I pressed the button and muted the phone on my side so he couldn't hear anything. I didn't want to give anything away and hoped that he was stupid enough to start talking before waiting for Mateo to say why he was calling. Mike had a habit of doing that and I was praying that he would be as predictable as I remembered.

"Hey, are you on your way, or did you already get lost?" he asked.

I stayed quiet, waiting him out.

"Shit, I can't hear a thing. Must be the shitty reception out here. We're at the abandoned shed that we talked about. Text me if you need directions."

The phone disconnected, and I smiled at how easy that was.

I opened Mateo's text messages and rolled my eyes at the ones at the top of the thread that he had recently received. You know, the ones that were from other girls that *weren't* his wife. I found Mike's name and opened the thread. My stomach sank as I read the last text message from Mateo to Mike. It was quick and to the point: *dealing with the problem now.* I shook my head to clear it. I had to stay focused on what really mattered right now.

I needed to confirm that *Mateo* had heard him on the phone and acknowledge that he was heading to the shed. I tried to think of what Mateo would say but had no idea how they talked to each other. I decided to just keep it short and simple.

Mateo: On my way.

I waited until I saw that the message was read before I exited out of the message. I pulled my hands inside of the sleeves of my shirt and tried to quickly wipe down the phone to get rid of my fingerprints. I didn't have time to deal with his body right now, but I also didn't want my DNA all over it if someone randomly found him, before I got back to take care of this. Not that I had any idea *how* to take care of it. After I wiped it down several times, I bent down and tossed it under the car. I had the information that I was looking for, so I no longer needed it.

Now that I knew that Mike was with Wyatt and Mateo was dead, I didn't have to sneak through the building anymore. I made a quick pitstop in the bathroom before going to my office to grab the things that I needed. I pulled my gun out from the safe and checked to make sure that it was fully loaded before tucking it in the back of my jeans. Once I had everything that I needed, I grabbed my keys and jumped in my truck. Now I just had to pray that Wyatt would still be alive by the time I got to him.

THREE STRIKES, YOU'RE GONE

Twenty Four
Wyatt

Not much had changed for me other than where I was sitting. I was still tied up and had the marks on my wrists from where I had been pulling at the rope, trying to break free. I chewed at the inside of my cheek in frustration when my master plan of trying to escape was quickly thwarted by a patch of black ice. Everything was going perfectly—Mike was still on the ground, trying to recover from the kick to his chest. Mateo was nowhere to be seen. All that I had to do was run from the back of the van to the front, and hope that Mike was stupid enough to leave the keys in the ignition.

Unfortunately for me, the long patch of ice that ran along the side of the van was my undoing as I slid Bambi style and hit my head. By the time that I was able to try to get back on my feet, Mike was already back on his and standing over me. There was nowhere to run at that point, and he knew it.

He had grabbed me by the rope and yanked me up, shoving me against the van until I caught my balance. I was surprised that we both didn't take another tumble on the ice. Luckily, the van was pulled over off the side of the road far enough that it was a quick walk to the shed, not that the abandoned shed in the middle of nowhere was an ideal place to want to be.

The door was barely hanging on the hinge, swaying with the wind as it whipped past us. Mike pushed it open and shoved me inside, not caring as I stumbled in and tripped on a piece of wood that was splintered up on the floor. He cast a quick glance at me before turning his attention to the small window by the door, keeping an eye out for someone. Or maybe some*thing*? At this point, everything that had already happened was so fucking wild and unbelievable that I wouldn't be surprised if a yeti came down from the mountains and ate us all alive.

The inside of the shed was dark and damp from the recent snowstorm, making everything smell mildewy. It was a small space with nothing inside and a few broken windows. I decided to get out of his way and sat down on the floor against the wall, shivering as the cold air blew around me. Thankfully, there was a small amount of light that had trickled in through the missing glass—enough to see what was around me. Aside from the resident rat that was dead in the corner a few feet away, there was nothing but cobwebs and dust.

I was starting to feel helpless, wondering where Kayce was and whether she was okay. I always thought of myself as a strong man, but here I was, sitting in the corner of an empty room, hiding like a damn pussy. Maybe it was the likely concussion that was keeping me down, but my body just didn't have the energy that I needed right now to try to fight back. I closed my eyes for a brief second, ready to just give up.

This was never how I had expected to die. Hell, I had imagined a whole different path for my life altogether. I had hopes and dreams, just like any kid, but I never thought that they would all come crashing down and end when I was twenty-five. A lot had happened in a year and I still couldn't wrap my head around the failure that was knocking on every door. It seemed like no matter what I did, I couldn't find success. I could feel the tears sting my eyes as I swallowed the harsh truth in the thoughts that were running through my head. As the guilt of disappointing my father started to build up, I saw an image of him that sent a chill right through me.

I had to fight, I couldn't give up. Out of all of the things that he had taught me growing up, it was that we always fight for the things that we want. And right now—I wanted Kayce. I needed her more than I needed the air around me to breathe.

More determined and focused, I started looking around again. As I looked closer, I found a sliver of glass laying on the floor, over in the corner. It wasn't that far from where I was sitting, I just needed to get to it without drawing attention to myself.

As quietly as I could, I started slowly scooting over toward it. I had to play my hand right this time and couldn't afford any more mishaps. I was only a few inches away when I heard the sound of a loud vehicle outside. I waited to see if Mike had heard it too but was relieved when I saw him with his head down, focused on his phone. The noise got louder as whoever it was got closer. Mike lifted his head, turning his ear in its direction at the same time that it stopped.

I slowly released the breath that I had been holding and scooted closer to the glass. Without drawing attention to myself, I carefully pushed it underneath my leg before resting my hands in my lap on top of it.

The wind picked up and whipped past the shed, howling through the room as we heard a car door slam outside. Mike's face lit up in excitement as he rushed over to the front door and opened it. Another gust of snow blew in, taking him by surprise as he turned his head to catch his breath. He held his arm up to cover his mouth before looking outside again, but another gust came through and he pulled back to avoid it.

I listened closely, trying to hear what was going on and praying that Kayce was okay. For all I knew, it could have been Mateo showing up with her dead body. I had to force those thoughts out of my head and try to focus on getting out of this mess.

Once the wind stopped for a moment, Mike stuck his head out of the door again. He pulled back in surprise, then leaned further outside to get a better look. When I heard the car, it sounded like it was at the back of the shed—not the front, where the van was parked. I felt a spark of hope, wondering if it was Kayce. She knew the area from that dreadful night, and she was smart as fuck. It would make sense for her to park in the back to stay hidden and give her the advantage.

"Son of a bitch," Mike muttered, pulling his jacket tighter against him as he stepped outside and pulled the door shut behind him.

That was it—the moment I had been waiting for. I picked up the piece of glass, ignoring the burn as it cut into the palm of my hand the harder I gripped it. It wasn't as sharp as I needed it to be, but I could feel it cut through the rope. In less than a minute, I had my hands free and tucked the rope into my pocket. I laid the glass down beside me and made sure it was hidden in case I needed it again.

I waited for Mike to come back in, but after several minutes had passed, I started to wonder what was going on. My nerves were already shot, but I could feel the anxiety clawing its way up my back, making my body tense as I waited out the unknown. I wanted to get up and make a run for it, but I had no idea whose car I had heard outside. It could have been Mateo showing up with Kayce, or it could be a group of mobsters that Mike is doing some shady business with. Who the fuck knew what I was in the middle of at this point.

Just as I was about to get up to go sneak a peek out the window to see what was going on, I heard voices outside and sat back down. The door flung open and Kayce stumbled in as Mike pushed her from behind. Our eyes immediately locked on each other, making sure we were both okay. I wanted to run over and hold her, to pull her as far away from Mike as I could, but I couldn't let him know that I had gotten out of the rope that I was supposed to be tied up with. There was still too much unknown, and I couldn't risk either of our lives by trying to be the hero just yet.

Mike wiped his nose on his jacket sleeve, leaving a smear of blood behind. I raised an eyebrow at Kayce, and she just shrugged while trying to keep the smirk off of her face.

"Sit your ass down next to your boyfriend," he demanded, nodding to where I was. I lowered my hands even further between my legs, keeping my knees up as a shield so he couldn't see them. Kayce walked over and sat down beside me. Her eyes quickly scanned my body before returning to the spot on my head where I had been hit earlier. Her brow furrowed as she stared at it before she looked at me and mouthed *I'm sorry.*

"Where's Mateo?" he asked her, as he continued to wipe at the blood that was dripping down his face. She shifted her attention from me back to where he was pacing back and forth by the door. A loud vibrating noise filled the room around us, and I wondered if it was Kayce's cell phone. I prayed that Lacey wasn't trying to call her right now because I knew that she would call over and over until she got her on the phone, and that could be deadly for us.

"He got pinned down," she said lightly. "He was crushed he couldn't be here."

Mike glared at her before pulling his cell phone out of his pocket and answering it. I felt my shoulders relax some when I saw that it was his phone that had been vibrating, and not hers.

"Yeah?" he huffed into the phone, walking back over to the door. "It's the same place as before."

"Are you okay?" I whispered quietly in her ear, making sure Mike didn't hear us.

"I am," she sighed. "You?" Her eyes went back up to the bump on my head.

"Yeah, I'm fine." I smiled and desperately wanted to reach over and grab her hand but didn't. I was just thankful that she was alive and from the looks of it, she didn't seem to be hurt. I prayed that she wasn't because if either of them did anything to her, I would go to my grave making sure that they paid for it.

"If you passed the windmill then you're almost here," Mike snapped at whoever he was talking to. I took the opportunity to focus on Kayce while he was distracted.

"Your head looks pretty bad," she whispered, concern laced in her tone. She lifted her hand to touch it but pulled away as I jerked back. I had no idea how bad it looked, but it fucking hurt like hell, not that I was willing to admit that to her.

"It's okay, really," I assured her as I kept an eye on Mike. He finished his call and slid his phone back into his pocket.

"Did you pass out?" she asked, not worried about Mike being done with his phone call. Maybe she hadn't noticed, or maybe she just didn't care?

I nodded, unable to say anything more as Mike turned back to look at us before opening the door. As another gust of wind whipped past as I heard car doors slamming. Not just one door, but two or more. Whoever it was had parked out front, and there was definitely more than one person.

The cold air forced its way inside the room as he held the door open. Two men walked in, neither of them acknowledging Mike, other than a shoulder check from the taller, skinnier guy.

When they turned to face us, I immediately recognized the shorter one as Brent, Kayce's ex-boyfriend. He looked at her, a tight smile on his face, before glancing at me. For a moment, it looked like he was worried about her as he worked his jaw back and forth and took in the situation before him.

"So, why are we here?" Brent asked Mike assertively, his eyes shifting from him back to Kayce.

"Because I have something that you want," Mike said dryly, walking over to where Kayce was sitting. He reached down and pulled her up off of the floor by her jacket. I clenched my fists, ready to pop up and clock him for putting his hands on her, when I remembered that no one could know that I wasn't tied up anymore.

Kayce stumbled from the force and caught herself before Mike grabbed her by the back of her hair. He reached into his coat pocket and pulled out a knife, holding it to her throat.

"Kayce?" Brent laughed hysterically. "You did all of this because you thought you could use Kayce to get what you wanted?"

Apparently, I had been sorely mistaken when I thought that he had been concerned for her when he first came in. Her eyes narrowed at him as she gave him a look that I never wanted to be on the receiving end of.

Mike's features hardened as Brent laughed at him.

"No offense, Kayce," he paused and held his hands up. "But she isn't of any value to me. I don't know what you thought you were going to get by kidnapping her."

"I just figured that maybe her *life* was worth something to you," Mike replied angrily. I could see his hand shaking as he tried to control himself. "But if not, then maybe I need to show you that I'm not fucking around anymore!"

He forced her to walk across the room, towards Brent, as we he kept the knife pressed to her throat. They were standing in front of Brent and the other guy when Mike reached into his jacket and pulled out an envelope, still keeping his grip on Kayce.

"Take it," he instructed, extending it to Brent.

With a dramatic eye-roll, Brent grabbed the envelope and opened it. His jaw tightened as he pulled the contents out and flipped through the pictures that were inside. He didn't say anything as he handed them to the other guy and kept his eyes on Mike. The room was eerily quiet as his friend looked through them before he chuckled and wiped at his nose.

"What do you want?" Brent asked sternly.

"Five million, in my account, by tomorrow." Mike pulled harder on Kayce's hair, making her gasp in pain.

"We fire you for embezzlement, and you think the best way to get revenge is to blackmail us for five million dollars? You're out of your fucking mind," the other guy laughed, handing the pictures back to Brent.

"I'm not playing!" Mike shouted, his voice booming through the small room. "I will release those photos to all of the magazines and tabloids—your career will be over. I will ruin you!"

The tension was mounting as the two guys looked between each other, not saying a word. This seemed to piss Mike off even more as the vein in his forehead throbbed while they ignored his outburst.

I tried to make eye contact with Kayce, but her head was forced up as Mike kept his grip on her. The knife was pressed so hard against her throat that I could see the red mark from where it had already nicked her. My anger was ready to boil over with every second that she stood there with him. I needed to get to her, but I was outnumbered and couldn't trust that Brent was on her side. He had already made it clear where she stood, why would I think that he would let her walk away from this if I saved her from Mike?

"You know, Mike, we don't take well to being blackmailed and threatened," Brent warned, stepping to the side.

In an instant, the guy beside him reached behind him and pulled out a gun. Without any warning, he aimed it straight at Mike and pulled the trigger. The bullet whipped past Kayce's head—barely missing her, and went straight through his forehead. I jumped up and rushed over to Kayce, pulling her away from him as his body hit the floor with a loud thud and the knife landed at my feet. She turned and curled into my chest, looking away from the gruesome scene in front of us. I watched Brent carefully as I waited for him to make his move.

THREE STRIKES, YOU'RE GONE

Twenty Five
Kayce

I felt like I was living in a nightmare that I couldn't wake up from. I wished that I could hide forever as Wyatt held me, but I also knew that neither of us could trust Brent or Dray. I forced myself to pull away from him and turn around. I looked down at Mike's dead body beside us, the puddle of blood getting closer to where we were standing.

There was a stare-down between the men as nobody moved or spoke. I took a moment to catch my breath, as I tried to figure out what was going on at this point. If Mike was working with Mateo to blackmail Brent and Dray, and now both of them were dead, then maybe this whole thing could just be over? It was wishful thinking but worth a shot.

I watched as Dray wiped at his nose again. Obviously, some habits never die for others either. He looked high as a kite, just as I remembered from the last time that I had seen him. It was hard to believe that the night we all swore to forget was the very thing that brought us here again.

The knife that Mike had been using was still lying on the floor between all of us. Without thinking twice, I bent down and grabbed it. I saw Dray move the gun in my direction before Brent's hand reached over and pushed it away. My heart was racing as I stood next to Wyatt and handed it to him with shaky fingers while keeping my eyes on Brent and Dray. I felt confused by Brent's behavior, and it made me even more uneasy than I was before. He hadn't seemed to care that Mike had kidnapped me and was trying to use me against him, yet he quickly pushed the gun away so I wouldn't get hit if Dray pulled the trigger.

An awkward silence lingered between all of us for a few more minutes before Brent finally spoke.

"Does anyone else have copies of these?" he asked, holding the envelope up in front of me.

"I have no idea," I admitted. "I didn't know about them until he started leaving them at my office a few days ago."

Brent nodded but said nothing.

"I wasn't a part of this and I didn't tell anyone about the photos or the notes he had left me," I added. I felt Dray's eyes on me and squirmed the way that I always did when he was around. He was one of those people that could naturally make you uncomfortable without trying. It was the pure evil that ran through him and tried to creep into your soul every chance it got.

"Then why is *he* here?" Dray asked, jerking his head toward Wyatt.

"He got caught up in it by accident. I'm working on his truck and he got stranded while here for work. He was at my shop when Mike came by. Mike had the wrong idea and brought Wyatt here. He doesn't know anything about what happened, and it will stay that way," I lied. I felt Wyatt's hand drop from my waist and knew what he was doing. If we were going to act like nothing was going on between us, other than me fixing his truck, then he couldn't touch me the way that he was.

"Look, there's nothing to worry about anymore," I pleaded, my voice rising when I realized what they were thinking. " Mike was the one who wanted to release these photos—not me. Can't we all just walk away and go our own way like we did last time? I think I've already proven that I won't say anything…"

"It's not that easy," Brent muttered, running a hand over the scruff of his jawline.

"Sure it is," I laughed nervously.

"No, it's not," he snapped. "Even if he doesn't know what happened before, he saw what just happened with Mike. How do we know that he's not gonna go snitch on us and tell someone?"

"I have a lot to lose if anyone got word of this," Wyatt said, speaking up beside me. All eyes, including mine, turned toward him.

"I'm the relief pitcher for the Colorado Cougars. If word got out that I was involved in something like this, I would be removed from the team, and my career would be over. Trust me, no one wants this to go away and never be spoken of again more than I do."

Brent and Dray exchanged a look between the two of them that I couldn't read. I hated that Wyatt was even pulled into this mess, to begin with, and I couldn't wait for it to be over.

"Well then, you'll know how important it is to tie up loose ends," Brent said, reaching into his pocket and pulling out a needle.

My eyes went wide and I stared in disbelief as I watched him turn around and plunge the syringe into Dray's arm before taking the gun from him. Now that Brent had Dray's gun, I felt even more anxious that I didn't have mine. I had reached for it when Mike attacked me outside, and during our struggle, it fell to the ground, lost in the thick snow on the way to the shed. *You don't take a knife to a gun fight...*

"Dude! What the fuck?!" Dray yelled as he jerked away and shoved Brent off.

"Problems have to be taken care of, and that includes you," Brent replied nonchalantly, stepping back and folding his arms over his chest. "Soon, things will be cleaned up, and I won't have to worry about all of these little *issues*."

"Why did you do that?" I shrieked as I watched Dray stumble toward the door.

"He was already high from a couple of hits he took on the way over here." He shrugged one shoulder and looked over at him. "I just helped top him off."

"With what?" I gasped. I knew that it was stupid to ask but there wasn't any point in trying to pretend that we didn't see what he did. He was roping us in and dragging us down with him. If he was willing to get rid of Mike and Dray, I knew what our fate was.

"Heroine. It'll be the quickest, and honestly, aside from the trouble breathing, he'll be too high to even know what's happening. I'm doing him a favor if you ask me."

I stepped back, unable to believe what I was seeing and hearing. Even though Brent and I weren't serious when we dated, I thought I knew him better than this. I never would have thought that he was this evil.

"Dray's had this coming for a long time," Brent explained, even though no one had asked. "He's been in a downward spiral ever since Stella died. Which is funny," he snorted, "because he killed her. And then I had to clean up the mess. But, I did it because we were going places, and I was finally getting where I needed to go in my career. We were selling out at international venues and we had a stellar tour lined up for next year—the sky was the fucking limit!"

He pumped his fist in the air excitedly as Dray leaned against the wall and started to slide down it. I tried to keep from looking at him as he gasped for breath, knowing that he was overdosing on the lethal combination of drugs in his system.

"That's the funny thing though—it was all just temporary. I needed everyone to keep their shit together for a little while longer while I got things set up, then they could ruin their lives however they wanted to. Mike had some great connections and made some killer deals for us, but now, I don't need him anymore. He started to get in the way and was too nosey for his own good, worrying about what business I was getting into and whether or not it was good for *everyone*. And Dray—well Dray has been a drag for far too long now. But the thing about him is that drummers are a dime a dozen. I just needed to get Jolted on the map, and then, I could easily find another drummer to replace him."

"You're a monster," I muttered under my breath, even though it was loud enough for him to hear me.

"Why? Because I look out for myself? I know what I'm worth and I'm willing to make whatever sacrifices that I need to get what I want. I'm the lead singer of the hottest fucking band in America right now and *nothing* is going to stop me."

I turned my head away from him in disgust and caught a glimpse of Dray hunched over, his head down as foam poured out of his mouth. His skin was turning blue as his eyes settled in the back of his head.

"Two problems down, two to go," Brent said bitterly, as he looked at Dray and laughed. He raised the gun and aimed it at us.

"Which one of you want to go first?" he asked, moving the gun back and forth between us.

"Ladies first," Wyatt said coldly, gently pushing me to the side. I turned to look at him, unable to believe what he had just said. Was *everyone* going to betray me today?

Brent tossed his head back, laughing hysterically. I looked over and saw Wyatt grip the knife at his side. His face was hard and his attention focused on Brent. Out of nowhere, he lunged at him with such force and speed that I almost missed it. I couldn't see much of what was happening as Wyatt's body blocked my view. There was a scuffle as Brent tried to fight back and push Wyatt off of him, but at that moment, Wyatt was stronger and used his full force to shove Brent up against the wall. His body leaned slightly to the right as his arm turned, and I saw the horror on Brent's face as Wyatt plunged the knife deeper into his stomach. Wyatt stepped away slowly, walking backward to where I was standing as we watched Brent slide down the wall, leaving a streak of blood along the way. I covered my mouth with my hand as I tried to keep the scream from escaping my lips and filling the silence as his body crumpled to the floor with a heavy thud.

THREE STRIKES, YOU'RE GONE

Twenty Six
Wyatt

I watched as Brent fell to the floor, not bothering to check him to see if he was still alive. While I had never killed anyone before, I was confident that the stab wound to his internal organs was enough to do the job. Besides, we didn't have time to waste with that right now. There were things we needed to do before we got the hell out of there before any more villains decided to show up.

I reached down and dug my cell phone out of Mike's pocket. A quick glance at the screen showed that there were seventeen missed calls and thirteen unread text messages. There was probably an equal number of voicemails too, but I would have to deal with those later. There wasn't time right now. We needed to get moving and were wasting seconds that mattered.

"We need to get out of here, Kayce," I said gently, placing my hand on her elbow as she stood there, covering her mouth with her hands. "Can you help me find the keys? We need a vehicle…"

My mind was scattered, trying to think through everything at once. All it took was for me to forget one tiny detail and this whole thing could blow up in our faces.

"Kayce!" I snapped, starting to lose my patience.

Her head jerked up, eyes filled with tears as her body trembled. I scolded myself for being so hasty with her. It wasn't like she was in an abandoned shed filled with dead bodies every day. Hell—neither was I. I forgot to account for the fact that she was likely in shock—anyone would be and that I needed to be gentle with her. It was hard to keep that in mind when I was scrambling, trying to figure out how to get us out of here and to somewhere that was safe.

"My truck is outside," she stammered, her hands slowly reaching down to pat her pockets. She reached in and pulled out her keys, handing them over to me.

"Thank you," I said as I took them from her. "We've got to get out of here, okay?"

"Okay," she whispered, looking around the room as if she was missing something.

"What are you looking for?"

She bent down and started picking up the pictures that were scattered on the floor.

"Don't worry about them," I said softly as I placed my hand on her shoulder.

"But if someone finds them…" Her voice trailed off, the thought forgotten for a brief moment.

"They won't," I assured her while helping her back up. "Where did you park?"

"Behind the shed."

"Okay, go get in the truck and I'll be right behind you."

Her eyes widened with a mixture of fear and curiosity.

"You're not coming with me?"

"I need to take care of something first. Please go wait for me in the truck," I urged. "I promise, I'll be right behind you."

I waited until I heard her close the door behind her before I turned and looked at the gruesome scene in front of me. While we could just run and leave here as if nothing happened, I couldn't guarantee that someone wouldn't stumble upon the decomposing bodies at some point. On top of that, I had to assume that there would be evidence of Kayce and I being here—whether it be fingerprints or a strand of hair, it wasn't worth risking it.

I rushed over to Dray and felt around in his pockets, making sure to avoid the mess that had cascaded down his hoodie. I didn't know much about drugs given that I was never into them, but I was willing to bet that he had a lighter on him given he reeked of pot on top of whatever he had done on the way over.

My fingers pushed through the tight fabric of his jeans, forcing their way into his pocket. After a few seconds, I felt something hard, cold, and metal. I pulled it out and grinned when I saw that it was a Zippo lighter. I jumped up and ran over to the photos that were laying on the floor by Brent. I flipped the top back and pushed my thumb down until the flame appeared. Holding the lighter steady, I carefully held the photos over it until the fire spread to them. I let them fall to the floor, watching as the flames licked the old, rotted wood. Next, I burned anything else that I could find, hoping that it would spread quickly. Unfortunately, it was an old shed with nothing in it and the inside had already been exposed to the snow which would make it more difficult.

It wasn't a brilliant plan, but it was the best that I could come up with while rushing to get the hell out of there. I watched as the flames danced around the floor and climbed the walls, sticking to the parts that were still dry. I pulled my hands through the sleeves of my hoodie and quickly wiped the zippo before tossing it on the floor next to Dray.

By the time I got outside and trekked through the thick snow to the truck, Kayce was already inside, warming up in the driver's seat. I climbed into the passenger side and buckled up. We didn't say anything, just a silent look, asking if each other was okay before she put the truck in drive and got out of there.

I would have offered to drive, but Kayce looked like she needed it more than I did. Instead, I unlocked my phone and scrolled through the list of text messages and missed calls from my mom, Buck, Grant, Lacey, and a number that I didn't have saved in my phone. There was too much to try to deal with all at once so I tackled the biggest item first: my mom.

I pressed the button to call her and held the phone to my ear while I shifted in my seat. I hated talking on the phone in front of other people, but it wasn't like I had much of a choice at the moment. If I didn't get back to my mom right away and let her know that I was okay, she was guaranteed to be in her car and on her way to look for me within the next ten minutes. Her last three texts had confirmed it.

"Wyatt Eugene Walker—where the hell have you been, and why aren't you answering your phone?!" she yelled through the phone. I pulled it away from my ear for a second, the shrill tone of her voice, when she was pissed, was too much for me to take with the pounding headache I had from getting hit so many times in one day.

"I'm sorry that I missed your calls, mom," I started slowly. "But I'm okay. You don't have to come down here."

"Too late," she snapped. "Buck and I are already on the road."

I looked around us at the blanket of snow that was falling around us. Kayce was used to driving in this kind of weather, but even she was going under the speed limit and had to use her high beams to see more than two feet in front of her.

"Mom, please turn around and go home. This storm is intense and you guys should not be driving in it."

"I'm not stopping until I make sure that you're okay."

I grounded my teeth in frustration, knowing that she wouldn't stop until she had some sort of proof that I was fine.

"Are you driving, or is Buck?" I gritted my teeth. I hated this idea but if it meant that she would turn around and go home, then I would do whatever it took to keep them safe.

"Buck is driving. For whatever reason, he wouldn't let me. He insisted that he drive us there," she scoffed as if it was the most ridiculous thing she had ever heard.

"Okay, I'm going to FaceTime you so you can see that I'm fine. But you need to promise me that you'll turn around and go home once you have seen for yourself that there's nothing wrong."

I glanced at Kayce, noticing the way she flinched at my words. I knew that there was dried blood on my head from the first time I had been hit, but I had no idea how bad the rest of it was. She tried to give me a reassuring smile before returning her focus to the road.

"Fine, but I will make no promises until *I've* decided that you're okay."

"Deal," I muttered and pulled the phone away from my ear so I could press the button to change the call to a FaceTime call instead. I held the phone in front of me, waiting for her to show up on the screen.

Even though she tried to force a smile, I could see the wrinkle lines in her forehead as she leaned closer to her phone. I expected her to gasp or let out a shriek, but instead, she stayed calm and her features became harder to read.

"Buck, can you please pull over?" she asked politely. I swallowed hard and looked out of the window. It was rare that my mom was this calm and collected when she knew that I had gotten myself into some sort of trouble. I almost always preferred the angry, screaming side of her because then I knew that she was just mad in the moment and that she would forget about it sooner than later. When she was calm that usually meant that she wasn't going to forget anytime soon.

I could hear Buck in the background as he agreed. My mom waited patiently for the car to come to a stop before turning her phone to Buck.

"Which one of you is going to go first and tell me what the hell kind of trouble you got into this time?"

Buck and I stared at each other for a second, neither of us bothering to answer her.

"Well?" she prodded impatiently.

I felt bad that Buck was even getting brought into this, yet I had no idea what he had told her. Did he mention to her that I had asked him to look into Mike? That couldn't have been that big of a deal, could it? There was no way that he knew anything about what had happened. No one did.

"Buck wasn't involved in any of this," I said, noticing the way that his features hardened before he looked over at her.

"Then why was he getting information on someone for you?" my mom asked, turning the phone back to look at her. "And what on earth happened to you?!"

"There was a fight, that's all," I lied. I couldn't tell them the truth, especially with Buck being a cop. There was no way that I could ever burden him to carry this secret for me of what I'd done. No, that would be something that I would take to my grave and never speak of ever again.

"Why did you get into a fight? With who?"

I could feel the irritation start to build again, each question forcing me slightly closer to the edge.

"Look ma, I really don't want to get into it right now. Okay? I'm fine, I just have a knot on my head and a terrible headache."

"You're just as stubborn as your father was," she sighed. "Fine. We'll turn around and go home. But promise me that you'll get to a doctor and have that bump on your head looked at…"

"I'll deal with it later, mom."

My attitude was getting more sour by the second. I knew where she was going with it and she knew how much I hated to talk about it.

"The doctors said, one more hit and you could—"

"I know, mom!" I snapped angrily into the phone. I looked away to avoid seeing the look of hurt that flashed across her face.

"Okay," she whispered, holding her hands up in front of her. "I won't push you. But keep an eye on it and don't be a dummy. If the pain starts to get worse, you better get your butt to a hospital and this time—call me."

"I will, mom, I promise," I assured her before wrapping up the call and hanging up.

I didn't feel like discussing it, so I was relieved when Kayce kept her attention on the road and didn't bother asking me about it. I turned my focus to the voicemails so that I could clear the notifications. I deleted the messages from my family and almost deleted the last message from an unknown number before deciding against it.

I held the phone up to my ear and waited for the message to start.

"Hey, Wyatt, this is Rudy Villanueva from the Colorado Cougars. I wanted to chat with you about the recent progress update that came in from your doctor. Give me a call when you have a chance."

I felt my blood pressure start to rise, the weight of the day starting to take its toll on me. I deleted the message and let my phone drop into my lap as I bit my fist and looked out the window.

"Everything okay?" Kayce asked, glancing at me for a quick second.

"Yeah, it's fine."

I didn't want to take my bad mood out on her. It wasn't fair and she had been through plenty of heavy shit today as well. It was already late, the sky eerily bright from the snow that had gotten thicker the closer that we got to town.

"How's your head feeling?" she asked cautiously as she slowed down for a red light.

"Not you too," I moaned, pinching the bridge of my nose between my fingers to push the headache away.

"I'm not trying to nag you," she laughed. "I'm genuinely concerned."

"I'm fine. Thanks," I said, forcing a smile that was reluctant to appear.

"I'm not a doctor, but I don't think you should be alone tonight—just in case." She rushed the words out, and I couldn't help but notice that she seemed nervous.

"What are you suggesting?" I asked, turning slightly in my seat to face her.

"I'll buy us dinner, and maybe you can come stay with me tonight… You know, so I can keep an eye on you with your lumpy head."

I laughed and felt some of the tension start to lift from my shoulders. She was afraid to be alone, and it felt oddly satisfying that she wanted me to stay with her for comfort.

"Deal," I said happily. "But—I have two conditions."

"Oh great," she replied sarcastically, easing on the gas pedal as the light turned green. "Let's hear what the diva wants this time…"

"Diva?!" I shrieked, pulling my hand up to my chest in mock exasperation. She laughed and looked over, her eyes immediately finding the cuts along my wrists from the rope. I lowered them and tried to pretend she hadn't seen them. "I'm not the diva, however, I'm also not budging on my requests."

"Okay, let's get this over with," she teased, driving slowly as she turned onto Main Street.

"First—I need to have some Tasty Pig tonight. Barbeque is the equivalent of nature's first aid. It'll make everything better."

"That's doable. What's the second item on your request list?"

"I'll tell you when we get there."

Ten minutes later, we were in line at The Tasty Pig, thankful that they were still open when everything else had already shut down from the storm. It would have been nice to go home and have it delivered but unfortunately, they never jumped on the modern train of food convenience.

"I guess it's a good thing that I wanted barbeque," I said, looking around at the empty parking lots around us. "There weren't any other options, even if we wanted them."

"Yeah, The Tasty Pig is one of the few businesses that will stay open for pretty much anything and everything. The owner has a house close by, so they never worry about the weather since they can just walk home if they need to. It's actually that little house, right over there," she said as she leaned closer to the steering wheel and pointed to the house sitting on the corner of the side street that was behind us.

The car ahead of us pulled forward and Kayce placed our order. As she was talking, I dug out my wallet and got my debit card ready. When she pulled forward, I handed it to her, watching her narrow her eyes as she looked at it.

"What's that for?" she asked with a quirked brow.

"My second requirement. I'm buying dinner."

She opened her mouth to speak, but I held my finger up to stop her.

"Look—I get to buy dinner because if not, then it'll feel like this weird prostitution thing where you buy me dinner and lure me back to your place. I don't know what you've heard, but I'm not that kind of guy."

Her face flushed red as I winked and pushed the card toward her. She reluctantly took it and handed it to the cashier at the window, after they gave her the total. A few seconds later, they handed it back to her, with a receipt. I tucked both of them into my wallet and reached over to grab the bags of food from Kayce.

"It'll be just a second," the cashier said. "We're just waiting on the peach cobbler."

I laughed hysterically at the look on Kayce's face as she turned beet red and sank back against her seat.

"I stand corrected," I laughed. "Apparently, you are trying to buy your way with me tonight, aren't you?"

She rubbed her lips together in an effort to not say anything. I could see the comeback sitting on her lips and wished that she would say it. Instead, the cashier slid the window open and handed her the last bag that had the cobbler in it. Kayce handed it over to me without looking and drove off.

Twenty Seven
Kayce

By the time we got back to my apartment, the snow was blowing so hard in every direction that you couldn't see more than an inch in front of you. We sat down on the couch to eat but the tension was thick in the air between us as the events of the day sat heavily on our shoulders. There was a lot that we needed to talk about, but I had no idea where to start.

I set the boxes of food in a line on the coffee table and opened the lids, allowing the heavenly smell to float out around us. It felt almost dream-like, sitting on the couch next to Wyatt, eating dinner while the snow fell peacefully outside. Never mind the dried blood on his head from getting hit earlier or the cuts on his wrists from where they had tied him up. If you looked past the physical evidence that we were wearing, you could pretend that we hadn't spent the day in a blood bath with a handful of people who wanted us dead.

"You okay?" Wyatt asked gently, handing me a paper plate.

I took it and set it in my lap, pulling a deep breath in before I trusted myself to speak and not have a meltdown.

"Yeah, I think so," I replied, turning my head to look at him. "Are you?"

He shrugged dismissively so I didn't push it any further. I didn't blame him for not wanting to talk about it. I wasn't chomping at the bit myself.

"Do you want some ribs?" I asked, changing the subject as I picked up the container from the far end of the table and held it in front of him. He smiled and scooped a few onto his plate with his fork.

I served myself before setting it back on the table and then went about filling my plate with the rest of the food. We didn't bother to talk after that. It was just two people who were quietly enjoying a much-needed meal. My stomach rumbled, a gentle reminder that I hadn't eaten anything since this morning with Wyatt before everything crashed down around us. I glanced over, pleased that he was devouring his food as quickly as I was, so he couldn't judge me for being such a piggy.

Once we were finished, we leaned back against the couch, too tired to move. Part of me wanted to get up and take a shower to wash the day off of me, but the other part of me was too tired and sore to get up to make the effort.

I still hadn't told Wyatt what had happened, and honestly, I had no idea where to start. It sat there with the other topics that we were strategically avoiding with our silence.

He lifted his hand and rubbed the side of his head, wincing as he pulled his hand away.

"We really should take a look at your head," I said, turning to face him. "Lean over so I can see it better."

He scooted closer and leaned toward me, angling his body so his chest was lined up against mine and his arm pinned me on the other side. I could smell the subtle scent of his cologne as it teased the edges of my mind, bringing the memories of the other night back to the surface.

It seemed so strange that it was just a few nights ago when everything now felt like it was longer. Today was so long and exhausting that I was sure it had been at least a week and not just a few hours.

I gently reached up and pushed his hair back away from the cut on the side of his head. There was a large knot sticking up beside it that faded into his hairline and disappeared. My fingers tenderly traced along it as I tried to see how bad it really was. As I got closer to his temple, I felt him flinch and jerk away.

"Sorry," I apologized softly.

"It's okay," he said as he looked into my eyes. "It's just a little tender."

"I can see why. It looks like he got you pretty good."

I pulled my hand away, afraid that I would start running my fingers through his hair if I didn't.

"Yeah, they both did," he chuckled, even though there was nothing humorous about it.

"Both?" I asked, pulling my brows together.

"Mike got me the first time, then while you were gone, Mateo got me the second time."

Hearing his name on Wyatt's lips sent shivers down my spine.

"You know Mateo?" The words almost stuck in my throat as I tried to force them out.

"Not really. I knew his wife, Mandy."

A faint blush crept up his cheeks as he tucked his chin and looked away.

"You slept with his wife?!" I gasped, putting two and two together.

He grinned sheepishly as his eyes slowly made their way back up to mine.

"I didn't know she was married."

I raised an eyebrow and waited for him to come clean. I had known Mandy long enough to know that there really was a good chance that she hadn't told him that she was married, but there was a very small one that someone in town wouldn't have said something and ratted her out.

"I was in Eastern Point on business, so was she," he explained with a shrug.

"Man, Lacey was right about you, wasn't she?" I laughed, feeling more relaxed now that we were talking and not avoiding the heavy elephant in the room.

"Hey, that one wasn't my fault!" he said, putting his hands up in front of him defensively.

We laughed together for a few minutes. It felt so good that I didn't want it to end, even if it was from talking about Wyatt having an affair with another woman.

"How did Mateo end up finding out anyway?" I asked, genuinely curious.

"Turned out that he was supposedly there for business, but his *colleague* looked like she was paid by the hour, if you know what I mean."

I rolled my eyes and grinned, knowing exactly what he meant.

"There's something—" I started saying at the same time he said, "Do you—"

We both stopped and waited for the other to finish their sentence.

"Go ahead," I offered, suddenly feeling too nervous to tell him about Mateo.

"It was nothing," he replied with a half-smile that pulled at the dimple in his cheek. "I was just going to ask if you wanted me to clean this up?" He looked down at the empty boxes on the table.

"Nah, I'll take care of them in a little bit. I'm too tired to care about that right now."

"Why don't you relax, and I'll clean this up?" he offered, reaching forward to grab the boxes at my end of the coffee table. The light caught the cuts on his wrist, making my stomach clench in response. I hated that he had these injuries because of me.

I reached forward and gently pulled his arm away, making sure not to touch his wrist.

"Leave them," I said quietly. "Really. They'll still be there tomorrow."

I could see the tension in his neck as he rolled his head back to relieve it. What had started out as a good day for him with getting Junior's commitment quickly turned sour because of me.

"Why don't we go take a hot shower, then get ready for bed?"

His eyebrows lifted in surprise, a cheeky smirk splitting his cheeks.

"We?"

"What?" I pulled my head back in surprise. "I said *you*. Not *we*." My mind was racing, trying to remember if I had just said that or if he was messing with me.

"You totally said *we*," he assured me, the stupid grin still plastered across his face. "First you try to bribe me to come over with dinner, then you add in the peach cobbler—which we've yet to eat by the way. Then you ask me to take a shower with you… I gotta say, maybe Lacey should have been warning *me*."

I sat there with my arms folded over my chest, refusing to give in and admit that I had said it. There was no proof either way, but he was having way too much fun believing that I did.

"I did not lure you over here with food and the promise of showering together," I said matter-of-factly.

"Well, then, I guess it was just your natural charm and hospitality that pulled me away from my cozy room at the Honey Lodge hotel tonight."

I fought the smile that was tugging at the corner of my lips, threatening to spread across my face when I pictured him trying to get comfortable on those hard-ass beds. I had never stayed there myself, but it was a running joke around town about how old and hard the mattresses were, yet there was never any talk of them getting new ones.

Out of nowhere, a huge yawn took over, making me realize how exhausted I was.

"Come on," Wyatt said, standing up and holding his hand out to me.

I tilted my head to the side, confused.

"Let's go take a quick shower, then we'll get to bed. It's been a long day."

THREE STRIKES, YOU'RE GONE

Twenty Eight
Wyatt

Kayce tilted her head back, letting the water run down her face and chest. I stood next to her, my fingers itching to follow the droplets of water as they rushed down her stomach. The water was relaxing, while the heat of it burned the cuts on my wrists. I didn't complain and tried not to act like a pussy about it.

I had told Kayce to go first so that way there was enough hot water. If it ran out by the time she was done, then I would be the one to take a cold shower—which I obviously needed with the erection that I had no way of hiding. Thankfully, her eyes were closed as she scrubbed the shampoo bubbles out of her hair so she hadn't seen it yet.

Not that it should be surprising that a man had a hard-on while showering with a beautiful woman. I didn't know a man in his right mind who could be around a naked, wet, woman and not have a bulging boner. Unless he was gay—then I guess he wouldn't care much about the naked woman. But I was neither gay nor crazy, and my dick was making sure that I knew it.

Her eyes fluttered open after she leaned her head forward and wiped the water off of her face. She looked breathtakingly beautiful. Completely natural—no make-up or silly filters that most girls had started to rely on for their constant selfies on social media. That didn't show you what someone really looked like. This did.

I studied her face, even though she gave me an odd look while I stared intently at her. She had high cheekbones that complimented her beautiful smile. It was perfect—like the kind you would see in a magazine ad. Straight, white teeth, and full, pouty lips. As I looked closer, I saw a small cluster of freckles on her cheeks that I must've missed this entire time. Or maybe I just hadn't gotten close enough to notice them before.

"You're being creepy," she stated before squirting a blob of conditioner in her hand, then ran it through her hair. It smelled sweet with a heavy vanilla scent that lingered in the air.

"I'm not creepy," I laughed, leaning my shoulder against the shower as I crossed my arms over my chest to keep from touching her. "I'm just admiring the beauty before me."

She stopped mid-rinse and looked at me as if I just said that two plus two equaled eighteen.

"What?" I laughed, suddenly feeling self-conscious.

"Nothing," she giggled. "But, if you have a thing for my shower, then I'll move and get out of your way." She wiggled her eyebrows as she squeezed around me and gently pushed me toward the water. I loved the feeling of her hands on my back as I stepped forward and let the hot water hit my face and chest. I closed my eyes and took a moment to enjoy it.

"The showerhead has different pressures," she laughed, "You know, in case you're into that sort of thing."

I turned around, running a hand down my face to wipe the water away before I looked at her.

"Trust me, I don't need a damn showerhead."

Her face flushed red as our eyes locked onto each other.

"All I heard was head," she muttered, taking a step closer.

I could feel the heat and electricity pulsing between us as the small gap between our bodies closed. Her chest rose and fell heavily against mine as her fingers reached down and trailed along the length of my shaft.

My dick twitched in response, ready for a release but not yet. I wanted to take my time with her, to enjoy every second. To watch her face as she came undone from my touch as I fucked her senseless.

I ran my hand down her side and over her hip before reaching back and cupping her ass. She gasped in response, her eyes darting up to look at me. Her lips parted as I leaned down and kissed her, my tongue greedily pushing its way into her mouth. I wanted to taste her—no, *needed* to devour her like I was on my death bed, and she was my last fucking meal.

She deepened the kiss, reaching up to wrap her arms around my neck as my dick pressed against her hip, desperate to be inside of her. Her breasts pushed firmly against my chest, our bodies perfectly lined up and ready for each other.

As quickly as it started, it ended when she pulled away and stepped back.

"I'm sorry," she whispered. "I don't think we should be doing this."

Without another word, she turned and got out of the shower. She quickly wrapped a towel around her body before she walked out and closed the door behind her.

Twenty Nine
Kayce

I sat on the couch with my knees pulled to my chest as I waited for him to come out of the bathroom. I felt terrible about what had just happened, but something about the way that he looked at me forced me to pull back. It was more of a natural reaction—step back and put my guard up before anyone had the chance to get close enough to hurt me. But I had seen the way his face fell when I got out of the shower and walked away.

It wasn't his fault and I couldn't expect him to know what was going on in my head. After everything that we had been through today, it felt nice to forget long enough to distract ourselves from the reality of it all. The problem was that both of us were used to using the same coping mechanism—sex, which used to work when we were single and carefree. Not that we were dating, but it felt different with Wyatt. I was already feeling myself fall for him, and that was even more terrifying than the things I had been through today.

A few minutes later, the pipes squeaked as he turned the shower off. It was warm in the apartment after I cranked up the heater, but I still couldn't shake the chill that had settled in my bones. I rubbed my hands together to try to warm up as my nerves frayed, when he opened the door and walked out.

He gave me a sheepish grin, almost as if he was unsure of how to act around me now. I hated that in a split second, I had completely ruined the light-hearted, fun vibe that we had found with each other.

"Hey," I smiled and waited for him to come sit beside me on the couch.

He was wearing a pair of sweats and a t-shirt that fit so perfectly around his body that I wanted to curl up next to him and sink into his comforting arms. I pulled at the string on my hoodie by my neck, wondering if it would be easier to just cover my head and pull it shut so I didn't have to look at him and deal with any of this.

"Hey," he replied warmly as the cushion next to me dipped with his weight as he sat down.

"I'm really sorry about what happened—"

"Don't be," he interrupted, holding his hand up to stop me from continuing my sentence.

I looked down, too uncomfortable to look up at him as I made my confession.

"I got scared," I blurted out, keeping my eyes on the piece of lint across the room on the edge of the rug by the wall. "I didn't know what to do, so I walked away."

He nodded his head and ran a hand down the scruff on his jaw from missing a few days of shaving.

We sat there for a few moments, neither of us speaking.

"Why were you scared?" he asked suddenly, turning to face me. His eyes were soft and sympathetic as they studied me.

"I don't know," I exhaled loudly with frustration. "It just felt— different. I don't know how to explain it. I wanted someone to comfort me and make everything go away for just a little while, but then when you looked at me, I realized that it felt…"

"Different," he repeated with a smile.

"Exactly. And I don't know why or what it means, but I knew that it was better to stop it before things went any further."

"I get it," he sighed. "I really do. Because things felt different for me too."

He reached over and lifted my chin with his finger. Our eyes locked and that same feeling from the shower started tingling in my stomach again.

"I like you Kayce," he continued, still holding my chin between his fingers. "And I think that you like me too."

I bobbed my head in agreement, too afraid to say the words out loud.

"But it's new for both of us. Or at least for me," he laughed, pulling his hand away so I could move from my frozen position. It was like his touch had some magic spell on me. "I've been with my share of women—hell, I've been with more than my fair share, but I've never met anyone like you before, and that scares the shit out of me."

I ran my tongue along the backside of my teeth as I tried to process what he was saying. It was something I had done since I was a little girl. Usually, it would help me to clear my head and find the right answer, but sitting here next to him as he stared at me with those eyes—I had never felt more foggy-brained in my life.

"What if this is just some sort of coping mechanism?" I asked, jumping ahead and speaking my thoughts before thinking them through. I saw the confusion on his face as he raised a brow in response to my random question. "I mean, what if what almost happened between us in the shower was just our way of escaping reality for a little while. Maybe that's why it felt different?"

Deep down, I knew better. I knew that this wasn't just some random thing that we were doing to pass time and forget the unthinkable. It was the very thought-out and deliberate thing that we both wanted to do because there was this insane chemistry that sizzled between us whenever we were next to each other.

"Is that what you think this is?" he asked calmly, not sounding offended or upset by it.

I paused for a moment and tried to force the words out of my mouth. I needed him to believe that I did. Then, he would walk away, and I could deal with my feelings for him on my own, after he went back to Haven Brook. It wasn't like this was something we could continue, even if we wanted to, because we didn't even live in the same town. Sure, it was only a few hours between Easterville and Haven Brook, but I couldn't imagine that either of us was going to be good at long-distance relationships when we avoided commitment at all costs to begin with.

"No," I admitted, betraying myself. "I don't think that is what *this* is." I moved my finger between us before he reached up and grabbed it, pulling my hand onto his lap.

"We don't have to label anything right now, Kayce. It's enough just to say that we like each other, and that maybe, this is more than just a fling."

His words were exactly what I needed to hear to calm the storm that had been brewing inside of me.

"Okay," I agreed, rubbing my thumb across the top of his hand.

His grin spread across his face, showing off the sexy dimples that I couldn't get enough of.

"Okay," he repeated with a laugh before reaching over and pulling me across the couch so I was leaning against his chest. He wrapped his arms around my waist and rested his head on mine. The warmth from our bodies was enough to send my body into complete shutdown as a yawn tore through me and made my eyes water.

"It's been a long day, we should get to bed," he offered when he noticed.

I didn't bother saying a word since my mouth was busy with another yawn. He chuckled behind me as we made our way to my bedroom and climbed into bed. I set my phone down on the nightstand beside me, looking for the cord to the charger when it started ringing. I groaned when I thought that it might be Lacey wanting to check in and see how the day had gone. Then I realized that it was late and there was no way that she would be up and calling me at this hour unless something was wrong.

I checked the caller ID and froze when I saw the name displayed on the screen. My fingers trembled as I picked it up and stared at it.

"What's wrong?" Wyatt asked, leaning over to touch my shoulder.

"It's the police," I whispered. I swallowed hard and slid my finger across the screen to answer it. The last thing that I needed was for them to show up at my apartment if I didn't take the call. While it was late and I could say that I slept through it, it would be terrible to have to talk to them about anything in person. I was a terrible liar and had always been told that my flushed cheeks gave me away.

"Hello," I croaked out, my voice getting stuck in my throat.

"Hey, Kayce, sorry to wake you. It's Dan," he said, assuming that I had been asleep and that was why I had sounded weird. That's the nice thing about small-towns though—everyone knows each other on a first-name basis and no one ever assumes that you were part of a mass murder earlier that day.

"No biggie," I lied, nervously biting my finger while Wyatt listened from the other side of the bed. "What's up?"

"Well, I was driving by your shop earlier, doing my nightly rounds, and I noticed that it had been broken into. The window up front was busted."

"Oh, yeah," I said lightly, finally releasing the breath that I had been holding. "Sorry that you had to bother with that, unfortunately, that was from the weather and I had tried to deal with it this morning. I boarded it up the best that I could but wasn't able to get anyone out to replace it because of the storm. Hopefully, it will hold up for another day or two."

"Yeah, um, I think there's a bigger problem than that," he said awkwardly. "The boards weren't up on the window anymore so I went ahead and checked it out."

Shit. This was it. I held my breath and waited for him to say it as Wyatt's eyes frantically searched my face for a clue as to what was going on.

"Okay?"

"The problem," he continued, "is what I found in the garage."

My mind was racing as I desperately tried to remember where Wyatt and I had left the photos from Mike. Were they on my desk? Did we leave them on the table in the garage? Were they the photos that Mike had with him at the shed? Why the fuck hadn't I gone back there to deal with Mateo before someone found out about it? I was so stupid!

I could hear him clear his throat on the other end and knew that he was waiting for me to respond.

"What did you find?" I asked stupidly, closing my eyes as I waited.

"A body."

THREE STRIKES, YOU'RE GONE

Thirty
Wyatt

There were flashing lights bouncing off the walls and onto the trees outside of Kayce's shop, when we pulled up. There wasn't much time for her to explain in detail what had happened or why Mateo's body was in her garage, but she insisted that the less that I knew—the better.

"Thanks for coming, Kayce, I'm sorry to have to drag you out this late and in this weather," an older man in a police uniform said, hugging her before glancing over at me.

"I'm sorry that this happened to begin with," she muttered before realizing what she said. "Dan, this is Wyatt Walker. He's Lacey's future brother-in-law and is in town to recruit Junior Soto for the Haven Brook University baseball program."

She looked up at me with a smile that begged me not to correct her if any part of that statement was incorrect. I extended my hand and shook his as he gave me a warm smile.

"Let's get inside where we can talk without losing a limb to frostbite," he said, leading the way.

We walked carefully through a handful of officers and the crime scene unit that was busy taking pictures of the broken glass that was still scattered on the outside of the building. I was disappointed that the wood I had used to fix it earlier wasn't strong enough to withstand the storm after all. The opening in the window was completely exposed, with a pile of snow that had started to accumulate inside.

We made our way into the garage where there were even more people scattered about and crime scene tape wrapped around the project car in the back of the room. I saw Kayce's eyes immediately go over to the area, but it wasn't curiosity that shone in them. It was fear.

"You don't have to go over to where the body is," Dan said, breaking the silence between us. "I can confirm that it is Mateo Villareal."

"Do you know what happened?" I asked, knowing that I had a better chance of getting information than Kayce did right now. She was a nervous wreck and I prayed that Dan didn't start getting suspicious as to why. Since I still had no fucking idea what happened, I could easily play along with whatever he could tell me.

"They're still conducting their investigation, however, it looks like a break-in that went terribly wrong. I have no idea what he was trying to steal, but we found a cell phone under the car that we believe he was trying to get to before the car fell on him."

Kayce turned and looked away, tucking her chin to her chest. It wasn't a look of admission, but it still made me wonder if she was responsible for this. I looked over to where they were working and waited for the heavy-set cop to move out of the way so that I could see what had everyone's attention. Finally, he stood up and walked over to talk to another cop. For a brief moment, I had a completely unobstructed view of Mateo's body that was crushed under the car that had been knocked off of the jack that it had been on earlier today.

I stole a glance from Kayce and slightly raised my eyebrow to ask all of the questions that I knew she couldn't answer. Subtly, she nodded her head yes while pretending to cough, before she turned and looked in the opposite direction.

"So what happens now?" I asked Dan who was looking down at a report that someone had just handed him.

"Well, for now, we continue with the investigation and make sure that it's thorough and complete. But honestly, I don't think we're going to find much other than what we already have. It doesn't appear that anyone else was here when it happened, so there are no witnesses. The window up front was already broken, and according to Kayce— temporarily fixed. Now the wood might have been ripped off by the wind with that terrible storm, or it might have been an easy target for someone who counted on everyone being at home because of the weather. I'm sticking with an attempted robbery that went bad."

"Do you need anything else from Kayce right now?" I prodded. I knew that we were both tired and likely to slip up and say something that could get us in hot water the longer that we stuck around.

"No, I don't imagine so. Just keep your phone on you and I'll be in touch. I would also recommend taking the day off tomorrow, since I don't know when we'll be able to clear everything out and give you your shop back."

I saw her eyes quickly dart over to the table where I had been sitting when I found the pictures earlier. I knew that she had to be thinking the same thing that I was—where had we left them?

"I left my duffle bag in your office earlier, I'm gonna go grab it," I said to Kayce, gently grabbing her elbow to get her attention.

"Okay," she said quietly, not drawing any attention to it.

I rushed off, stepping past the officers that were still moving around in the lobby as I jogged down the hallway and opened her office door. I walked around behind her desk and picked my duffle bag up off of the floor. It was obvious that no one had been in here since they found Mateo's body because the pictures and envelope were still sitting on her desk. I quickly grabbed them and unzipped my bag, pushing them into Junior's folder that was sitting on top of my stuff. I zipped the bag shut and slung it over my shoulder, looking around to make sure there was no other evidence that we were leaving behind.

"Can I help you?" a man's voice asked.

I looked up, my heart feeling like it had jumped out of my chest and into my throat. A plainclothes officer stood in the doorway, arms folded over his chest as he studied me. I tried to regain my composure as I shifted the bag behind me in some subconscious, desperate attempt to conceal what I was hiding. My eyes quickly took him in, noticing the gun on one hip and the badge on the other.

"I just came to get my bag," I said, patting it for good measure. "I'm here with Kayce," I added, when he didn't blink or budge from his spot.

"No one is allowed back here," he replied in his official police tone. "This is a crime scene."

"I apologize, I wasn't trying to interfere," I stammered, suddenly feeling my nerves shoot through the roof as he pinned me with his look. "I had mentioned to Dan that I had left my bag in here and that I was coming to get it."

He nodded his head, the muscles in his neck pulling tight with the movement. This guy looked like he ate steroids for breakfast, lunch, and dinner.

"Alright, then you won't mind if I check it before you go," he said, staying put as he continued to block the door.

"Of course not," I said through somewhat clenched teeth. I was screaming internally, begging for some sort of miracle intervention to get me out of this one.

I walked out from behind the desk, feeling the weight of the bag heavy on my shoulder. Every step that I took felt like I was one inch closer to having everything blow up in my face. This was it—this was how everything was going to end for me. I would end up going to prison for crimes that I didn't necessarily commit, and then, my career would forever be down the drain. Unless, there was some sort of professional baseball team in prison.

I was almost to Robocop when I saw Kayce and Dan come down the hallway and stop just outside of her office.

"Hey, did you get what you needed?" Kayce asked, looking up at the beast of a man beside her. "What's up, Logan?"

I closed my eyes to keep from rolling them. Why did it not surprise me that Kayce would know this meathead?

"Just caught this guy rummaging around in your office," he stated, with a nod in my direction. "I was just about to go through his stuff. Make sure he wasn't taking anything that didn't belong to him."

"Seriously?" she said sarcastically, before she nudged him out of the way. "He's Lacey's soon-to-be brother-in-law. He's practically family."

She stood beside me with her hands on her hips and glared at him. I had to give it to her. For someone as small as she was, she sure packed a lot of sass into that little, tiny body.

"The boy is fine, let him go," Dan said from the hallway. "They need you to go help outside."

Logan gave me one last glare before he turned and followed Dan out of the office and down the hallway.

"Are you good?" Kayce asked, glancing at her desk.

"We're good," I confirmed, patting my bag to let her know that I had what she was looking for.

We kept our heads down and quickly made our way outside and into her truck. The drive back to her apartment was quick now that the worst of the storm had passed through already. Even if I wanted to ask her about what had happened with Mateo, I was too exhausted to stay up and listen.

We made our way back to the bedroom, where I tucked my duffle bag under the bed, then crawled in and fell asleep listening to the loud snores of the incredible woman next to me.

Thirty One
Kayce

I rolled over and felt a hard body next to me, forgetting for a second that Wyatt had stayed the night. My fingers felt cold against his warm back, and I wondered when he had stripped down last night without me noticing. Knowing me, I was already passed out and snoring before he even reached the bed.

Feeling a little silly, I gently lifted the sheet to see if he had fully stripped down like he had done last time or if he was still wearing his pants.

I looked over, holding it slightly in the air, waiting to see if he had felt the cold air on his skin. I didn't want to wake him, and I definitely didn't want to get caught red-handed. He didn't move, so I lifted it the rest of the way, disappointed to find that he was wearing his sweatpants. He was rolled onto his side, facing away from me, so I almost missed it when he mumbled into the pillow.

"Are you checking to see if I'm naked?" he asked sleepily, slowly rolling over onto his back and turning his head to look at me. I let the sheet fall from my hand and tried to pretend that I hadn't just been caught doing exactly that.

"You know, you can just ask if you wanted to see me naked," he teased playfully, opening his eyes to look at me. I could feel the blush covering my skin and tinting it pink in the mid-morning sun that was filtering in through my curtains. I couldn't remember the last time that I had slept in this late, but I also couldn't remember the last time that I had been this exhausted.

"I wasn't trying to see if you were naked," I scoffed, picking up my cell phone from the nightstand to distract myself, so I didn't have to make eye contact. It was bad enough that he knew that I was lying because he had just caught me in the middle of it. I didn't want him to have the satisfaction of seeing the guilt branded across my face.

I had a few unread text messages from Lacey that had come in this morning, but other than that, nothing was needing my attention. I don't know what I expected. Somewhere deep down, I had this nagging feeling that someone would find out what I had done to Mateo, and I would get a call from Dan, letting me know that they knew what really happened.

"Then why were you lifting the sheet and looking at my crotch?" he asked as he rolled onto his side and propped himself up on his elbow.

"I thought I felt something tickle my leg." I set my phone on the nightstand and laid down on the pillow, pulling the blankets back up to my chin as an added layer of protection to keep him from reading more into what he already knew was the truth.

"So, you checked to see if it was my dick tickling your leg?" he laughed hard and let his head fall back as he enjoyed himself at my expense.

"You're impossible," I muttered, frustrated that he wasn't letting up on my blunder this morning. I could have come clean and just admitted what I had been doing, but that would have been too easy, and apparently, I didn't do anything easy these days.

"Alright, I'll stop giving you a hard time," he conceded.

I pushed the blankets off of me and swung my legs over the edge of the bed. It seemed like a better idea to put some distance between us before I got tempted to reach over and see just how good he could tickle me.

"But, I will promise you one thing," he added, rolling over and climbing out of bed. I turned to look at him, waiting for him to continue. "It wouldn't be your leg that you would have to worry about it tickling."

He tossed me a playful wink before grabbing his hoodie from the floor and slipping it on as he walked out of the room and into the living room.

I grumbled and ran a hand through my hair. I totally walked into that one, and after last night, I deserved the mounting sexual tension that was frustrating me.

I grabbed a hair tie from the nightstand and pulled my hair into a messy knot on top of my head. There were plenty of things for me to worry about—my hair wasn't one of them.

Wyatt was sitting on the couch, looking at something on his phone, when I walked out of the bedroom. He didn't look up from his phone, so I went about my business and started a pot of coffee. At this point, I was sure that even *my coffee* needed coffee this morning.

My body was sore and achy, but I was thankful that I didn't have the physical marks to show what had happened like Wyatt did. The knot on his head turned a nasty purple-black color and looked a little more swollen today than yesterday. I wondered if maybe I should convince him to go to the hospital to have it checked out when my phone rang with a call from Lacey.

I looked over at Wyatt, who was still busy on his phone, so I slid my finger across the screen to answer it. I didn't pay attention until the last minute that it was a FaceTime call and not a regular phone call until I saw Lacey's face on my screen. She went from smiling and happy to see me to major mom mode with squinted eyes as she tried to look closer at me to see what was wrong.

"Good morning to you too," I muttered when she didn't say anything, just kept staring at me.

"Why aren't you at work?" she asked, tilting her head to the side.

"I took the day off," I said with a shoulder shrug. I waited anxiously by the coffee maker, hoping that it would work its magic, and put something stronger in my coffee for me today. Lord knew that I needed it.

"*You* took the day off?" She tilted her head to the other side, a look of concern still stretched across her face. "Are you sick?"

I pulled my head back in surprise and shook my head.

"Why would you assume that I'm sick? Just because I haven't showered or gotten ready on my day off?" My tone was a little more hostile and aggressive than I had wanted it to be, but my mood was quickly growing sour.

"No, I just know that you don't ever take days off. It's ten o'clock on a Thursday, and you look like you just rolled out of bed," she replied softly. "I just wanted to make sure that you're okay."

"I'm fine," I assured her. I set my phone down for a second while I poured myself a cup of coffee, wondering if I should pour one for Wyatt as well. I didn't want to tell Lacey that he was here with me— again. How was I going to explain that?

"Okay, well, I wanted to call and talk to you about next month. Are you going to be able to make it down?"

I picked up my phone and took a drink of coffee, trying to figure out what she was talking about. My brain was too tired to try to think through the endless possibilities of why she would want me to go to Haven Brook next month.

I was about to answer when I heard Wyatt's cell phone ring loudly from the couch. I froze in place, my mouth slightly hanging open as I wondered if she had heard it.

"Whose phone is ring—" She pressed her lips together as she stopped talking once she realized what she was about to say. My face turned red in embarrassment as I glanced over at him, completely oblivious to my conversation with Lacey as he answered his phone.

"He stayed over?" she asked quietly.

"Let me call you back," I said quickly, not giving her a chance to respond before I hung up. Wyatt had stood up and was standing by the window, looking outside as he raked a hand through his hair. I couldn't imagine that it was one of his brothers calling, given how stressed he looked by whoever he was talking to.

I pressed the button to call Lacey back, this time making sure to avoid FaceTime. I wanted to have privacy for my conversation, yet I found that I wasn't able to walk away from his. What if it had something to do with what happened yesterday? I needed to know if there was trouble heading our way because I couldn't get past the idea that somehow we had managed to escape everything without anything more than some minor injuries. Things like that never happened for me, so I was sitting idly, waiting for the other shoe to fall.

"Okay, do you want to tell me why Wyatt is at your apartment, and you're not at work today?" Lacey asked when she answered the phone.

"It's a long story," I murmured as I stirred the creamer around in my cup with a spoon. I was too distracted to focus on what she had said while I tried to hear what Wyatt was talking about.

I tuned Lacey out as she mentioned something about a double wedding and how she could have Connie get busy on ours. Wyatt was still at the window with his back turned to me, but his shoulders were tight with tension.

"Yeah, I know what the reports say," he replied heavily, the agitation in his tone strong.

His head dipped down to his chest, a look of defeat washing over him.

"I know what it means," he bit out angrily. "What are my options?"

I lifted my mug to my lips and carefully took a sip, my curiosity peaked as to what he was talking about. There was no doubt that it had nothing to do with yesterday, but whatever it was seemed to be upsetting him.

"So, basically, you're saying that it's your professional medical opinion that I will never play professional baseball again."

I felt my heart sink when I heard the words, fully understanding what was going on and how devasting this news was for him.

"Did you hear a word that I said?" Lacey asked, a hint of irritation in her voice.

"I'm so sorry, Lace. I was distracted for a moment," I apologized. I turned my back to Wyatt to give him the privacy that I should have given him all along. "Can you tell me again?"

She sighed dramatically on the other end, the sound of her breath heavy in my ear. I knew that she did it on purpose because she knew how much I hated it. I couldn't blame her. I was being a terrible cousin to her by not listening or making the time for her the past few days that I should have.

"I said that Mia and Jade are trying to convince me to have a bachelorette party. I told them that I don't need one since I've been married before and I'm knocked up with twins, but they're insisting that we do *something.* I was hoping that maybe you could help me come up with an idea of something fun that we could do?"

I felt myself smiling as I listened to her talk, the familiarity of our close relationship a comfort that I didn't realize that I needed. Part of me wanted to confide in her and tell her what had happened, but I knew that I couldn't. This would be another secret that I would have to take with me to the grave. I just hoped that Wyatt would do the same.

"I think it would be great for you to do something fun to celebrate before the wedding. Since the weather will still be bad for a few more months, it will be hard to do anything outdoors. But you could always have a fun slumber party—a girl's only night. We could rent movies and make popcorn, and stay up super late—"

"You do remember that it's me that we're talking about, right?" she joked. "I'm asleep by seven-thirty every night. Eight o'clock if I'm feeling a little wild that night."

"Well, then, I guess we're going to have to do a tea party and Parcheesi. I'll make sure to get you back to the senior center before supper at four o'clock."

I took a sip of coffee and waited for her to snap.

"I happen to think tea is a fabulous idea," she said sarcastically. "But I'd rather play Monopoly."

I snorted and felt the burn of the coffee as it shot out of my nose and all over the counter in front of me. I set my cup down and reached over to grab a handful of napkins.

"Are you okay?" Wyatt asked from across the room, walking over to where I was standing.

Great. I rolled my eyes at how embarrassing this was as I looked down at the splattered coffee on my white hoodie.

"Yeah, I'm fine. Sorry to startle you," I mumbled as I held the phone between my ear and shoulder and continued to wipe at the stain on my shirt with the napkin.

He nodded his head slowly as if he didn't believe that I was okay. A few seconds later, he walked away and went back to his phone call.

"What in the world was that all about?" Lacey asked.

"I was taking a drink of coffee when you mentioned Monopoly, and it came shooting out of my nose when I remembered the stupid strip-Monopoly you told me that you and Grant played," I explained, tossing the dirty napkin onto the counter.

"Oh, yeah," she giggled. "I forgot about that… Well, okay, I didn't forget about it. I think that's actually when I got pregnant. His boat and my shoe made one hell of a—"

"Stop!" I shrieked, not wanting to hear the rest.

"Maybe you should play a game with Wyatt today since you're both there and you have the day off," she suggested casually.

"Yeah, I don't think so," I said dismissively, not wanting to get into the details about him and me.

"Why not? If he's sleeping over at your apartment, I'm guessing you guys are getting along pretty well and pretty much doing it nonstop at this point, right?"

"Not technically."

I watched as Wyatt got off of one call, only to take another. He seemed to be rather popular this morning, and I wondered if this was what a regular workday looked like for him. I knew that he was supposed to get back to Haven Brook as soon as he had Junior's commitment, but that had been delayed due to the crazy blizzard that had just passed through. Maybe they were letting him work remotely while he was stuck here?

"What's going on, Kayce? You seem off."

"It's nothing, really." I rushed the words out too quickly to make them sound believable. Lacey knew me better than my own mom and would instantly pick up on the lie.

"Go somewhere where you can talk," she instructed while waiting silently for me on the other line.

I grabbed my cup of coffee and went to my bedroom, glancing at Wyatt on my way. He was still preoccupied, so I didn't bother him as I went inside and closed the door behind me. I climbed up on my bed and set the coffee down beside me on the nightstand while I got comfortable.

"Okay, spill it," Lacey said.

"It's a long story and one that I can't get into," I said wearily.

"Does it have something to do with the knot on Wyatt's head?" Lacey asked, catching me off guard.

"How did you hear about that?"

"Grant just got off of the phone with Connie. Apparently, she saw it when they were Face Timing after he went missing for a while, and no one could get ahold of him. He convinced her to stay put and not drive in the storm, but she called Grant to ask if he and Chase could go down to Easterville this weekend to pick him up and bring him back home."

I felt my stomach sink as I thought about him leaving.

"There was an incident and a small altercation," I said vaguely, not getting into the details. It was up to him what he wanted to share with his family, but we definitely needed to talk about things this morning to make sure we both had our stories straight.

"Is that why he stayed the night?"

I loved how she assumed that he had stayed the night, but also, how else was I going to explain why he was at my apartment at ten in the morning on a day when I should have been at work?

"Yes."

"But you can't talk about what happened?"

"No."

"Okay," she said with a breath. "I won't push you about what happened as far as why he has a knot on his head, but I am going to ask what's going on with you guys. You seem so standoffish about him when I ask, but yet you guys have spent a ton of time together in the few days that he's been there."

"I don't know, Lacey, it's complicated," I groaned, not wanting to think about it.

"Why? Do you like him?"

"Yes. A lot."

"More than Brent?"

His name sent a chill through me, along with a brutal reminder of the big secret that I couldn't talk to her about.

"More than anyone," I whispered. I pulled the pillow that Wyatt had slept on up to my chest and cuddled it, smelling his cologne.

"Oh, Kayce," she cooed, giddy with happiness. "That's wonderful! You're finally in lov—"

"Don't you dare say it," I warned.

It felt like saying Beetlejuice. Once you said it out loud, nothing but bad things were going to come.

"Alright, alright," she laughed. "I won't push you to say it, but I am so excited to hear that it's happening. And so soon, too!"

She hit the nail on the head without even trying.

"It is too soon, isn't it?" I asked, chewing on my nail. "I've only known him for three days, Lacey. THREE. DAYS."

"Yeah, and you guys have obviously gone through something together—that you can't talk about, but something that pushed you guys even closer. Life works in mysterious ways, but I believe that everything happens for a reason. Like Wyatt taking this job and getting his first recruit in Easterville. Or how you came to his rescue with his truck and letting him stay the night at your apartment when he couldn't get his hotel room situated. Whatever it is that you guys went through, it might just be the one thing that solidifies the bond you've already created."

"I don't know," I sighed heavily. There was so much that had happened in such a short time that my head felt like it was spinning.

"He doesn't even live here, Lacey. I can barely commit to having this tiny apartment, how would I ever be able to do a long-distance relationship?"

"You *could* just move to Haven Brook… I mean, Annie and I would love to have you here with us, and I know I would love for you to be here when the new babies are born."

I thought about what she was saying. It wasn't like I had anything significant to keep me in Easterville, other than my parents still lived here, and I had my own shop. But then again, my parents were starting to travel more now that my dad was retired, which meant that I hardly saw them anymore. On top of that, my shop only did well because it was the only automotive repair shop in town. If a man decided to open up a shop of his own, I would easily be out of business the first week.

But it was ridiculous to think that I would pack up everything I have and move to another town for a man that I've barely known for three days. Who did that sort of thing?

People in love. I rolled my eyes at the thought and dismissed it just as quickly as it had popped into my head.

"I can't just up and leave, Lacey. You know that."

She waited a few minutes before responding, knowing that this was a sensitive subject for me every time she had asked.

"I know. But sometimes things change, and we find ourselves doing crazy stuff we never imagined we would."

I heard footsteps on the other side of the door and wondered if Wyatt was looking for me.

"Well, I hate to run, kiddo, but I have to get going for my doctor's appointment. Call me if you need anything."

"Okay, I will. Let me know how my future nieces or nephews or both are doing."

She laughed and agreed to text me with an update when she was done. I hung up and climbed out of bed, grabbing my cup of cold coffee from the nightstand. When I opened the door, Wyatt was sitting on the couch, his head in his hands.

I didn't want to let on that I had been eavesdropping on his conversation earlier, so I had to pretend that I didn't know what was wrong. I set my phone and coffee cup down on the counter and then walked over to where he was sitting.

Gently, I rested my hand on his shoulder and waited for him to look up at me.

"Are you okay?" I asked softly.

He looked around the room as if he was searching for the answer.

"I don't know," he muttered, still seeming lost.

"Did you get bad news?" I walked around and sat down next to him on the couch.

He rocked back and forth for a few seconds, his jaw clenched as he thought about it.

"No, not bad news. Life-changing news."

I held my breath and waited for him to drop the bomb that had been silently ticking inside of him.

"I just got offered a professional scouting position with the Arizona Rattlers. It's my dream job to work for a professional baseball team since my career as a player is officially over, but I would have to…." His voice trailed off, fading into the silence as I processed what he was saying.

"Move to Arizona," I finished for him. The knot in my stomach grew tighter as it moved up higher to wrap around my heart.

Thirty Two
Wyatt

My heart had felt like it was beating out of my chest with the excitement of getting the job offer. I had applied for the position shortly after several doctors confirmed that it would be unlikely for me to continue to play baseball, but when I didn't hear anything for a few months, I gave up and applied for the job at Haven Brook University.

Never in a million years did I think that I would be given the opportunity to work alongside some of the best athletes in the world, and yet now that I had it, I wasn't sure what to do with it. I saw the look on Kayce's face when I told her that the job would require me to move to Arizona. The way her eyes watered and how she blinked the tears away before they could fall. None of that was lost on me. In fact, it was the reason that I was coming down from my high and thinking of reasons that I should say no and stay in Colorado. It felt strange to be so worried about what she thought, but secretly, I had hoped that she would be as excited about it as I was.

I was about to talk to her about it when her phone rang, and she excused herself to take the call in her bedroom. I could tell that she was upset, but I couldn't put my finger on the reason why. I was starting to feel restless and needed to clear my head.

My phone vibrated against my thigh as it rang. I pulled it out and answered it, seeing Noah's name on the caller ID.

"What's up?" I asked with a little more irritation than needed.

"Woah, I should ask you the same," he joked.

"Nothing, it's just been a long day," I replied, running a hand down my face. I needed to shave. It had only been a few days since I had taken the time to clean up before I met with Junior, but the scruff on my jawline was already irritating me. I liked to take pride in my looks, and this gruff-messy look wasn't for me.

"It's not even eleven in the morning. How is it already a long day?"

"It just is," I sighed heavily, not wanting to get into any of the details on the phone.

"Alright, well, Chase and I are heading to Easterville in an hour or so to pick you up. Should be there around five or six, depending on what the roads are like on our way over there."

I could hear Kayce's voice from under the door. Something about it made me want to stay and talk to her, but I knew that I had to do the right thing. And given how upset she looked a few minutes ago, the right thing was to walk away before I hurt her even more. Maybe some distance between us would be what I needed to clear my head and get back to normal.

Fuck if I even knew what normal was anymore. In four days, everything that could go wrong had gone wrong. Not to mention the crazy shit that went down yesterday. Maybe Lacey was right about Easterville being a place you needed to escape from. The real problem was that I wanted Kayce to run away with me.

"Are you still there?" Noah asked when I hadn't answered him.

"Yeah," I coughed to clear that throat that suddenly felt constricted. "You guys don't have to come for me. I can find a way back."

"We were given orders," he said with a hint of humor.

"Orders?"

It took a second before it hit me—my mom.

"When did she call?" I asked. I stood up and walked over to the window, looking at how peaceful it looked outside with the snow covering the roads.

"About twenty minutes ago," he laughed. "She insisted that we bring you home so she can keep an eye on the knot on your head. Which, by the way, what the fuck happened to you anyway?"

"It's a long story," I mumbled.

"Alright, but if it has to do with you knocking up one of your former one-night stands, please leave that shit in Easterville. We don't need any more of that here."

I laughed and shook my head, remembering the ordeal Noah had gotten himself into with Cindy, a one-night stand that went crazy and kidnapped his girlfriend.

"Nothing like that," I assured him. There was no way that I could tell anyone what really happened. Kayce and I still needed to talk about it to make sure we kept our stories straight.

"Thank God," he chuckled. "Send me the address to your hotel, and I'll text you when we're almost there."

I heard the bedroom door open and looked over to see Kayce walk out.

"I'm not at a hotel," I said with my eyes locked onto hers. "I'm at Kayce's apartment. Ask Grant for the address, he can get it from Lacey."

The line was quiet for a second. Kayce was standing still by the couch, her phone clutched to her chest as she watched me.

"Wyatt, you son of a bitch," Noah laughed. "You slept with—"

I pressed the end button and hung up, afraid that Kayce would hear what he was about to say.

"Is everything alright?" I asked as I slid my phone back into my pocket and walked over toward her.

She slowly nodded her head.

"That was Dan, the officer from last night," she explained. "They found drugs in his system with the toxicology report. Apparently, he was pretty high when he *broke in*. They believe that he accidentally knocked the jack out while trying to get something from underneath the car. The case is closed, and I should be able to go back to the shop later today or tomorrow morning at the latest."

"Closed?" I repeated, unable to believe it myself.

She bobbed her head in agreement.

"Wow. That's a relief," I said, still processing the news. "But I have to ask, Kayce, what really happened yesterday with Mateo?"

I sat on one end of the couch and patted the other, offering her to sit with me. She curled up into a ball on the other side and wrapped her arms around her knees.

"Right after you got hit—the first time, Mike dragged me down the hall by my hair. He was trying to get the door open, but it was stuck. He had to let go to mess with the lock, and when he turned around to grab me again, I punched him in the face and took off running. I thought I was in the clear and snuck around to the back entrance of the garage, where I keep a spare key. I could hear voices, so I hid under the table until the front door closed. I thought they had left. I was coming to find you, but when I got up, Mateo was right there, waiting for me.

"I didn't have a chance to run before he held me by my throat. By the time he let go, I was gasping for air and didn't have the strength to run. I was still freezing from being outside for so long, my body was just too weak. So, I led him to the back of the garage where my project car is, and I slid underneath it. I knew that he wouldn't easily be able to catch me unless he climbed under after me. I purposely antagonized him to get him mad, so he wouldn't have time to think about it. Once he was under the car, I got out as quickly as possible and pushed the jack out from under the car. He was dead in an instant."

Her bottom lip slightly trembled as she told me what happened. I sat there in awe of this incredible woman who was so strong and independent that she did what she had to do to survive. Knowing that she had done all of that by herself made my heart full.

"How did you know where I was?" I asked, trying to put together the rest of the puzzle.

A blush spread across her cheeks as she guiltily looked away. This immediately piqued my interest.

"Kayce?"

"I um… I might have stolen Mateo's phone to get the information from Mike."

"How did you get into his phone? Wasn't it locked?" I asked, remembering Mike's comment about how I should have better privacy settings enabled on mine.

"It was," she admitted. "But I got lucky because it was set with fingerprint access."

My eyes went wide with shock as I listened.

"Don't worry," she laughed nervously. "It's not like I cut off his finger and put it in my pocket for future use. I just unlocked the phone and then changed it to a four-digit password that I made up myself."

I nodded in approval. She was definitely smart and quick thinking—there was no doubt about that.

"I'm impressed," I said proudly. "You did really well with thinking on your feet and getting creative to find answers to your problems."

"Thank you." She smiled the first genuine smile that I had seen in days, and I found how much I had missed it.

"It still seems crazy that everything just happened yesterday. It feels like it was weeks or months ago." I looked down at the cuts on my wrist, making note that I would need to hide those from my family until they healed. Thankfully, it was still bitter cold outside which was the perfect excuse for wearing long sleeves and hoodies.

"I know," she sighed heavily as she leaned back and let her knees rest against the pillow beside her. "I would never have imagined something like this would happen, but I'm thankful that it's over."

I didn't say anything because it felt like I would jinx it if I did. While things felt like they were over because no one was actively trying to kill us, I had no idea if we were that lucky. Two members of a well-known rock band were soon going to be reported missing, along with their former manager. People were bound to start talking about that, and what if it led back to Kayce and me? Did anyone know that they were coming to Easterville? Was anyone looking for them?

"About earlier," I started, my voice feeling a little shaky as I worked up the courage to talk to her about it. "You seemed a little upset when I told you that I got offered the job in Arizona."

She looked up at me, her golden-brown eyes darkening as the sunlight shifted position in the room.

"I'm sorry that I wasn't more excited for you earlier. I've been feeling a little tired and run down today," she lied. "But I'm very happy for you, and I think you'll love it in Phoenix. There's plenty of hot women out there. Literally and figuratively," she joked.

I felt the sting in my heart as her words stabbed right through it. Did she really think that I was that shallow that I would want to go there to find another woman? How could she not know how hard this felt to think that I would have to leave—whatever this was between us— behind if I took this job? It soured my stomach to think that by going after my dream, it was going to also create a new nightmare. One where I had to live in a world without Kayce in it because there was no way she would go with me.

THREE STRIKES, YOU'RE GONE

Thirty-Three
Kayce

It had been twenty minutes since Wyatt left with Noah and Chase. I had offered to take him by his hotel to grab his stuff and check out before they got here, but he insisted that they would do it before they headed back to Haven Brook.

The afternoon was more painful than I had imagined after he told me that he was leaving. I had selfishly hoped that he would be here until his truck was fixed, but it was silly of me to think that he didn't have a life back home that he needed to get back to.

Maybe it was for the best that he left when he did. I could feel myself getting closer to him, and that scared the shit out of me. While he had tried to assure me that what we felt for each other was real and not just a reaction to the trauma we had endured yesterday, it didn't really feel that way after he easily packed up and left with his family.

Everything felt chaotic around me, so I grabbed my jacket and left to get some fresh air and dinner since I was in no mood to cook. I passed by the shop and felt a pain in my stomach when I saw the crime scene tape still wrapped around the building. Dan had said that they were trying to move as quickly as possible but that it might not be ready for me to go back until tomorrow. I couldn't honestly say that I was looking forward to going back.

My shop had been a part of me for so long that I thought that it defined who I was. I needed people to see me as a strong, independent woman who enjoyed working on cars, but I don't know that anyone ever saw me as anything other than the daughter of Mel and Betty—the son they always wanted but never had.

The gossip had never bothered me growing up, and I was happy spending time with my dad and grandpa as they taught me everything they knew. So what if I didn't want to sit around and play Barbies and have tea parties? I could take an engine apart and put it back together wearing my fanciest princess dress without missing a step.

I pulled into the parking lot of Taco Bell and waited for my turn to order. My phone rang, and I ignored it, not having the desire or motivation to answer it. The car in front of me moved forward, so I scooted along with it. I had just finished placing my order when my phone rang again. I knew that if I didn't answer it, Lacey would just keep calling until I did. I waited until after the cashier had given me back my credit card and handed me my bag of food before I answered the phone.

"Kayce! Did you see the news?" Lacey shrieked. It wasn't the excited tone she had when Chris Hemsworth was on tv. It was the one she used to use when we were little, and she would share secrets with me about her dad.

I felt a chill run down my spine as I pulled forward and turned onto Main Street.

"No, what news?"

"That singer you were dating- the one from Jolted—he's dead!"

I slammed on the brakes, sending the bag of food flying across the seat and onto the floormat of the passenger side of the car as I stopped at the red light. I hadn't been paying attention and didn't realize it had already turned yellow long before I came barreling up to it.

"What?!" I gasped. Surely, she had to be mistaken. There was no way that the news already knew about his death. How could anyone know? Unless someone was around and saw us? Or unless he told someone where he was going.

"Hold on, I'm listening to the story now," she said. I waited impatiently for her to tell me what was being reported as the light turned green. I carefully headed back to my apartment.

"It said that Brent Fallows and Dray Long were found in an abandoned shed, along with their former account manager. According to the other band members, Mike, their manager, had recently been fired for embezzling money from their fan club. Brent and Dray had planned to meet up with Mike to recover the stolen funds when something went wrong. They haven't released the details of what happened, but police were sent out after someone called in to report an abandoned structure on fire."

"Oh my God," I whispered, covering my mouth with a hand as I turned into the parking lot and found a spot close to the stairs by my apartment.

"I'm so sorry," she said sympathetically. "I know that you guys haven't been together for a while, but I thought you should know."

"Yeah, thanks for calling to tell me."

I rushed up the stairs and went inside, desperate to get out of the cold. My stomach growled, reminding me that I had once again neglected to feed it consistently for the past few days. I tossed my keys and purse on the counter and took my food to the couch.

"Are you okay?" Lacey asked softly as I unwrapped a chalupa and set it in my lap.

"I'm fine, really," I assured her and took a bite.

"Are you eating?"

"Yeah," I said as I moved the food around with my tongue. "I was starving, and you caught me while I was out grabbing dinner."

"Are you eating chalupas?"

I swallowed my bite and laughed.

"Is there ever a time when I'm *not*?"

"That's true," she laughed. "Maybe I'll have chalupas at my bachelorette party, so you'll be sure to make it."

I rolled my eyes and took another bite. It wasn't the worst idea and probably would be an easy way to lure me there.

"Have you decided when you're going to have it?"

"Grant and I talked about it last night, and since we're not doing the traditional bachelor and bachelorette parties, we're just going to do them that Friday before the wedding. That way, everyone that comes in from out of town can be there for all of it in the same weekend."

"You mean me. So *Kayce* can be there for all of it," I laughed and took another bite.

"It's important to me, and I don't want you to miss any of it," she said light-heartedly.

"I know, and you know that I would never miss anything if I could avoid it."

"I just don't want you to have to miss so much work and fall behind," she added with her mom tone.

"You don't have to worry about me, Lacey. I promise, I'm an adult and can manage my bills and taking a few days off from work. I will be there."

I could hear the sound of my chewing as I waited for her to say something.

"I didn't mean to upset you."

"You didn't," I fibbed and took another bite. I hated that this was something that we talked about often. She constantly worried about me and whether or not I should keep the shop open. It wasn't that I was wild and carefree with my money. No one in town valued what I did, and lately, I had more lulls than busy days.

"Okay, well, I won't keep you so you can enjoy your food. But call me soon so we can chat and catch up?"

I thought about everything that I desperately wanted to talk to her about and felt frustrated when I realized that I couldn't. Not only did I have to keep the stuff about Brent a secret, but I also didn't want to unload my problems with Wyatt on her either. I had no clue whether he had told any of his family about his new job offer, and I sure as hell didn't want to be the one to slip and tell Lacey. She would tell Grant and his entire family would know before he even made it back to town tonight.

I promised her that we would sit down and talk this weekend, knowing that it would be enough to keep her from pressing me about what was going on between Wyatt and me. By that time, he would already be home and likely would have already told his family about his new job in Arizona. Then I wouldn't have to tell Lacey what was wrong. She would already know why my heart was broken.

Thirty Four
Wyatt

I hadn't spoken to Kayce after I left her apartment on Thursday. Part of me tried to convince myself that it was for the best, while the other part of me wanted to ram my head into the wall for a brief escape from the pain that I was feeling from leaving her. But wasn't that what I was planning to do anyway if I decided to take the job in Arizona?

The weekend was a blur, filled with plenty of beer as I tried to drink away the nagging voice that told me to call her. I had heard from the grapevine—aka Lacey told Grant—that one of Kayce's ex-boyfriends had been killed in a fire. Grant didn't know many of the details, and I didn't bother to ask because I didn't want him to think that it had anything to do with my obsession with Kayce. Instead, I got on my laptop and found the article without having to do much digging. There was suspicion that Brent had been stabbed before he shot and killed Mike; however, they were having a hard time collecting evidence due to the fire. The good news was that they didn't believe anyone else was involved as two of the band members went to recover embezzled funds from the recently fired band manager.

The entire thing looked like a big, steaming pile of shit, and I was glad that they weren't bothering to dig any deeper. Between a random car that passed by and called in the fire and the other band member that reported them missing, no one seemed too concerned by the incident.

I sat in my recliner with the paperwork for the new job sitting on the table beside me. I had picked it up several times to fill it out, and each time I would think about Kayce and set it back down. I tried to force myself to focus on the football game playing on the tv but couldn't seem to muster the enthusiasm to pay attention to who was playing. My depression was starting to sink to a new low.

My mom had sent me a text message earlier, asking me to come over for family dinner. She tried to get all of us together every Sunday, but it didn't always work out with everyone's busy schedules. For whatever reason—maybe all of the stars were perfectly lined in the fucking sky—everyone was free for this one, and I was the last person she was waiting on.

It wasn't like I could decline because I was grumpy and didn't want to go. That would never fly with my mom, nor should it. But I also couldn't show up, mopey and depressed, and talk about how I broke Kayce's heart, and therefore broke my own. I hadn't told them about the new job yet either, which felt odd as I was now the one with all of the secrets in the family.

My phone dinged with a new message. I groaned as I reached into my pocket to get it.

Kayce: Did you see the news about that tragic accident with Jolted?

Just seeing her name on my phone had me pushing the foot rest down so I could sit up straight. My fingers quickly moved across my phone as I typed.

Me: I did. It's so unfortunate.

I didn't know what else to say. We both knew that we had to keep our messages about this vague, and I knew what she was asking when she sent her message. Did I see that we were in the clear? Yes, I had seen that.

It felt good to talk to her, even if it was just a quick text message. I didn't want to stop, but I also didn't know what to say.

Me: How are you?

It was such a lame message when I really wanted to ask her a thousand different things. I needed confirmation that she was okay and that I hadn't really broken her heart the way that I feared I did. She didn't deserve it, and I couldn't shake the feeling that she was just as torn up as I had been the last few days.

Kayce: I'm good. How are you?

I rolled my neck back on my shoulders, feeling the tension across them.

Me: Honestly?

I waited for a few seconds as the dots bounced at the bottom of the screen as she typed.

Kayce: Yes.

Me: I feel terrible about how we left things between us.

Kayce: Me too.

Me: Can we talk? There has to be a way for us to work this out?

I stared intently at my phone for a few minutes, waiting for her to text me back. Just as I had given up hope that she would respond, I got her message.

Kayce: I don't think that there's anything for us to work out. Our lives are too different, and neither of us should give up the things we want to try to make this work.

Kayce: Your truck will be ready next week. I'll call and let you know when you can come pick it up.

I tossed my phone onto my lap and closed my eyes as I leaned back in the chair. A few seconds later, I felt it vibrate with another text message and quickly grabbed it, hoping that she had already changed her mind about what she had said.

Grant: Dinner is in 30 minutes. Get your ass over here.

I blew out a heavy breath along with some choice curse words as I got up and got ready.

Forty minutes later, I was sitting at the table at my mom's house, listening to everyone talk as they got situated. Jade and Noah were at one end of the table, getting their son, Asher, situated in his high chair. My older brother Chase was at the head of the table, where my dad used to sit, helping Mia get their girls situated. Riley was giving them sass about how she was a big girl and didn't want to sit in her high chair. I laughed when my mom reminded him that he was worse at two years old and that he better be prepared for when Millie caught up to her big sister's attitude.

It felt good to be around my family and see my brothers settling down as they started their own families. For a while, Noah and I had joked about how we would be the ones to stay single and have all of the fun while Chase was settling down with Mia. But then Noah met Jade, and everything changed after that. Even Grant fell quickly for Lacey. I was fine being the only single one out of the bunch, but now as I looked around at how happy everyone was, it made me want that same happiness too. Hell, even my mom had secretly been dating someone without anyone knowing. It seemed like it was only time before I would find someone to settle down with, but my career seemed to have another idea.

"How did your doctor's appointment go?" my mom asked Lacey as she scooped some green beans on her plate before passing the bowl to Buck.

We hadn't spoken about the information that I had asked him for on Mike, and I prayed that he hadn't heard about what happened on the news. Buck was a quiet man, and I trusted that he wouldn't say anything unless it was when we were in private. And even then, I still hoped that he would avoid it.

"It went well," Lacey said as she leaned over to put a piece of fried chicken on Annie's plate for her. It was incredible how much Annie looked like her mom. I was curious to see what the twins would look like and if either of them would look more like their mom or dad.

I always felt like Chase and Grant looked like my dad, but I never thought I looked like my mom or dad. For years I had worried that maybe I had been adopted, but my mom assured me that I wasn't. My curiosity always got the better of me, and I wondered what my dad would look like as he got older.

"They'll do her twelve-week ultrasound in two weeks," Grant added as Lacey got distracted with Annie. "I'm hoping we'll be able to find out the gender soon after that. They're doing the genetic testing at that appointment and said that they could tell the gender with the bloodwork they'll be collecting anyway."

"We are not finding out," Lacey chuckled and gently elbowed him in the ribs when she was done helping Annie. "I want it to be a surprise."

"Finding out you are pregnant was a surprise. Finding out it is twins is a surprise. I think we've had plenty of surprises already," he teased, planting a kiss on her cheek.

"Well, then you won't mind waiting for one more." She pursed her lips and narrowed her eyes at him, and it immediately reminded me of Kayce. I looked down and pushed my mashed potatoes around with my fork.

"How's the new job?" Buck asked me, changing the subject as everyone began eating. I felt my cheeks turn red as I panicked, wondering how he found out. My mom turned to look at me, her brows pulled together in confusion.

"How did you find out?" I asked, wondering if Kayce had told Lacey about it.

Buck slowly lowered his fork to his plate and looked at me with the same confusion my mom had.

"Umm, you told us about it, son," he said cautiously. "We all knew that you were taking the position with the university. Your mom even checked on you a time or two while you were in Easterville."

I wanted to smack myself in the head for being so dense. Of course, that was what he meant.

"Oh, yeah, um, it's going well. I got the kid's commitment," I said quickly before anyone could question why I was acting so strange.

I shoved a bite of chicken into my mouth and chewed, hoping that it would be the end of the conversation and someone else would start talking.

"What's going on, Wyatt?" my mom asked, turning to look at me after setting her fork down next to her plate.

All eyes were on me as my heart thudded in my ears. I could feel the sweat dot along my forehead and wondered if this was what it felt like to be in a police interrogation room.

"Nothing," I blurted out, my voice cracking in the process.

She tilted her head slightly to the side and said nothing. Her eyes searched my face, confirming that I was lying as I blushed the harder she stared at me.

"Okay, fine!" I exclaimed, slamming my hands down on the table. "I got offered a new job, and that's what I thought Buck was asking about. I haven't told anyone about it, so it caught me off guard when I thought he knew."

"What new job?" Grant asked, leaning forward to listen.

"Why didn't you want to tell us?" Chase asked right after him.

I pulled in a deep breath, trying to calm myself so I could speak without looking like an idiot again.

"I had applied a while back and never heard anything, so I figured they weren't interested. I got a call on Thursday from the Arizona Rattlers, offering me the scouting position that I had interviewed for last year."

I swallowed hard as I turned and looked at my mom. Her eyes were wide with surprise, her hand fiddling with her necklace as she processed my words.

"When did you interview?" she asked quietly.

"Last year. When I said that I was meeting with the rehab specialist in Phoenix, I was actually there to interview for the position."

"And you never bothered to tell me?"

"I'm sorry, I didn't mean to upset you. I knew that you would have told me not to rush things, to wait and see if my shoulder got better."

She pressed her lips into a thin line and turned forward in her seat. She picked up her fork but held it in the air before taking a bite. I could see the wheels turning in her head as she tried to figure out what she wanted to say.

"You're right. I would have told you to wait. But only because I knew how much playing baseball meant to you. Not because I wouldn't want this other opportunity for you."

She took a bite and kept her attention focused on her plate instead of me.

"I know you want the best for me. You all do. But this job means that I would have to move to Arizona."

I saw the look on everyone's face as I said it. The realization of why I had kept this a secret finally hitting them.

"Is this what you want to do?" Noah asked gently.

"It would be my dream job," I admitted, feeling guilty for it.

"Then you should take the job," Grant said from the other end of the table.

"You have to do what's best for you," Chase added. "Besides, Mia and I will need a vacation to someplace warm soon. We can come to visit and show the girls what warm really means."

"We all support you, Wyatt. You know that," Buck said as he squeezed my mom's hand.

"I know," I sighed heavily. It felt better having them know about the job, but that still didn't solve my biggest dilemma. "But it's not that easy. I can't make up my mind on whether or not I should take it."

"Why not?" Grant asked.

"Because maybe it's better if I stay in Colorado," I blurted out. I wasn't ready to talk about this. Not yet, and definitely not with my family.

"What's in Colorado that is worth giving up on your dream?" my mom asked, turning to look at me again.

My face fell, and I closed my eyes. I could see the look on her face when she realized what it was. She had seen it with my brothers and Noah.

"Oh," she whispered. "I see."

I looked up and found Lacey watching me, a look on her face that I couldn't quite figure out.

"I knew it," she said quietly, her eyes never leaving mine.

THREE STRIKES, YOU'RE GONE

Thirty Five
Kayce

It had been over three weeks since I had talked to Wyatt. The last message I had gotten was a quick text, letting me know that he had taken the job in Arizona and that he wouldn't have time to come get his truck for a few more weeks. He offered to pay me to have it stored somewhere until he could come for it and apologized that things were so busy and chaotic for him right now.

Whenever I talked to Lacey on the phone, we both avoided any conversations about Wyatt. She didn't give me any updates on him moving to Arizona, and I didn't bother asking for one. He had made up his mind, and as of February 1st, he would be starting the next chapter of his life. He was moving forward—which was something that I needed to do as well.

I, on the other hand, was sitting at my desk, drinking a cold cup of coffee and staring at the stack of bills that I couldn't afford to pay. I almost laughed when I saw his offer to pay me to keep his truck in my garage a little bit longer because he didn't want to cost me any new business by having it sitting there, in the way. If I thought business was slow before, it was even slower after word got out that someone had been killed here. Small towns were just funny like that. It didn't matter whether people thought I had killed Mateo or not; they had already made up their mind that they wouldn't give me their business from there on out.

My parents had offered me to move back home with them, and while I hated the idea, I didn't have much of a choice. My rent was due in a week, and my bank account was sitting at a measly four dollars—not even enough to buy a few chalupas as one last "pity me meal."

It was almost one o'clock, and my stomach growled loudly, thanks to my daydream about chalupas. I opened my desk drawer and rummaged around, looking to see if I had any hidden snacks that I had forgotten were in there. My phone vibrated across my desk, distracting me from my food search.

"Hey," I said, sitting upright as I answered Lacey's call.

"What are your plans this weekend?" she blurted out with a hint of panic in her voice.

I almost laughed, thinking about how I had no plans because I had no money to do anything.

"I have no plans," I said lightly, trying to force the stress to roll off my back.

"Well, you do now," she informed me with a little more cheer.

"I do?"

"Yes. I'm getting married *this* weekend."

I felt the excitement that I had started to feel deflate.

"The wedding is supposed to be three weeks away. On Valentine's Day. Remember?" I asked, wondering if pregnancy brain was making her crazy.

"I know, I know," she groaned. "But my dress barely fits, and I *really* want to wear my mom's wedding dress. It's important to me, Kayce. So if I don't get married this weekend, then I won't be able to wear it. These babies are making me *huge,* and they're supposed to go through another growth spurt again soon."

"Okay," I said quietly, frantically trying to figure out how to get out there with a quarter tank of gas and no money. It would be nearly impossible unless I found some way to come up with cash—and quick. "You know I wouldn't miss it. I'll be there."

"Oh, thank goodness." She let out a breath, and I could hear the relief in her voice. I was glad that at least one of us was feeling less stressed because I, on the other hand, was way more stressed than before, if that was even possible.

I was chewing on my nail, lost in my own thoughts, struggling to figure out how I was going to pull this off and make it happen.

"Kayce?" she asked, and I wondered if she had asked me something and I had missed it. I had a terrible habit of doing that, but usually only when Wyatt was around.

"Yeah?"

"I've already transferred some money into your account for this weekend," she said sternly. "I don't want to hear about how you don't need it or how you can handle things on your own. This was a last-minute decision on our end, so I wanted to make sure that it didn't put any stress on you. There's enough for food, gas, and for you to have a girl's day with us for the bachelorette party on Friday."

"Friday? As in two days?" I gulped, not even realizing that today was already Wednesday and that she really was throwing a total curveball at me.

"Bachelorette party on Friday—we're going to go get manis and pedis, then go for massages, and then we'll have a nice lunch and relax. The boys will be doing their own thing while we do ours. After that is the rehearsal dinner, and Saturday is the wedding."

"Wow," I said, completely impressed with how organized she sounded. "It looks like you have everything figured out. I'm really happy for you, Lace."

"Thanks." I could hear the smile in her voice. "Wyatt's mom, Connie, has been a total life-saver, as well as Mia and Jade. I can't wait for you to meet them!" she squealed. "They're so amazing, and I know that you will just love them as much as I do."

"I can't wait either. It'll be a fun weekend."

I thought about how I felt about seeing Wyatt again. My stomach was flipping back and forth, which matched what my brain was doing at the moment as well.

"Do you think you can take off tomorrow and drive down early? You can stay with us, so you don't have to get a room. We have the guest room already set up," she offered.

I looked down at the blank calendar on my desk and almost laughed.

"Yeah, I can leave tomorrow. I'll let you know when I'm in town."

We hung up, and I leaned back against my chair as I thought about what all I needed to do before I left. Finally, I grabbed my purse and keys and headed out to the store.

Thirty Six
Wyatt

"Did you get the contract signed for your new lease?" my mom asked as she moved about the kitchen, putting the food from lunch away. I had come over to help her with the last-minute wedding details for Grant and Lacey after she called me in a panic that they had moved up the date.

While I knew that it was more stressful for my mom to put everything together and make it perfect, I was secretly relieved that it had been moved up to right before I had to leave for my new job in Arizona. I couldn't imagine that they would be as lenient with giving me time off after only being there for two weeks, and it broke my heart to think that I would miss my brother's wedding. Or maybe, it was more that I was worried that I would miss seeing Kayce.

I had no idea if she was going to show up or not. It wasn't like I could ask Lacey without having another heart-to-heart conversation about why I was being such an idiot and not calling her. I knew that she deserved better than what I could give her, which was why I was walking away from her. It didn't do any of us any favors to pretend that whatever this had been between us—could work out.

"Yeah, I signed the paperwork, and they'll have my keys at the front desk when I get out there."

"I still can't believe you're leaving in a week."

She smiled, but I could see the sadness underneath it.

"Me neither." I leaned back in the wooden chair at the table and crossed my ankles.

"Are you having second thoughts about going?" she asked cautiously, while washing a plate.

That was a hard question to answer with no right answer. Did I want to go after my dream and work for a professional team? Yes. Did I want to pack up and leave everything I had come to know as my home for the past twenty-five years? No. Was I ready to explore and broaden my horizons? Yes. Did I want to walk away from Kayce and never see her again? No. And that was the part that kept me up at night, reconsidering whether I was making the right decision.

"No," I lied, staring down at my shoes to avoid meeting her eyes. She would know I was lying—hell, she probably already did. But at least I could say that I didn't look her in the eye and lie to her. That was better, right?

"Grab a towel and wipe down that table," she said, changing the subject for me. I loved that she knew when not to push, and this was one of those times. "If you're gonna sit there, you may as well make yourself useful."

I chuckled and got up, grabbing a clean towel from the drawer. I sprayed some cleaner on it and began wiping the table down when I heard the front door open. I assumed that it was Buck coming home but was surprised when Grant and Lacey walked in.

"Hey, what are you guys doing here?" I asked as I walked over to hug Lacey.

"We were out doing some last-minute wedding shopping," Lacey explained as she shrugged out of her jacket as Grant helped her. "And I started to feel funny, so we came here so I could take a break and maybe help Connie?"

"What's wrong? Are you okay?" my mom asked, wiping her wet hands on a towel before rushing over to see Lacey.

"I'm okay, just feeling a little tired, and I think walking around so much was aggravating the babies. I had a couple of Braxton-Hick contractions, and Grant freaked out," she laughed, looking over her shoulder at him with a playful smile.

"You don't *know* that they weren't real ones," he replied, looking past her to my mom.

"Why don't you sit down, and I'll get you a glass of water. We'll see if that'll help those pesky guys go away," my mom teased, leading Lacey to the table with her hand on her lower back. I stepped to the side and pulled a chair out for her.

"I'm sure that it's nothing, really." She sat down and winced as she leaned forward and cradled her stomach.

"See—that's not nothing," Grant said with panic in his voice.

My mom looked between them, unsure of what to say. I could see the doubt on her face and could tell that she was worried that these might not be fake contractions either.

"Why don't I run Lacey over to the hospital and have them take a look?" I offered, clapping a hand on Grant's shoulder. "Mom's going to need your help with some of the wedding stuff anyways," I added when he gave me a strange look.

My mom tried to hide her grin when she realized what I was doing.

"I can take her to the hospital," Grant objected, looking between all of us as if we were crazy for thinking that he couldn't.

"I know, big brother, we don't doubt that you can." I squeezed his shoulder gently. "But Lacey needs someone who will stay calm and *not* send her into labor right now. So, how about I take her to get checked out, and you help mom with the doilies or whatever girly project she has on her agenda today?'

I felt the sting of the towel after my mom whipped it at my arm, giving me a fake evil glare for making fun of her. I laughed and ducked when Lacey tried to swat at me with the towel I had left behind on the table.

"See, there's plenty of violence, so it's like a *manly* girl project. It's right up your alley!"

I laughed and moved out of the way as he turned to put me in a headlock.

"Gotta be faster," I teased, reaching up to wrap him in one first. "How are you ever going to survive in a house with four kids if you can't even catch me?"

That one got him riled up as he tried to get out of the hold that I had him in. I heard another groan and looked over to see Lacey bending forward again as my mom gently rubbed her back. Grant and I immediately let go of each other and stopped horsing around.

"You better get going," my mom said calmly, keeping her eyes on Lacey. "My keys are hanging by the front door. Take my car."

I nodded and turned to Grant. I could see the look of helplessness that was on his face.

"It's okay, I'll take care of her," I assured him. "Keep your phone on you so I can call with an update, okay?"

He shook his head and helped Lacey stand up before walking her out to the car. I was thankful that everything happened at my mom's house because it didn't look like Lacey was in any position to be climbing up and out of Grant's truck. Thankfully, my mom had a comfortable little Sentra that was easy for Lacey to get in.

I gave a quick wave to my mom and Grant as I made my way to the hospital.

"You didn't have to take me to the hospital," Lacey said as I reached over and turned down the radio. "But thank you. I don't think I have the energy to keep Grant calm today," she laughed. "He's already so stressed out with getting everything done for the wedding, I can't imagine what he'd be like at the hospital if he thought something was wrong with the babies."

"No worries. I'm glad that I could help."

I drove slowly, making sure to stay right around the speed limit and to drive as carefully as possible to the hospital. Luckily, it wasn't that far of a drive, and the roads were already clear after the snowstorm that barreled through a few nights ago.

"I'm going to miss you when you leave," she said softly, turning slightly in her seat to look at me. "I know that Grant is going to miss you too."

I could feel the burn in my throat from her words. It was hard to think about moving and leaving everything behind. More importantly, it was *who* I would be leaving.

"I'll miss you guys too," I replied as I focused on the road. "But hopefully, you guys will come to visit when the babies are a little older?"

"You know we will."

We didn't say anything else until we got to the hospital. I offered to run inside and get a wheelchair, but she swatted the idea away as she pushed past me and made her way to the front desk. She explained what was going on, and then we were asked to have a seat.

A few minutes later, a nurse came to take Lacey back. I offered to go with her, unsure whether she wanted her privacy or wanted the support. I was surprised when she asked me to go back with her. We followed the nurse down a long hallway, then into a room with a bed that raised up too high for Lacey to sit on. There was another woman in the room, standing next to the bed, entering information on the computer. I was about to help her up when I saw the tech push the keyboard away before she reached over and pushed the button to lower it.

Lacey sat down and lifted her shirt as she was asked. I turned away to give her some privacy and kept my head turned when I heard the sound of gel being squirted. I prayed that this wasn't one of those vaginal ultrasounds where they stick the probe up inside of the girl because if it was, this was about to get *real awkward, real fast.*

"You can look now," Lacey laughed, followed by a giggle from the nurse.

I turned and looked at the screen that they were both staring at, feeling my heart swell when I saw two very distinct babies on the monitor. It wasn't like when people showed you pictures of their babies, and you had to guess which end was head or tails. The image was crystal clear, and these cute little tadpole-looking creatures were my nieces or nephews or some combination of both.

My cheeks split as the grin spread across my face. I turned to look at Lacey, wondering if she was seeing the same thing that I was. She burst into another fit of laughter when she saw the excitement on my face.

"It's pretty amazing, isn't it?" she asked quietly.

I nodded and turned back to look at the screen, not wanting to miss a single second of it.

"So, I saw that you've been having some discomfort today?" the tech asked, glancing over her shoulder at Lacey as she kept moving the wand around on her stomach.

"Yeah, I think I was having Braxton-Hicks contractions. My soon-to-be husband was worried, so I agreed to come and get checked."

The woman smiled back at me, likely assuming that I was Grant.

"When are you getting married?" she asked as she turned her attention back to the monitor.

"This weekend," Lacey said excitedly, resting her arms over her head. "We were planning to get married in three weeks, on Valentine's Day, but my dress is getting a little too snug, so we moved it up."

"How exciting! Congratulations, you two!"

"I'm not the husband," I blurted out randomly, feeling my cheeks flush immediately.

I looked over at Lacey to see her arching a brow at me. I could see the humor on her face and knew that she was trying, yet again, not to laugh at me. Apparently, I was the comedy relief for everyone today.

The ultrasound tech stayed quiet. Either she hadn't heard me or was polite enough to pretend that she hadn't. She finished up and set the wand back in its holder before reaching over and wiping the gel off of Lacey's stomach.

"Everything looks fine. Both babies are very active and have plenty of fluid around them, which is a good sign. I'm going to hook you up to a monitor that will monitor any contractions, as well as the babies' heartbeats. The midwife will be in to check on you shortly, and we'll have a better idea of what's going on then."

I stepped to the side to allow her room to get everything set up. When she was done, Lacey had so many bands wrapped around her stomach with cords everywhere that I couldn't imagine that she was comfortable. A few minutes later, a nurse came in with a Styrofoam cup filled with ice water that she asked Lacey to drink.

Once we were alone, I stood off to the side, too afraid to go near her, so I didn't accidentally bump any of the monitors that were hooked up. She looked tired as she leaned her head back and closed her eyes after taking another drink of water.

"What a way to spend the last few days before the wedding, right?"

"It'll all work out, don't worry," I said gently, trying to reassure her.

"As long as the babies are okay, that's all that matters," she said, opening her eyes.

"They'll be just fine. And then we'll get back to putting together the wedding of your dreams."

I smiled when I saw her face light up with excitement.

"I'm so excited about the wedding, I just can't wait! It'll be so nice to have the family all together as we get married. Liam and Annie are just thrilled that they get to be in it, and they're over the moon that Kayce will be spending the night with us when she gets here tomorrow!"

I felt the weight of her words as they smacked me straight into my heart. She continued, not realizing what she had said or that she was rambling on about how happy she was that Kayce was coming to Haven Brook. She wasn't the only one.

Thirty Seven
Kayce

The drive to Haven Brook wasn't bad. I had gotten up surprisingly early, given how late I had been sleeping lately. Ever since Wyatt left, I no longer had the desire to get up and out of bed in the mornings, and I hated that part of my life. I needed a change—something to make me feel like *me* again. Not the sad, lonely, depressed me that signed the paperwork to sell her business this morning before getting on the road.

My hand had trembled as I scribbled my name on the papers, knowing that I didn't have any other options. Aside from taking out a loan to pay my bills for a few months and flashing people on the street corner to try to draw up new business, I was out of ideas. Now I was twenty-five years old, single, unemployed, and getting ready to move back in with her parents. Life was just freakin' peachy.

The only good part about my day so far was the breakfast burrito that I had grabbed from Jumping Joe's and the latte that I had treated myself to from the new coffee shop that had just opened in the next town over. I'd spent the first three hours listening to every sad, break-up song that I had on my phone, then shifted gears to a party playlist to try to get myself hyped up for the weekend. It was a wedding, and I was the maid of honor, so I needed to get my shit together.

I saw the sign for Haven Brook coming up and reached over to grab my phone. Without getting too distracted, I found her name and pressed the button to call her so I could let her know that I was almost there.

"Hey, are you getting on the road?" she asked happily.

"I'm actually getting ready to get *off* the road," I said with a smile as I slowed down and pulled off onto the off-ramp. "I just got off the freeway and should be at your house in fifteen minutes."

"You're here? Now?!"

The way her voice went shrill had me worried that maybe I shouldn't have come so early. I had hoped to come in and help her with any last-minute stuff for the wedding. Instead, it seemed like I was possibly adding to the stress that she was already dealing with.

"I'm so sorry," I rushed out. "I should have called before I left to make sure that this was okay with you. Don't worry about me—I will keep myself busy until tonight—or whenever you're free."

"Kayce—" she snapped, pulling me out of my panic. "Don't be ridiculous. I'm happy that you're here early. I just didn't believe it, you surprised me," she laughed.

"Are you sure?"

"Yes," she groaned. "Now, get your butt over here so I can give you a hug!"

"Okay, I'll see you in a few."

I was smiling for the first time in weeks as I headed to the only person who could ever calm me with just a hug.

Ten minutes later, I was parking in front of their house. I paused for a moment to look at it, completely blown away by how beautiful it was. Lacey had sent me plenty of pictures of it when they were having it built and after it was done, but I hadn't been back to Haven Brook since then. When I was here last, most of my time was spent at the hospital with Lacey after her dad tried to kill her.

I opened the door and climbed out, grinning when I saw Lacey come running out of the door, her baby bump on full display as Grant followed after her.

"You shouldn't be running," I called over to her, walking around to the passenger side of the truck to get my stuff.

"That's the same damn thing that I just told her," Grant grumbled, trying to catch up with her.

"Oh shush," she snapped over her shoulder at him. She waited for me to grab my duffle bag out of the truck before she wrapped her arms around me in a great, big hug.

I let my bag drop to the sidewalk and wrapped my arms around her. It was at that moment that I realized just how *okay* I was not. I hugged her tighter, desperate for the comfort that she was giving me as the tears spilled down my cheeks. My shoulders shook as I crumbled in her arms, unable to hold it together any longer.

"Oh honey," she whispered. "What's wrong?"

She pulled back and looked at me as she held my face in her hands. We were standing so close that her warm belly pressed against me. I reached down and rubbed a hand over it, amazed by the life she had growing inside of her.

"Look at this perfect belly," I said in awe. I looked up at her as she wiped my tears away. "You look stunning, Lace. Such a beautiful bride-to-be and a glowing mama."

Now it was her turn to cry. The tears ran down her cheeks as she swiped them away with the back of her hand. Grant smiled and gave me a quick nod before reaching down to grab my bag. He carried it inside and closed the door to give us some privacy.

"Look at you," Lacey commented as she ran a hand through my hair. "This color looks amazing on you. I really love this cut. It's so cute and frames your face perfectly!"

I felt my cheeks flush from the compliment. I was worried about making such a drastic change—well, drastic for me anyways. The purple in my hair had faded, and I felt I needed something *normal* for once. I decided to go with a dark ash brown, but that didn't feel like enough of a change, so I called my friend and had her help me cut six inches off. My hair felt lighter and touched the top of my shoulders, which I found was a better length for me.

"Thank you," I replied nervously, tucking my chin to my chest. "I wanted to make sure that you had good pictures from your wedding without having some crazy girl with bright hair."

I laughed and tugged at a piece of hair.

"You know that I don't care what color your hair is. All that I needed was *you*."

We linked our arms and went inside to get out of the cold. Lacey gave me the official tour of the house and showed me to the guest room, where Grant had already left my bag on the bed for me. The room was packed full of boxes with stuff for the wedding, so it was a little hard to see anything but the bed. It was a beautiful house with plenty of room. But, in an odd way, it made me feel sad as I thought about them starting their new life together as a family.

"The bathroom is down the hall, but feel free to use the one downstairs if this one is tied up. Liam and Annie fight over who gets to use this one, so it might be easier just to use the other one," she laughed as we walked out of the bedroom.

THREE STRIKES, YOU'RE GONE

We were walking down the stairs when I heard voices. I knew that Grant was home but didn't know that anyone else was there. I was about to take a step when I looked up and saw Wyatt walking out of the kitchen with Grant. My heart skipped a beat as I missed a step and landed hard on my ass.

Thirty Eight
Wyatt

"Kayce!" I ran over and reached a hand out to help her up. "Are you okay?"

I could see the embarrassment on her face as it turned bright red, but I didn't care. I continued to hover around her, looking her up and down to make sure she was alright.

"I'm fine. Thank you." She pulled her hand away as soon as she could and leaned against the side of the wall, furthest away from me.

For a moment, I had barely recognized her. She looked completely different—not that she wasn't hot as hell with her long, dark purple hair that she had a few weeks ago. But the way that the dark brown color made the gold in her eyes sparkle, I found myself hypnotized.

"Hey, Wyatt," Lacey said from behind Kayce. I stepped back to let them finish walking down the stairs and scooted off to the side. My hands felt sweaty, and my stomach was starting to knot up from seeing Kayce. I felt like a teenage boy who had just said hi to his crush for the first time. While I had thought that time apart would be good for us, I was finding that it hadn't been. If anything, it had made the longing that I had for her even worse.

"Hey," was all that I was able to get out as my eyes wandered back over to Kayce. She tucked a strand of hair behind her ear and wrapped her arms around her stomach while she avoided looking at me. I knew that she was feeling as awkward and uncomfortable being around me as I was around her. I just didn't know if it was because she was trying to fight the pull between us that I was feeling, or if maybe it was because she no longer felt anything.

"What are you doing here? I thought you were packing today?" Lacey asked as she walked past me and led Grant to the living room by the hand. Kayce lowered her eyes and sucked in a deep breath when she heard it, which led me to believe that I was right after all. She did still feel something for me, or she wouldn't care if I was leaving.

"I came by to check on you," I replied, glancing over at Kayce before I walked into the living room and sat in the recliner off in the corner.

"That's so sweet of you, thank you," she gushed, leaning back against Grant on the couch. "I'm doing much better. Thank you again for taking me yesterday.

Kayce narrowed her eyes and tilted her head to the side.

"What happened yesterday?" she asked Lacey, completely ignoring me as she sat down in the recliner next to me—which happened to be the only empty seat in the room unless she wanted to sit on Lacey's lap.

"I wasn't feeling well, so Wyatt took me to the hospital to get checked out. The babies are fine, and it turned out that I was just a little dehydrated, which was causing some contractions. Some rest and a couple of gallons of water, and I was feeling ten times better."

"You need to rest and take it easy," Kayce scolded, earning a scowl from Lacey.

"You sound just like Grant," she teased, playfully elbowing him in the side.

"At least someone does," he snorted. "Maybe you'll listen to her since you don't listen to me."

"I listen to you!"

The room got quiet for a few minutes before Lacey burst into laughter, and we all joined in, knowing that it wasn't true.

I found myself staring at Kayce, watching the way her eyes wrinkled in the corners as she laughed. It was killing me being this close to her and not being able to touch her. I had only had a small taste of her, and I needed more. I wanted to devour her in every way possible.

"What are your plans for the day?" Grant asked me when the laughter finally died down.

I looked at Kayce, wondering what her plans were, before blurting out, "I don't have any."

"Good, then you can help us set up for the wedding."

I could feel his eyes on me, and I knew what he was thinking. He had already made it clear when I was in Easterville that he wanted me to keep my hands off of Kayce. And now, it appeared he was going to do everything in his power to make sure that I didn't go anywhere near her while she was here.

"You know that I'm always happy to help," I replied smugly, matching his look from across the room. I wrapped my hands around the end of the armrests and stared him down.

"Okay, okay, enough of the chest match, you two," Lacey scolded and pushed off from Grant as she stood up. "We do have a lot to do before the wedding, and Wyatt, if you're able to stick around and help us, we would greatly appreciate it. However, I know that you need to get your stuff packed, so we won't have any hurt feelings if you can't."

I nodded and smiled, loving how Lacey always took control and put Grant in his place.

"I'm going to take Kayce to grab a bite to eat, and then we're going to head over to The Vine. Chase said that we can store stuff in the back and start decorating tomorrow afternoon when they close. First, I need to go see what we have and what we still need to get. Grant, you and Wyatt can work on taking the rest of the stuff from upstairs over. Otherwise, Kayce won't have a place to sleep tonight."

"What about us? Don't we get lunch?" Grant asked with a grumpy face. Lacey smiled as she reached up and patted his cheek a few times.

"There is stuff in the fridge to make sandwiches," she teased. "Or if you're lucky, maybe your brother will fix you something when you go drop stuff off."

"You know that I would rather *eat sandwiches* with you," he whispered in her ear, too loud, so I was able to hear as well.

"Ugh, get a room," I groaned and walked past them.

Kayce laughed and watched them for a few seconds before she looked away. I desperately wanted to talk to her, but not in front of them. I needed to find a way to get her alone and tell her how I felt about her. Not that it would change anything, but deep down, I hoped that it would.

"Come on, let's get going. Noah promised me a few meals before I leave, so lunch is on me today," I joked, clapping him on the back before heading upstairs to start packing up the boxes.

THREE STRIKES, YOU'RE GONE

Thirty Nine
Kayce

"That was so good, but now I'm stuffed," I said as I leaned back in my chair and pushed my plate away.

"Slow-Mo's will do that to you," Lacey laughed and raised her hand to get the waitress's attention.

I had heard her talk about the food here plenty of times, and even Wyatt had mentioned it when I asked if they had any good barbeque places. But no one told me that their southern comfort food could put you in a food-induced coma. My stomach was as hard as a rock, and I was uncomfortably full after devouring a plate of fried chicken and mashed potatoes.

"I might be too tired to work now," I joked, relieved to see the smile on Lacey's face. Thankfully, even though there was still a lot left to do, she didn't seem that stressed out about it. Which was helpful given that she had been in the hospital the day before and hadn't told me.

"It's okay, we have the easy job. The guys have the hard part."

The waitress came over and slid our ticket onto the table before clearing the empty plates. I reached over to grab it. Lacey frowned as she swatted my hand away and swiped it across the table to her. She was digging in her purse for her wallet when her phone rang.

I leaned back against the booth and closed my eyes for a minute while she answered her phone. I felt strangely calm now that I was in Haven Brook, and I tried to justify that it was because I was with Lacey and that it had absolutely nothing to do with Wyatt.

"No!" she gasped, clasping her hand over her mouth as she closed her eyes. "You've got to be kidding me…."

I stared at her, waiting for her to finish.

"Okay," she sighed heavily, tapping her fingers on the table as she shook her head. "There's nothing else that we can do. Can you guys get everything packed up and take it back to the house?"

I could feel the stress radiating from her and worried that she was going to work herself up too much and end up back in the hospital.

"Keep me posted, and I'll try to see what I can come up with as a plan B."

She hung up the phone and set it on the table. Her brow furrowed in disappointment as she stared out of the window.

"What's wrong?" I asked, reaching over to touch her hand.

"That was Grant. A pipe burst in the kitchen at The Vine, and we can't store anything in the back breakroom because the floor is flooded. Chase and Noah are working on getting it fixed, but they don't think the room will be dried out anytime soon.

"You said that they're closing early tomorrow so you guys can start setting up, right?"

"Yeah, but there won't be enough time for us to pack everything up from the house, take it over there, and get it set up. Plus, we have the bachelor and bachelorette parties, the rehearsal dinner—there's just too much. It's not going to work," she sniffled.

"It will work, Lacey, I promise. We just have to break it down into smaller pieces and go from there. Okay?"

She nodded her head and wiped at the tear that had slid down her face.

"Okay."

"So, the guys are taking everything back to your house now, right?"

"Yeah, they'll put it in the—" Her face fell as she realized what she was going to say.

"Lace, it's okay. They can put it in the guestroom. Just have them move my bag to the living room, and I'll sleep on the couch tonight. My dress is still hanging in the truck, so I'll move it into the guest bathroom. Everything will work out."

"You can't sleep on the couch, it'll be so uncomfortable, and it's loud in the morning when the kids get up."

"It'll be fine."

"Okay. It'll be fine," she repeated.

"Tomorrow after they close, we can have everyone help move everything back from your house to The Vine. Since they'll be closed, we can put stuff up front and just unpack and decorate at the same time. I'll go back after the rehearsal dinner and finish whatever we don't get done before then."

"Crap!" she exhaled, letting her head fall back. "They're not going to be able to do the rehearsal dinner for us if the pipe isn't fixed by then. What if it's not fixed by Saturday? We can't have our wedding there with no running water and broken pipes!"

"Deep breaths, Lace," I reminded her. "It will all come together."

I felt her relax as I squeezed her hand and prayed that I wasn't lying.

We got into her car and headed over to The Vine to see if we could help the guys pack stuff up and take it back to the house.

"Are you okay?" Lacey asked me randomly, looking over at me before turning her attention back to the road.

"Yeah, I'm fine. Why?"

"Because I know you better than that," she said softly.

"Everyone is moving forward with their lives, and I'm stuck in this rut," I sighed, looking out the window. "It's not even a rut, per se. It's like I'm moving backward. I have no job, no money, and I'm moving back in with my parents, who are busy traveling the world and enjoying retirement. Everyone is finding their way, and I'm drowning in the deep end."

"What do you mean you don't have a job?" Lacey asked as she turned into the parking lot of The Vine.

"I haven't been able to get any business for the past three weeks. I don't have any clients lined up, and people would rather go two towns over for service than to come to a shop where someone died."

"That wasn't your fault," Lacey said, putting the car in park and turning to look at me. I had told her in very vague detail about what had happened with Mateo. Not what *really* happened, just what the police had said happened.

"You know as well as I do that it doesn't matter in small towns. They weren't that impressed with a female mechanic, to begin with, this just gave them another excuse to go elsewhere."

"Okay, so how do we find new clients? Can you run a special in the paper?"

I loved where her heart was, and I almost hated breaking the news to her. She was one of the few people who had ever believed in me and pushed me to go after my dreams.

"It's not that easy." I paused and forced out the breath that I had been holding. "I signed the paperwork to sell it this morning. I am officially jobless as of February 1st."

"Kayce, I'm so sorry. I can talk to Grant and see if we can loan you—"

I put my hand up to stop her.

"No, but thank you." I pulled my shoulders back and tried to find the confidence that I needed. "I'll be fine. I just have to find my way."

She smiled warmly at me, making me believe that I meant what I had said. The back door of The Vine opened, and Wyatt walked out. My heart skipped a beat when he looked over and locked eyes with me. It was at that moment that I knew that finding my way wasn't going to include him, and that broke my heart.

<u>Forty</u>
Wyatt

"Is that it?" I called over my shoulder while pushing the stack of boxes as far over as I could. There was barely enough room to move without knocking something over, and I wondered how Kayce was supposed to sleep in here tonight.

"Yeah, that was it," Grant confirmed from the hallway.

I carefully backed up and made sure not to bump anything on my way out of the room.

"I thought you guys were having a small wedding," I noted, scratching at the scruff on my chin. "That's not what a small wedding looks like."

"Tell that to Lacey," he laughed and leaned back against the wall. He slid down it and sat on the plush carpet. Tired from moving boxes around all day, I did the same.

"What time do Liam and Annie get home from school today?" I asked, wondering when the house would get back to the loud, somewhat chaotic state that I missed.

"They're actually going to moms for a sleepover. She and Buck went to pick them up from school, and then they were going to the store to get snacks for the movie marathon tonight."

"They really do love movie night, don't they?" I smiled as I remembered doing something similar with my parents and brothers when we were growing up. I tried not to talk much about our childhood because it had never been easy to open up about what happened when my dad died. Even though they had never said it, I always felt like Chase and Grant had looked down on me and blamed me for his death. *If I were older, I would have known what to do. Had they been there, they would have known what to do. Dad might still be alive.*

"Honestly, I think it's Buck more than the kids. Mom doesn't keep a lot of sweets in the house, so he uses it as an excuse to buy stuff for root beer floats and sundaes. On top of all of the candy that the kids insist that they need. I think they're all in on it together."

"I'm glad that mom has Buck in her life. I haven't seen her this happy since…."

My voice trailed off as I fought the urge to talk about what was weighing so heavily on my mind.

"Since dad died," Grant finished for me.

I gave him a sad smile, feeling bad for bringing him up right before his wedding. I was the worst at bringing everyone down with me, and this was just another example of that.

"Dad would be happy," Grant said, catching me off guard. I tilted my head in confusion.

"About mom finding someone to spend the rest of her life with. He'd be really happy about that."

I nodded in agreement, knowing that he was right. My dad was a wonderful man, and he loved my mom more than anything. He didn't have to tell us, we could just see it.

"He'd be happy for you too," he added, tapping my leg with his boot. "You're going after your dreams and what makes you happy. He would be proud of you for being so strong and independent."

His words clutched at my heart and squeezed hard around it.

"I don't know that I'm even happy," I muttered, scrubbing a hand down my face. I felt the prickle of hair and made note that I needed to shave and clean up before the rehearsal dinner tomorrow night. Not only did I want to look nice for their wedding photos, but I also found that I wanted to impress Kayce, as useless as it might be.

"Why not?"

Grant was never one to push or prod me, which I have always appreciated. I always imagined that he would be closer to Chase because they were closer in age than we were, but surprisingly, our relationship seemed to be the strongest. I was there for him when his wife, Renee, lost her battle with cancer. He was there for me when I battled deep depression after hearing the doctors say that I would likely never play baseball again after several intensive surgeries to save my life.

"I don't know," I sighed, cracking my knuckles. "How does anyone even know if they're happy? Maybe we just pretend to be happy, but we're all secretly dead inside and can't feel a thing."

"Well, that's a little deep," he chuckled. "And pretty dark."

I looked up at him, my face stoic. His smile faded, and he nodded.

"Happiness isn't some elusive thing that you have to chase after or wonder if it's real. You know when you've found it."

I quirked a brow and studied him. He had to be shitting me with this so-called advice.

"Do you know how you can tell whether or not you've found it?"

I waited for a minute before I decided to humor him.

"How?"

"You're miserable when it's gone."

His eyes softened as he smiled, knowing that his words had struck a chord with me.

"What am I supposed to do? I can't ask her to pack up and leave her life behind to follow me. And I don't know that I could live with myself if I didn't take this job. I've had a hard enough time accepting that my career is over. I don't know that I'm ready to walk away from baseball altogether."

"Maybe I should have taken your advice from the start and stayed away from her," I sighed heavily, knowing that I wouldn't have been able to do that, even if I tried.

"Or maybe *I* was the one who was wrong. It seems you're both falling pretty hard for each other." He paused to stand up. "Who am I to get in the way of true love?"

He smiled and walked off down the hall, leaving me to sit and ponder whether or not he was right. I knew that I had fallen for her—and hard. But there was no way that it could be true love because a guy like me didn't deserve a woman like her.

Forty One
Kayce

I felt sore and achy from moving boxes, even though the guys handled most of it. I tried to help as much as I could while also keeping Lacey distracted so she would sit down at rest. Finally, around six o'clock, the guys were almost done getting the rest of the boxes loaded in the guestroom while Lacey and I went to pick up dinner.

The line at Paul's Pizza was long, but Lacey assured me that this was *the place* to go for pizza. She swore that it was the best pizza that she had ever had, and I found myself remembering my conversation with Wyatt about how Easterville had the best breakfast burritos. Maybe it was just something people did in small towns—brag about the best food they had.

The smell of the pizza floated out of the lid of the box as it sat on my lap the drive back to Lacey's house. I wasn't sure if Wyatt would still be there when we got back or if he needed to get home to finish packing. I hated that I cringed every time someone mentioned it, but it was a sore spot for me, and each mention of it only reminded me that he was leaving and I wouldn't see him again.

I felt like Sandy from Grease, crying over a boy who I had a minor fling with. But in the movie, she was desperately in love with him, and he loved her too. So much so that he was willing to change for her, even though he was ridiculed by his friends. In the end, she was the one who made the change to be with him, and they lived happily ever after. Or so you thought. Who knew what really happened after that. The problem was that this was real life and not some made-up fantasy from a movie. One of my favorite movies—but still, a movie.

We pulled into the driveway and waited for the garage door to open before Lacey pulled inside. I hated that I had butterflies in my stomach, secretly hoping that he would still be here. It wasn't fair that I had no way of knowing for sure, because it wasn't like I could look to see if his truck was still here. The damn thing was still sitting in my garage, serving as a constant reminder of the devilish man that drove it.

Once the car was parked, I unbuckled and got out, making sure not to drop the pizzas. I waited for Lacey to press the button to close the garage door before coming around to open the door to go inside. I could have opened it myself, but it felt weird to just make myself at home when I didn't live here. *You don't even have a place of your own anymore,* I thought sourly.

We went into the kitchen, and I set the boxes down on the island. Lacey grabbed some paper plates and napkins from the pantry and set them beside it.

"Pizza is here," she called loudly into the living room, not sure where the guys were. "What do you want to drink?" she asked, opening the fridge.

"Water is fine, thanks."

"We have beer and wine if you want some," she offered, leaning against the open door.

I felt the energy around me change as I looked up and saw Wyatt walk into the room.

"I'll have some wine," I said quickly, walking over to help her. Or maybe I was just trying to put some distance between him and me so I could try to think clearly.

"Do you guys want a beer?" Lacey asked as they pulled out their chairs and sat down at the table. Grant had moved the pizza box over and promptly jumped up to move it back when Lacey gave him a look. He grinned sheepishly as he took a bite of pizza and winked at her.

"Boys," she muttered under her breath.

"Yes or no on the beer?" she asked once more.

"Yes, please," Wyatt said, getting up to come get it himself. She smiled up at him as she handed him a cold bottle from the fridge.

"Here's two. Make sure you share," she teased and handed him another bottle.

"Yes, ma'am," he joked, making me smile.

I hated how much I missed him and seeing his stupid smile with those damn dimples.

A few minutes later, I had the bottle of wine open and was pouring myself a glass before joining everyone else at the table. The only spot available was between Grant and Wyatt. A Walker cookie if you thought about it, which I tried not to because it was wildly inappropriate. Not that I had any attraction whatsoever to Grant, I just couldn't figure out how to keep my legs closed around Wyatt.

We talked as we ate, the mood light and fun. I wondered what it would be like to live in Haven Brook and do this more often? How amazing it would be to see Lacey as we talked daily instead of just hearing her voice on the phone. Or watching Annie and Liam grow up while getting to know the new babies. When I stopped and thought about it, I didn't have anything waiting for me when I went back to Easterville. Everything that was important to me was sitting right here, at this table.

By the time dinner was over, my heart felt as full as my stomach. It was the perfect ending to an emotionally charged day. There were so many ups and downs throughout it that I wondered if we were on a roller coaster and when it would be over.

I helped clean up the kitchen as Lacey yawned. I could see that she was exhausted and needed to rest.

"I'll finish cleaning up. Why don't you go upstairs and rest?" I offered, gently rubbing her back.

The guys had run over to their mom's house to take Annie her pillow that she had left behind and couldn't sleep without.

"It's okay, I can help," she countered stubbornly.

I tilted my head to the side and put my hand on my hip.

"Okay, fine." She yawned again before hugging me and heading upstairs for bed.

I wiped down the table and island, then ran the empty pizza box out to the garage. I was trying to break down the box to get it to fix when the garage door opened, and Grant pulled in. The headlights were too bright for me to see if he was by himself or if he had already dropped Wyatt off at home. I turned my attention back to the box and pushed it down with all of my might as I tried to get it to fit inside the cramped bin.

"Do you need help?" Wyatt asked with a chuckle, walking up beside me.

I stepped to the side to let him have a try at it.

In one quick movement, he pushed the box down, forcing it to fit.

"I could've done that," I mumbled grumpily, folding my arms over my chest.

"I know," he said, humoring me.

Grant had already walked inside, leaving us behind in the garage. We walked side by side the short distance to the door.

"I thought Grant took you home," I blurted out randomly without thinking before I said it.

"Nope, I'm still here," he laughed.

My skin prickled from the heat as the blush spread across my chest and up my neck.

"I can see that."

"Did you want me to go home?" he asked, standing in front of the door but not bothering to open it.

I was reluctant to look up at him, afraid that if I did, the walls that I had been working so hard to build up would suddenly crumble.

He reached over and gently tipped my chin up with his finger. That single touch was all that it took to undo me.

I leaped forward, practically jumping in his arms like a crazed monkey as he wrapped them around me and lifted me to his hips. My heart was racing as I kissed him, my hands desperately pulling him closer as I needed more.

His back hit the door of the garage before he turned and pressed my body against it as I continued to straddle his hips. I could feel his erection pressing into me as he pinned me in place and ran a hand up my side. He slowly kissed my neck as he pushed my hair to the side.

"You look fucking gorgeous with the new hair," he growled in my ear, nipping it before he went back to planting kisses down my neck. "I want to take you home and fuck you so bad."

"Do it," I panted, my nails scratching down his back. "Take me home. Just one night—as friends saying goodbye or whatever. Just one last night," I begged. I didn't care how desperate I sounded right now. This was what I needed—what both of us needed. One night of pretending that things between us weren't about to get a whole lot more complicated.

Forty Two
Wyatt

I didn't bother going inside to look for Grant before I practically yanked Kayce out of the house and took her back to my place. He knew me well enough to know that when we didn't come inside after the first five minutes of being alone, we weren't coming in anytime soon.

I was thankful that Kayce had her truck because I was thinking with my dick right now, and unfortunately, he didn't know how to drive a car.

A few minutes later, we were inside my house, flinging pieces of clothes off left and right. There was something about her that I couldn't stay away from, and I could tell that she felt the same desperate energy that I did. I wanted to touch her and feel her body against mine, but I also knew that I needed to slow down and enjoy this night with her. I needed to treat it as if it was the only night we would ever get with each other because it likely was.

She reached forward to unbuckle my belt, and I reached down and grabbed her hand to stop her. Her head jerked up to look at me, confusion flashing across her beautiful face. Her hair looked darker in the dim light of my bedroom, making her look even sexier. I swallowed hard then licked my lips, ready to make love to her the way she deserved.

"What's wrong?" Her voice was so quiet that I barely heard her.

"Nothing," I assured her, rubbing my thumb across her hand as she continued to hold onto my belt buckle. "I don't want to rush tonight—even though I want nothing more than to be inside of you right now. I want to take my time and make love to you this time."

Her chest rose and fell heavily as she pulled her bottom lip in between her teeth.

"Okay," she agreed, slowly stepping away, closer to the bed.

I undid my belt and pulled it through the loops of my jeans while her eyes focused on every movement. I tossed it to the side, then kicked off my boots and stepped out of them. She was standing in front of my bed, wearing nothing but her black lace bra with matching panties. She looked like a fucking goddess, and I was ready to make a sacrifice.

I walked over to her, wearing nothing but my boxers, and wrapped a hand around her waist. I loved the sound of the gasp she made before I leaned down and kissed her. Gently, I lifted her ass, and she wrapped her legs around me without breaking the kiss.

Our bodies felt like they were made to fit as we moved fluidly around each other. I laid her on her back on the bed, my body pressed against hers. Her legs wrapped tighter around my waist as she tried to pull my pelvis closer to hers. I chuckled lightly, happy to see that I wasn't the only one who wanted this so badly.

I pulled away and rolled off of her. My fingers trailed across her stomach, then along her hips, before dipping into her panties. I felt my dick twitch when my fingers slid inside easily, knowing that she was wet and ready for me. She tilted her head back and moaned as I worked two fingers inside of her.

"You're so fucking wet, baby," I groaned, feeling her pussy tighten around my fingers. Fuck, I wanted it to be my cock right now. I felt ready to explode, the tension mounting.

"I want you, Wyatt," she said in a whisper. "Please, please. Fuck me, Wyatt," she begged as my fingers fucked her harder.

I couldn't take it anymore as I pulled my fingers out and stripped off my boxers. I bent over to reach into my nightstand for a condom when I remembered that I was completely out.

"Fuck!" I growled, startling her.

"What's wrong?"

"I don't have a condom," I muttered with disappointment.

She propped herself up on her elbows, blowing a piece of hair out of her face.

"It's fine," she said, shaking her head and laying back down. "I'm on the pill."

"Kayce, we don't have to do this if you don't want to. I can get condoms in the morning, before—"

"Wyatt, I want to do this. I haven't been with anyone else, and I get tested every year when I go for my annual check-up. Unless you don't want to."

"No, I want to," I rushed before she could get the wrong idea. "I just don't want to fuck this up tonight. I know how important it is to be safe, and I don't want to make you uncomfortable by doing something that you might regret in the morning."

"I appreciate that. But what I really want right now—is that." She looked down at my dick, and a mischievous smile spread across her face.

I made my way back over to her and laid next to her, giving her a chance to change her mind. This wasn't some random girl that I was hooking up with. She was way more than that, and I needed to make sure that she was fully comfortable with what we were doing.

She reached up and wrapped her hands around my neck, pulling me on top of her. Her tongue parted my lips and dipped inside as she arched her back and pressed her breasts against me. I reached down and pulled her panties over her hips and down her legs before tossing them to the floor. I could feel her nails scratching at my back as she anxiously waited.

Slowly, I slid inside of her, closing my eyes as the warmth and wetness of her pussy wrapped around my throbbing cock. I could honestly say that I had never had sex without a condom before, and now that I had been with Kayce without one, I felt even more addicted to her. I thrust harder, her legs spreading open to allow me to go deeper. Everything felt so fucking good and more intense without the barrier that I found myself struggling not to come right away.

She laid underneath me, her golden-brown eyes darkening as they locked onto mine. Her short hair fanned out across my pillow as her breasts bounced beautifully in her face as I drove harder inside of her. Everything about her was perfect, and I wanted to watch that gorgeous face as she came hard on my dick.

I reached down between us and started rubbing her clit with my middle finger, working it in a frenzy as I circled the swollen bud over and over again. I could feel her body responding, her back arching as her legs tightened around me.

"Come for me, Kayce," I coaxed, rubbing harder as I continued to thrust harder. I was close to a release and wanted to make sure she got hers first.

She whimpered and closed her eyes as she panted heavily before her pussy spasmed against my dick, my finger feeling the ripple of her orgasm.

"Fuck!" I growled as I pumped faster inside of her, my orgasm coming right on the heels of hers.

My chest was heaving as I laid on top of her, soaking up every second of being inside of her before it was gone.

Forty Three
Kayce

I laid in Wyatt's arms, resting my head against his chest. My fingers trailed lightly across his chest, tracing over the scars from when he was stabbed and the handful of surgeries that it took to save his life.

"I know that you must hate them, but I love these," I said sleepily, continuing in a circular pattern around them.

"My nipples?" he asked with a laugh, rubbing a hand down my naked back. I still had my bra on because I was in too big of a hurry to take it off.

"Your scar, silly," I giggled. "But I like your nipples too."

"I think yours are better," he teased, making me blush. "Why do you love my scars?"

I thought for a moment of what the best way would be to answer that question. There were so many reasons, and I wasn't sure that I wanted to confess all of them right now.

"Because these scars are the result of the selfless sacrifice that you made to save Lacey," I paused and pulled in a deep breath, trying to find the courage to say what my heart needed me to say. "And, because they are proof that your life was worth saving, even if it took the doctors several tries. They never gave up, and these scars should always be a constant reminder that you were meant to be here. To do great things and live the life after getting a second chance."

He said nothing, just pulled me closer to him, and kissed the top of my head. It was starting to get cold in the room, and I shivered against his body. He reached over and pulled the blankets on top of us. I felt completely relaxed as I quickly fell asleep next to him.

Between it being a long day and the emotional roller coaster that I had been on, I was dead asleep when Wyatt's screams woke me. I jumped up, clutching the sheets against my chest as I looked around for the source of danger. My heart was pounding, my pulse racing. I looked over and found him still asleep, his face tight in anger as he mumbled about saving someone.

"HELP!!! PLEASE, SOMEONE!! HELP MY DAD!!"

I felt my heart sink as I realized that he was having a nightmare about his dad. I didn't know what to do; I felt completely helpless. Lacey used to have bad dreams when she was a kid, and I learned the hard way not to wake her up in the middle of one. It seemed stupid because why would anyone want to stay stuck in a bad dream, but after my black eye from her accidentally punching me, I didn't question it again.

I waited for a few minutes until he seemed calmer. I was about to rub his shoulder to try to wake him when I saw the tears running down his face. My heart broke even harder when I realized how much pain he was still in after losing his dad. I gave it a few more minutes, and then I gently nudged him until he woke up.

"Hey," he croaked out tiredly. "Are you okay?" He rubbed his eyes and looked around the room, confused.

"You were having a bad dream," I said softly, brushing my thumb across his cheek to wipe the tear away.

"Sorry," he apologized, his shoulders tightening with tension again.

"Don't be. I'm sorry that you were having such a bad dream."

"It wasn't a dream," he said, then pulled his lips into a thin line. "I was watching my dad die again. It happens often, like a video that someone plays on repeat. I haven't found a way to stop it, but I hate when it happens."

"That's terrible. I can't imagine having to go through that over and over again."

I still felt just as helpless as I had a few minutes ago, only now, he was awake, and I had no idea what to say or do. I wanted to make him feel better or offer him comfort of some sort, but there was nothing that I could do to take this pain away, and I knew that.

"Is there anything that I can do for you?" I asked anyway.

"Just lay with me," he said with a cheeky grin as he lifted the blanket for me to climb back under next to him. "I like how it feels having your body against mine."

I laid down and curled up next to him, wrapping my legs around his as

I rested my arm across his stomach. I had seen him naked a handful of times now, but I had never stopped to admire this heavenly body that was capable of magic. And just like that, within a matter of minutes, we both had fallen asleep in each other's arms.

Morning came too quickly, and I groaned when my phone rang on the nightstand beside me. I was surprised that it hadn't died, given that I hadn't bothered to find a charger last night. Needless to say, my phone wasn't a priority of any sort last night.

I picked it up and swiped the button to answer it.

"Hello," I groaned sleepily, propping myself up on one elbow while holding the sheet against my body. I could feel Wyatt beside me as he reached over and pulled me back over to him.

"Do I even want to know where you are right now?" Lacey asked coyly.

"Umm. Yeah. About that…" I trailed off and didn't bother to complete my sentence when I heard her burst into laughter on the other line.

"I knew it," she teased. "I bet Grant twenty dollars last night that we would wake up and find you at Wyatt's house this morning."

"Now you're making money off of me?" I groaned, covering my face with my hand.

"Only twenty bucks. But if you can get your butt up and ready this morning, I'll use it to buy you breakfast."

My stomach growled loudly as if it heard the invite. Wyatt laughed and rubbed a hand over it. For a moment, I wondered what it would be like if we were to settle down. Would he want to have kids? Would he still be lying next to me in bed, rubbing my pregnant stomach the way I had seen Grant do to Lacey's?

"How long do I have?"

"Forty-five minutes. A minute later, and I will eat your head for breakfast."

I laughed at the thought, wondering if she was serious given that she hadn't laughed herself.

"Fine. I'll be there in forty-five minutes," I laughed and hung up.

"I have to get up and go meet Lacey for breakfast," I said, rolling over to look at him.

"I heard you have forty-five minutes," he said as he raised a brow.

"How long do you need to get ready?" He licked his lips and reached down to grab a handful of my ass.

"Twenty? Twenty-five tops," I mumbled as he leaned over and kissed my neck.

"Good, then I'll have time for breakfast before you go."

In one quick movement, the sheet and blankets flew up, and he dove under them, spreading my legs apart before nestling himself in between. I never got around to putting my panties back on, even after I had gotten up to use the restroom a few hours ago. His hands gripped my thighs as his tongue went straight to work, licking my slit before parting my lips and dipping inside. My back arched as I enjoyed every second of it, wanting more from this perfect man.

He continued his delicious torture of licking and sucking, building the perfect rhythm that brought me to the verge of orgasm. I could feel the tension building, the need for him getting stronger as I got closer. I reached down and grabbed the back of his head, pushing it harder against me as he sucked my clit until I came. My thighs clenched around him as my body hummed in pleasure.

He chuckled and came up for air, pushing the blankets off of us.

"What do you know? You *are* the breakfast of champions. Better than a bacon burrito from Jumping Joe's." He winked and smiled his half-smile that I loved so much.

"Now that's just blasphemy," I gasped, acting appalled. "Jumping Joe's is perfection."

"No, Kayce," he said, his tone turning serious. "*You* are perfection."

I felt my heart flutter as I listened to his words, the look on his face confirming that he meant it. I pulled my lower lip in between my teeth, unsure of what to say. I didn't want to mess up this moment between us by saying the wrong thing.

"You better go jump in the shower, or you're going to be late," he warned, moving over so I could get up.

I looked over and saw his cock, hard and waiting for me. Suddenly, I didn't care about breakfast or whether I got there on time.

"I know something else that would be perfect," I said seductively, turning onto my hands and knees as I popped my ass up in the air. His eyebrows shot up high on his forehead as he got my message, loud and clear.

He climbed over and swatted my ass cheek before sliding into me. I rolled my head back in response, loving the feel of his cock deep inside of me. His hands gripped my hips as he slowly started to pump. I spread my legs to let him in, moaning as I reached down to touch myself.

I had no idea how it was possible to be ready for another orgasm so soon, but the harder I rubbed, the closer I got. He felt so good as he thrust harder, forcing my breasts in my face as they bounced in response. I felt him unhook my bra in the back before pushing it down my arm. I slid out of it, making sure not to lose my balance as I held myself up while we continued.

He reached forward and rubbed my nipple between his fingers before moving to the other side. I was right on the verge of climax, and the extra stimulation was about to send me over the edge. I panted heavily as I held myself up with one hand and rubbed my clit with the other. He pounded harder and quicker, and I knew he was close. I waited as long as I could before I gave in and let my orgasm consume me.

It was the most intense feeling that I had ever felt, and every nerve ending in my body was on fire. I screamed his name as I came, feeling his body stiffen right behind me as he climaxed. We were both panting and sweating when we were done. I blew a strand of hair out of my face, knowing that I would definitely have to shower and clean up before I could go see Lacey.

"You're right," he said as he gently pulled out. "That was perfection."

I laughed and looked over my shoulder at him. When our eyes locked, I felt something that I had never felt before now, and it scared the shit out of me.

THREE STRIKES, YOU'RE GONE

Forty Four
Wyatt

I had been wearing a shit-eating grin the majority of the day, and no matter how hard I tried, I couldn't get rid of it. Kayce and I had taken a quick shower before she rushed off to go meet Lacey for breakfast, and I had spent the day with Grant, Chase, and Noah for the so-called bachelor party.

I wasn't sure why we were calling it that, especially since it was the middle of the day, and there was little drinking and zero strippers. But either way, I tried to focus on spending time with the guys before I left because I didn't know when I would be able to come back again. I was going to miss this, but more importantly, I was going to miss them.

The day flew by rather quickly, and before I knew it, we were lining up along the wall at The Vine as the minister went over what everyone was supposed to do tomorrow. Thankfully, Grant and Lacey had a smaller wedding party, and since I was the best man, that meant that I got to walk Kayce down the aisle since she was the maid of honor. I tried to keep my attention on what was being said, but I was distracted by her every movement.

Finally, after rehearsing it a few times, we were good to go, and everyone scattered about to set up for the big day. My mom and Buck had been there since this afternoon, getting everything ready, but there was still a lot left to do. Noah ordered some pizzas and offered everyone beer for helping out. The night passed by in a flash, but by the time we were done, everything looked perfect, and Lacey had tears of happiness when she left.

I wanted Kayce to stay around so we could talk, but she left with Lacey and Grant, giving me a quick wave on her way out. It wasn't like she needed a place to stay now that the guest room was cleared out. I knew that my time with her was limited and that I would have to make every minute of it count tomorrow.

I felt like my life was an hourglass, and the end was coming soon.

When I got home, I was too restless to go to sleep, so I stayed up late packing up more of my stuff to move to Phoenix. It was amazing the amount of crap we accumulated without even realizing it. I had started a box for donations, and that seemed to be filling up faster than the boxes that I would be taking with me. Maybe it was better to travel lighter and not have as much baggage to unpack when I got there.

By two in the morning, I was yawning every few minutes, and my body was begging for sleep. I gave in and laid down, smelling Kayce's perfume on my pillow from last night and this morning. While I would have imagined that it would have been some sort of trigger that kept me up even longer and kept me from sleeping, it surprisingly had the opposite effect. Something about feeling like she was there with me was so soothing that I fell asleep almost immediately.

I woke up the next morning feeling rested, even though I had barely gotten five hours of sleep—at most. I guess the difference was getting a solid five hours of sleep compared to getting a full night's sleep that was constantly interrupted by tossing and turning.

I cleaned up and jumped in the shower, ready to take on the day. Okay, so maybe not ready for the day, but ready to see Kayce again. I had been thinking about her nonstop, and even though she had insisted that the other night was just a one-time thing, I couldn't help wondering what it would be like if it were more.

The heavenly aroma of coffee floated through the living room while I gathered the stuff I needed and waited for Chase to come pick me up. I really hated not having my truck and having to have everyone drive me around, but there was nothing that I could do about it, so it was pointless to complain. I filled my travel mug with coffee and made sure the lid was on tight before I rushed out the door to the sound of Chase honking.

I raised an eyebrow as I swung my duffle bag over my shoulder and held my coffee in one hand while locking the door with the other. I jumped in the back seat, behind Noah, and buckled up as Chase started driving. I knew that we were heading to The Vine to finish setting up for the wedding, but I hated how long it would be before I would get to see Kayce. It was like sitting on pins and needles.

"You look bright-eyed and bushy-tailed this morning," Noah commented, turning to look over his shoulder at me.

"I slept good last night." I shrugged and looked out the window to avoid the knowing look that he was giving me.

"Must be nice," they both muttered, and I tried to hold back a laugh.

"Well, I don't have small children to keep me up at night," I added with a wink.

"Just give it time, then you'll be in our club of sleepless nights, and it won't be the kind you're used to," Chase warned playfully.

"Nah, that life isn't for me," I lied, remembering the feeling that I had when I was touching Kayce's stomach yesterday morning. It was so cute to hear it growl so loudly, making it known that she was hungry. But I couldn't help but think about what it would be like if she were pregnant with my baby, and that thought was seeping deeper and deeper into the back of my brain.

I had felt my voice crack and knew that they heard it when they smirked at each other but said nothing. We pulled into the parking lot a few minutes later, which meant that I was free from having to have this conversation with them. There was plenty of work to be done, and that meant no time to talk.

The hours flew by, and before I knew it, it was already three o'clock, and we were being told to get ready. Everything looked perfect, and my mom raved about how wonderful it was that everything had been pulled together at the last minute with all of the unexpected changes. The ceremony was at four, which meant that I only had an hour longer before I would get to see Kayce.

The guys got ready in the back room since the floors were still a little wet and everything was drying out from the broken pipe. Originally, the girls were supposed to get ready back here, but that had been another last-minute change. I got dressed in the bathroom and made sure to fix my tie before putting on my vest and jacket. The suit was classic black and white with a champagne-colored solid tie that matched the girls' dresses.

I was hanging out up front with my mom and Buck when I heard the front door open and froze, wondering if the girls were here early. It was only three-thirty, but I knew that they would be here at any minute to get ready and wait in Chase's office until the ceremony started. A few guests had already started to show up, so I knew that it could easily be another guest. But that didn't keep my heart from getting overly excited at the possibility.

I could feel my mom's eyes on me, watching intently, but I didn't care. My body felt the electricity that radiated between us the moment she walked through the door. It was as if nothing else mattered and no one else was there. I felt my heart skip a beat when I saw her and wondered if this was the feeling that grooms claimed to experience when they saw their bride walking down the aisle to them.

Her hair was pulled up on her head, piled loosely with a few curls that hung perfectly around her face. I loved that her makeup was minimal, giving her a soft romantic look that I loved on her. She looked gorgeous, and the shimmery material of her dress caught the light perfectly, making it look like she belonged in a damn fairytale. Aside from the fact that the dress fit her body perfectly and wrapped tightly around her hips and ass in a way that had me wanting to rip that damn thing off of her with my teeth.

She gave me a flirty smile before walking down the hallway with the other girls. It wasn't lost on me that Mia and Jade had seen how Kayce and I were looking at each other, and I knew that I would be hearing about it from Chase and Noah as soon as the girls had a moment alone with them to gossip. But in all honesty, I didn't care. The whole world could watch me stare at her right now, and I wouldn't bother to look away.

A few minutes later, Annie came in, announcing that Lacey would be coming in a few minutes and that we all needed to clear the room because no one was allowed to see the bride yet. I laughed at how demanding she was for such a little girl, but wandered outside onto the patio with the guys to allow Lacey to come in unseen.

It was almost time, and the seats were filling up fast inside. In all of the years that I had been coming to The Vine, I had never imagined that I would see my brother get married here. It was Chase's baby, so to speak, but it had been something that had become part of our entire family. His dream was something that held us all together and gave us a place to call home when we needed it.

By three forty-five, the men were taken back to where the girls were waiting, while Chase stood up front next to the minister. Everything looked perfect, and we had succeeded in turning their brewery into a beautiful wedding venue at the last minute. I felt my hands start to sweat as I looked for Kayce so we could line up the way we had last night during the rehearsal.

A few minutes later, she walked up behind me and wrapped her arm in mine as we got ready to go.

"You look great," she said, leaning in close to me. We were at the back of the line, behind the groomsmen and bridesmaids, which gave us a small amount of privacy—aside from Lacey, who was standing right behind us with Buck.

"Thank you." I leaned closer to her, getting a whiff of the vanilla in her conditioner that I loved so much. "You look absolutely stunning, Kayce."

She smiled as the blush flashed across her face. I didn't have time to say any of the other things that I wanted to before we were being led down the hall and out into the lobby.

I walked proudly with Kayce on my arm, ignoring the looks of everyone as we passed down the aisle. For once in my life, I didn't notice anyone other than her. The world could explode around us, and I would still be oblivious to anything but her.

When we reached the alter, I stopped and gave her a quick kiss on her cheek before she walked over to stand in front of Mia. I took my spot next to Grant and heard the chuckle escape Chase's throat behind me.

A few minutes later, everyone oohed and ahhed as Liam and Annie walked down the aisle. If ever there was an adorable ring bearer and flower girl, it was these two. They were totally hamming it up for the guests, making everyone laugh, including Lacey. She looked beautiful as she walked down the aisle with Buck, wearing her mother's wedding dress.

Her blonde hair was pulled back, out of her face, as the soft curls hung down her shoulders and back. Her stomach pulled the fabric of the dress tight against her bump, making her look even more beautiful if that was possible. I felt the tears sting my eyes and looked away, scolding myself for being such a pussy. I wasn't the kind of guy that cried at weddings—I was the kind of guy that avoided weddings like the damn plague.

I tried to keep myself focused on the wedding and being present in the moment. But no matter how hard I tried, I couldn't stop thinking about Kayce. I had to force myself to look down at the floor to avoid looking like some sort of creep that couldn't keep his eyes off of her.

After the ceremony was over and Grant and Lacey shared their first kiss, everyone applauded, and the wedding party made our way back to the back while my mom helped set everything up for the reception. It was hard having everything all in one spot, but if anyone could pull it off—it was my mom. And thankfully, they had a rather small wedding with guests that were happy to jump right in and help out.

It was noisy in the hallway as everyone crowded around Grant and Lacey to congratulate them. I waited my turn before squeezing in to hug Lacey.

"You look beautiful," I said while hugging her. "I'm so happy for you guys."

"Thank you," she replied sweetly. "I can't wait to do this again!'

"You're already planning your next wedding?" I asked, one brow raised. "I don't wanna sound like a dick, but maybe give it more than a few minutes before you decide it's not gonna work with my brother."

She laughed and rolled her eyes, swatting me on the chest.

"Not *me!*" she joked, still laughing. "I meant that I can't wait to do this again when *you* get married."

"Me?" I said, acting appalled that she would even consider such a thing. "Nah, weddings aren't my thing. I don't see myself settling down, and…" my words trailed off as Kayce came into view, standing off to the side as she looked down to talk to Annie.

Whatever Annie said to her had her laughing. She threw her head back, her eyes lighting up the way they did when she was truly happy. At that moment, I realized that I would never be able to do that for her. I was the darkness that would forever dim the light that deserved to shine within her.

Forty Five
Kayce

By the end of the night, I had twisted and shouted so much that my body was aching in protest. My heels had been thrown off at one point, and my bare feet were now black from dancing all night. Several times I had tried to pull Wyatt out on the dance floor, but something in him had changed after he talked to Lacey, and I couldn't figure out what. The playful, flirty Wyatt that I had loved being around the past few days was gone. In his place was grumpy, depressed Wyatt that wanted to sit in the corner and drink beer with a frown on his face.

The night wrapped up relatively early, per Lacey's request. They had rented a hotel room for the night, and the kids were staying the night at his mom's house, which left me by myself at their house. I wanted to ask Wyatt if he wanted to stay with me, but every time I worked up the courage, something would happen to stop me.

By the time I finished helping clean up, almost everyone had left, including Wyatt. I made my way back to their house and took a quick shower before turning in for the night. The next morning, I got my stuff together and left Lacey a quick note to let her know that I had gone back to Easterville. I wanted them to have time to themselves, and I had things that I needed to handle.

The drive back would have been quick, however, I decided to take the long way and stopped by the shed. I looked around to make sure no one was nearby before I parked my truck behind the shed and got out. The snow had melted quite a bit over the last few weeks, and I knew that if I had any chance of finding my gun before someone else did, I had to do it now. I tried to remember the area that I had been walking when Mike had found me, hoping that I was close.

I kicked the snow around in the spots where it hadn't yet melted, hoping to find it. After twenty minutes, I was just about to give up hope when I rubbed my foot over something hard. I bent down and pushed the snow out of the way, feeling relief as I found my gun. I picked it up and brushed the snow off of it before tucking it in the back of my jeans.

I should have gotten back in my truck and got the hell out of there, but the curiosity in me was too strong to walk away. Checking again to make sure no one was coming, I walked along the side of the shed and stopped at the window. There were black marks on the wood from where the fire had spread, however, the majority of it was still standing. Likely because the weather was so shitty, and there was so much moisture from the snow.

I sucked in a breath and held it as I turned and looked in the window. The blood was rushing in my ears, making it hard to hear if any cars were coming. I blinked my eyes and tried to focus, unable to believe that the horror scene that I had remembered so vividly before was now gone. Obviously, the police had already been here and collected the bodies, given that it was on the news. I guess I just didn't expect the blood and everything else to be gone as well.

Feeling somewhat relieved, I turned and walked back to my truck, satisfied that I had dealt with at least one of my demons.

When I got back into town, it was already one o'clock. There was plenty to do at home with getting my stuff packed up and moved to my parent's house, but I felt the need to go back to my shop before I did anything else. This weekend had been a nice escape from reality, but it was only temporary. I still had things that I had to take care of if I wanted to move forward with my life.

I pulled into the parking lot and felt the anxiety prickle at the back of my neck. No matter how much I had tried to convince myself that I wanted to keep this shop open and try to make it as the only mechanic in town, part of me desperately wanted to walk away from this chapter in my life. Maybe it was because it was now tainted with images of Mateo's dead body, but either way, I couldn't find my peace there anymore.

The window was still boarded up, but this time with a bigger piece of wood that covered the entire area. I hadn't bothered buying a new window because I couldn't afford it. I also found that I just didn't care. The drive and determination that I used to have died the day that I murdered Mateo.

I had to constantly remind myself of that gruesome fact. *I MURDERED someone.* It wasn't an accident—I couldn't play that card if I wanted to. It was very deliberate and on purpose. I guess you could say that it was self-defense, given that he had just tried to strangle me a few minutes before. I liked to think that anyone who had been in my situation would have done the same, but I wasn't so sure. Maybe other people would have called the cops and been lucky that they showed up on time. I wasn't one of those people.

I knew what it was like to call them and not have them come on time. To have to think on your toes because some asshole thinks that he can force himself on you and assumes that you're too weak to do anything about it.

The tears stung my cheeks as they spilled over and down my face as that night replayed in my head. While I had been drunk enough to block most of the details of that night out, I vividly remembered Mateo following me to the bathroom at the bar and pinning me against the sink as he tried to rape me. I screamed as loud as I could as I fought him off, but he was stronger than I was and covered my mouth with one hand while undoing his pants with the other. I sobered up immediately as the fear pulsed through me. There was an empty beer bottle next to the sink beside me that ended up being my saving grace. I couldn't remember a more satisfying feeling than the sound of the glass breaking before I took the broken bottle and sliced it down his face.

I shook my head and tried to clear away the thoughts, feeling more at peace for what I had done as I went to my office to finish the paperwork to sell my shop. I spent the afternoon packing up the items in my office and loading them into my truck. On my way home, I stopped by my parent's house and loaded them into the garage.

There was a lot of change surrounding me, but I kept trying to remind myself that it was good change and that I needed to embrace it instead of fight it. I grabbed a quick bite to eat as I headed back to my apartment to pack some more.

The days seemed to blur together when all I was doing was packing. Between my shop and my apartment, there was no normal for me anymore. My parents would be coming back from their trip to the Grand Canyon this weekend but were planning to leave again the following weekend. I couldn't keep up with their new travel schedule, so I stopped trying.

I sat at my desk and stared at the calendar that had the days crossed through that had already passed. Both my shop and my apartment's lease were up on February 1st, which was coming up on Monday. I had three days left in both and no motivation to do anything before I was officially kicked out.

My phone rang, vibrating across my empty desk.

"Hey," I said, answering Lacey's call. "What's up, *Mrs. Walker*?"

"Hi! It still sounds so strange to hear people call me that."

"Why? Did you keep your name instead of taking his?" I asked, wondering if I had just assumed that she would take his.

"No," she laughed. "I took his name, I just haven't gotten used to people calling me by it yet."

"Oh," I giggled, feeling silly.

"So, I was calling to see if Grant and I can come down this weekend to pick up Wyatt's truck?"

Her question was completely innocent, however, I felt it pierce straight through to my heart. I hadn't talked to Wyatt since the wedding last weekend and had contemplated asking him to come to get his truck because I was closing the shop. I had held off for as long as possible because I didn't want to admit my failure to him. It also stung that he wasn't bothering to come back for it himself, and I wondered if it was because he was avoiding seeing me before he moved to Arizona on Monday.

"Sure," I said, swallowing hard to get past the lump in my throat.

"Thanks. We're heading out tomorrow and leaving on Sunday."

"You're staying the night in Easterville?" I asked, surprised.

"Yeah, we're treating it like a mini honeymoon since we didn't take a real one. Grant is going to take me shopping in Glenview, so we're staying in Easterville. We'll grab the truck on Sunday when we head back if that's okay?"

"Yeah, that's fine." I let out the breath that I had been holding and wrapped up the call with Lacey. It wasn't that I didn't want to talk to her; I just couldn't do it with Wyatt stuck in my head.

Forty Six
Wyatt

"This feels like a terrible idea," I muttered from the back seat as I saw the sign for Easterville.

"It's not a terrible idea," Lacey countered. "It's a wonderful idea!"

"You're only saying that because it was YOUR idea," Grant laughed as he reached across the console to hold her hand.

"So are you saying that it's a terrible idea?" she scoffed, squeezing his hand.

"I wouldn't say terrible... but..."

"You're such a grumpus! You just can't stand the thought that your baby brother is finally in love and ready to settle down."

"I never said anything about love or settling down," I said with an edge to my tone. But just because I hadn't said it out loud didn't mean that it wasn't true. I was just scared shitless and refused to admit it as we pulled off the highway and headed to Kayce's shop.

"You Walker boys are so stubborn," she sighed. "But it's okay. That's what I'm here for."

"And what's that?" Grant asked with a smile.

Lacey looked out the passenger window for a moment as she thought about it.

"I'm here to make them realize how much they love each other and to make sure they don't make the same mistake I almost made when I thought about running from you."

"You definitely were a runner," he laughed, turning onto the street where Kayce's shop was. "I still check our credit cards every now and then, just to make sure you haven't booked a room somewhere."

"I did," she said as he put the truck in park. "I have a room to myself this weekend, so I can rest and relax and get all of the room service I want."

She winked before she got out of the truck and closed the door before he could say anything.

"Women," he muttered to me before we got out.

I stood next to his truck, looking at the shop and the boarded-up window that still hadn't been fixed, almost a month later.

"You ready?" Lacey asked cheerfully.

Just as I was about to say something stupid, my phone rang. I pulled it out of my pocket and looked at the caller ID.

"Go ahead without me. I've gotta take this call."

She folded her arms over her chest and cocked a brow at me.

"I'll be in as soon as I'm done, but I've gotta take this." I gave her my best *I'm not lying* smile and turned away to answer the call.

I glanced over my shoulder and saw them walking inside as I slid my finger across the screen to answer it.

"Hey, Julian," I said as calmly as I could. "How are things in Phoenix?"

"Warming up, which is a nice change from the cooler temps we've had lately. Though I'm sure it's nothing compared to the storms you guys have had recently," he laughed.

I felt a knot in the pit of my stomach as I talked to him. I was standing in the parking lot of Kayce's shop, talking to the man who held my career in his hands, and all that I could think about was the feisty girl inside who I couldn't get off my mind.

"The reason for my call," he said to clear the silence between us. "Is to confirm what time your flight comes in on Monday."

He continued talking about the rest of the details, but I couldn't focus on what he was saying. I didn't care about my apartment or when the moving vans got there. All I cared about was Kayce, and I realized that I didn't want to do any of this without her.

"I can't do this," I blurted out, scrubbing a hand down my face in frustration. The panic bells were ringing in my head, telling me to shut the fuck up before I ruined everything.

"I'm sorry, I don't understand. Do what?"

"I can't take the job. I'm sorry. I just can't move to Phoenix right now."

The silence on the other end felt thick around me. It was too late to take it back and tell him that I didn't mean it. In one moment of fear, I singlehandedly crushed my dream and everything I had worked so hard for.

"Okay," he said with a heavy sigh. "I'm sorry to hear that you've changed your mind."

"I—" The words caught in my throat.

"I wish you the best in your future endeavors."

That was it. It was over. He wasn't going to beg me to change my mind or ask me what happened. I was easily replaceable, and they would likely have someone by the end of the week who wanted the job and would drop everything to take it.

"Thanks," I mumbled before hanging up.

I chewed the inside of my cheek, frustrated by what I had just done. While I had given up on one dream, maybe it was because I was ready to go after another. Lacey was right; I had to stop running from what I wanted, which meant that I needed to talk to Kayce and tell her how I felt.

I went inside, stopping when I heard voices down the hallway in her office. I headed that way, unsure of whether she knew that I was here or not. Knowing Lacey, she would want it to be a surprise, though I wasn't sure that Kayce would think it was a good one.

"So, is he already gone?" Kayce asked. I could hear the vulnerability in her voice. She didn't want to ask, but she needed to know. "Is that why he didn't come back for his truck himself?"

"We were planning to come through here anyway, so we offered to help out," Lacey said softly.

"Well, it's perfect timing since I'm outta here on Sunday night."

"I'm sorry, Kayce. I know how hard this is for you." Lacey sounded sad, and I wondered what was going on. Where was Kayce going? Why hadn't I heard about her plans to leave?

"It's okay," she sighed heavily. "It's time to say goodbye to the old and make some big changes in my life. I guess I just wish that I would've gotten to say goodbye to him one last time."

I shook my hands a few times, trying to force away the nervousness that was washing over me. I couldn't just lurk in the hallway and eavesdrop all day. I needed to man up and go in there.

"I know, honey," Lacey started to say as I rounded the corner and stood in the doorway.

Kayce's eyes went wide when she saw me. She was sitting at her desk with her hair pulled into the messy bun that I loved when I first met her. Her hair was still the beautiful brown color from the wedding. The memories of that weekend had been tormenting me this week as I yearned for more.

"Hey," I said quietly, leaning against the door frame.

"Hey."

The world felt like it stopped moving as we stayed staring at each other. Grant and Lacey were sitting across from her, looking back and forth between us as they waited for one of us to say something.

"Well, now that you're here, I'll get the keys for you. I can pull the truck up front, then you should be ready to go."

She opened the desk drawer beside her and pulled out the keys. I could tell that she was feeling as uncertain about me being here as I was. The thing that I hated was that she didn't look happy to see me. She almost seemed pissed off.

"I'm not ready to go," I said dumbly, desperate to stop her from moving the truck. It felt like once she did, everything between us would be over. I would have my truck, and everything between us would be done.

"Well, I'm sure you remember the way to the gas station. Mrs. Ashby should be working today, so you can probably grab a room if you take enough candy."

"You know damn well that I'm not here to rent a room." My tone changed as my frustration seeped out.

"Then what are you here for?" she demanded with her hand on her hip.

I looked at Grant and Lacey, suddenly wishing that they weren't sitting there, watching this.

"We should give them some privacy," Grant said quietly to Lacey, bending to stand up before she reached over and swatted his hand.

"No, I'm staying until the end, and so are you," she hissed. "I didn't come all this way to miss the big moment." She was grinning so hard that I worried her cheeks were going to hurt.

"I'm waiting," Kayce said, pulling my attention back to her.

"I'm here for you." I shrugged as if that simple sentence should tell her the words that were wrapped so tightly around my heart that I couldn't say them.

She didn't speak, just stood there staring at me with her hand still planted firmly in her hip. It was apparent that she was going to make me work hard for this.

"I can't eat. I can't sleep. I lay down at night, and I smell the vanilla from your conditioner on my pillow. That's the only thing that calms me. But then I remember that you're not there with me, and I feel this sense of panic that I can't get rid of."

I pushed out a shaky breath, hating that I was having to bare my soul in front of everyone. But if it meant that she gave me another chance, I would strip down naked and bare it all.

"Kayce, we've been through some crazy shit in the little time that we've known each other. I know that you were worried that what you were feeling then was just a coping response to what had happened, but it's not that for me. I've been head over fucking heels in love with you from the very first night when you let me eat your cobbler."

I watched as her cheeks turned scarlet, and Lacey's jaw dropped. I couldn't help the cheeky grin that was spreading across my face as I raised a brow and challenged her to say something about it without further embarrassing herself.

She pressed her lips together and shook her head. Deep down, I could see that I was getting through to her by the way her lips twitched as she tried to hide her smile.

"By the way," I said, turning to Grant. "You guys need to get some barbecue from The Tasty Pig before you head back. And be sure to get the peach cobbler— it's to die for."

"Are you in love with me, or the cobbler?" Kayce asked, folding her arms over her chest.

"Both." I pushed off from the doorway and took a few steps closer to where she was standing. "And if you give me a chance, I'll prove it to you every day. Even if that means that we eat cobbler every night."

"That sounds like a promise you can't keep," she said warily. "It'll be a little hard to share cobbler when you're in Phoenix, and I'm here."

Her face fell as she said it, and I could see the sadness clouding her eyes.

"I'm not going to Phoenix."

I heard the gasp from Lacey and the curse word that flew out of Grant's mouth, but I kept my attention on Kayce as I took a few more steps toward her.

"What do you mean you're not going?" She took a step back as I came behind the desk and stood next to her. She pulled her shoulders back and refused to let her guard down just yet.

"I got a call from the team's manager, confirming what time my flight on Monday. I told him that I couldn't take the job."

"Why on earth would you do that?" Kayce asked, her eyes as big as saucers.

"Because baseball has always been my one true love, and until recently, I thought that was what my life was about. And then I met this beautiful, incredible woman, who I found I couldn't live without. It turns out that *you're* my one true love. Without you, nothing else matters."

She closed her eyes, and the room went silent. A few moments later, she opened her eyes and shook her head.

"Boys are so stupid," she sighed.

"Umm, thanks?" I furrowed my brow.

"You need to call them back and tell them that you made a mistake. A HUGE mistake. Then beg for your job back and let them know that you'll be there Monday morning."

"It's not that easy," I argued, feeling frustrated that this wasn't going the way that I wanted.

"Kayce, I love you, and I can't live without you. So that means that I'm giving up the job so I can stay here to be with you. Unless you don't want me to?"

I felt the panic start to rise inside as I took a step back. Was that what this was all about? Did she want me to go because she didn't feel the same way? Was I head over heels in love with someone who didn't love me back?

"No, I don't want you to do that," she said softly, lowering her voice.

"Got it," I snapped, running my hand through my hair as I looked over at Lacey and Grant. They were looking away from us, trying to give us privacy now that they saw the direction this was going.

Grant looked up and saw the look on my face. He gave me a subtle nod and leaned in to whisper something to Lacey before they stood up and walked out, closing the door behind them.

"I'm sorry, I shouldn't have come here and done this—" I apologized.

"Stop," she interrupted, reaching over to grab my arm as she pulled it away from my hair.

"I'm saying that you shouldn't have given up your dream job to stay here for me. Now that my shop is closing, I don't have anything holding me here. And not that you asked me to, but I would be willing to go with you to Phoenix... if you wanted me to."

I pulled back and studied her, waiting for her to tell me it was a mean joke. Instead, the grin on her face spread quickly as she waited for me to realize that she was being honest. She was willing to pack up her life and go with me.

"You know that I will have to travel—a lot, and that I'll probably be working a lot of weekends?"

She nodded her head yes.

"And it gets hot in Arizona. Like really, really hot."

"I get tired of the cold anyway," she laughed.

"Maybe you could travel with me when I go? And then we can explore whatever city I'm in when I'm done?"

"I would love to travel and explore with you, Wyatt."

I felt the calmness that I had been missing without her and knew that this was where I was meant to be.

"Now get on the phone and tell them that you want your job back," she said as she poked me in the chest with her finger. "I want to be nice and tanned this summer, so maybe we can find a place with a pool?"

I laughed and realized that I hadn't even told her that everything was already set up and ready to go for me.

"I think we can arrange that," I chuckled with a wink.

"Well, I guess I should get started on looking for jobs there right away. I'll have a little bit of money to help with rent for a few months from selling Wrenched, but I don't want you to worry about me not carrying my weight."

"Kayce, I'll take care of you. You don't have to worry about that." My heart swelled as I said it, knowing that I had never spoken truer words in my life.

"I would never ask that of you, and I really do like being able to take care of myself."

"I know you do. But from here on out, we're a team. We're going to tackle things together and celebrate all of the wins as they come."

"Starting with this one," she squealed as she reached up and kissed me.

Epilogue- Nine Months Later
Wyatt

"Hurry up! They're going to be here soon," Kayce squealed as she walked by and pounded on the bathroom door as I finished brushing my teeth.

I put my toothbrush away and rinsed my mouth. It was a huge day for us, and I loved the excitement that Kayce was feeling about it. I opened the door and caught her fluffing the pillows on the couch for the fifteenth time that morning.

"I think they're fluffy," I laughed, walking over and wrapping my arms around her waist. Her hair was shorter than before and colored dark red, matching the Arizona Rattlers jersey that she was wearing.

"I just want everything to be perfect," she said as she laid her head against my chest. Nine months of living together, and I still hadn't had my fill of her yet. I could feel my dick hardening against her ass, wondering if we had time for a quickie before everyone got there.

"Everything is perfect," I murmured against her ear as I ran my tongue up her neck.

"Your mom is going to be here in any minute now, so you better put that thing away," she teased as she bumped me with her butt, not helping my erection go down.

Just then, the doorbell rang, and Kayce took off running to answer it.

After I got up the nerve to call Julian back and beg for my job, he threw another curveball at me and offered me the head coach position instead of the recruiting one I had been initially offered. It turned out that the owner had heard about me from the Colorado Cougars and was impressed with my skills as a player. Given how long I had been playing and my love for the sport, he decided he wanted me to take over when the head coach decided to move to another team in March.

With the higher salary and Kayce's new job as a mechanic at the best automotive shop in Phoenix, we decided to forgo the apartment and bought a house with a massive pool in the back. That was probably the single best investment I had made in my life when I found out how much she enjoyed skinny dipping.

"I can't believe you're here!" Kayce beamed as she wrapped Lacey in a hug as they came inside. Grant held two car seats on each arm as Annie and Liam waited their turn to hug Kayce.

"Here, let me help you," I offered, reaching over to take one of the car seats from him.

"Thanks, they get heavy quickly," he laughed, following me inside and leaving the girls to linger in the doorway.

"Hello, princess," I cooed as I set the car seat down on the floor and pulled the blanket back to look at my niece. "Daisy Mae, you just get more beautiful every time I see you."

She smiled up at me and giggled as I tickled her foot. It was hard to believe that the twins were already going on four months old and getting bigger by the minute.

I turned to the other car seat that Grant set down beside her. I felt my grin pull across my face as I looked down at the matching outfits they were wearing. Daisy was wearing an Arizona Rattlers onesie with a fluffy red skirt, and Jackson had the same onesie with red sweat pants. It made me beam with pride when I felt how supportive my family was.

"Future MVP right here," I said as I leaned over and tickled Jackson's toes.

"How was the drive out here?" I asked, looking up at Grant as I sat on the floor with the babies.

"It was good. The new Excursion made it easier," he laughed.

"I can imagine, that's a beast of a vehicle." They definitely needed the room with six of them, including the two car seats, double stroller, and all of their luggage. It was probably the best investment that he had made in his life.

A few minutes later, the girls came over to join us. Kayce stood over my shoulder, looking at the babies as she squealed over how cute they were. I got up and moved out of the way so Lacey could get them out of their car seats as Kayce waited impatiently to hold them.

The doorbell rang again, so I rushed over to answer it.

"Hey!" I stepped back and held the door open for my mom and Buck to come in. Right behind them was Chase, Mia, and the girls. I knew that Noah and Jade wouldn't be too far behind them.

The house was quickly filling with noise as everyone moved about, hugging each other and saying hi. Finally, the entire family was back together, and it felt like home again. Only it was pushing ninety degrees here, and Haven Brook had a severe snowstorm warning back home. There were some things that I didn't miss.

I helped Grant and Lacey get set up in two of the guest rooms while Kayce showed my mom and Buck to the other one. Chase and Noah had rented a house close by for their families, knowing that we all wouldn't fit under one roof for the week. It was hard to believe that they were here for a whole week! I wished that I was on vacation with them, but if anything, I was going to be working overtime since it was the World Series and the Rattlers were in it.

Everyone came out to watch a few games and to have a much-needed vacation. Kayce had taken the week off to entertain everyone and had already planned out the things that she wanted to do, including an all-day trip to the zoo and a girl's day shopping at Scottsdale Fashion Square.

But today, today was a day for all of us to spend together. I didn't have to go in to work, and no one had anything pressing to do. The pool was ready and filled with plenty of giant rafts that Kayce insisted that we needed. We had plenty of food to barbecue and snacks to munch on throughout the day. One thing that I had learned about Kayce was that when she did something- she put everything she had into it. So we weren't just having a pool party and a barbecue. We were having the ULTIMATE pool party and an epic barbecue that would put The Tasty Pig to shame.

I thought that my life would always be plagued by the nightmares that haunted me for so long after my dad died. It turned out that I just needed a little bit of light in my life to lift some of the darkness. And that light was about to get a whole lot brighter when I asked Kayce to marry me.

****

Thank you so much for reading Three Strikes, You're Gone! I hope you loved the Haven Brook series as much as I enjoyed writing it! If you're looking for something new to read, I have a couple of picks for you:

If you want something action-packed, try my other
romantic suspense series, Dark Shadows

Five Steps Ahead (Dark Shadows Book 1)

https://books2read.com/u/38Q0gO

If you want small-town packed with plenty of feels, try the Stone
Creek Series

Chocolate Covered Mistletoe (Stone Creek Book 1)

https://books2read.com/u/3LRk9N

<u>Other Books By Samantha Baca</u>

<u>The Haven Brook Series:</u>
'Til Death Do Us Part (Haven Brook Book 1)
https://books2read.com/u/m2RJNR

The Cradle Will Fall (Haven Brook Book 2)
https://books2read.com/u/b6O0QE

The Ties That Bind (Haven Brook Book 3)
https://books2read.com/u/mqgoz8

A Very Haven Christmas (Haven Brook Book 4- Novella)
https://books2read.com/u/mvqGjj

Three Strikes, You're Gone (Haven Brook Book 5)
https://books2read.com/u/mvqL2z

<u>The Dark Shadows Series</u>
Five Steps Ahead (Dark Shadows Book 1)
https://books2read.com/u/38Q0gO

Ten Seconds Too Late (Dark Shadows Book 2)
Coming 2022

Against The Clock (Dark Shadows Book 3)
Coming 2022

Out Of Time (Dark Shadows Book 4)
Coming 2023

The Stone Creek Series (Novellas)
Chocolate Covered Mistletoe (Stone Creek Book 1)
https://books2read.com/u/3LRk9N

Candy Coated Promises (Stone Creek Book 2)
https://books2read.com/u/mldP5Y

Pumpkin Spiced Possibilities (Stone Creek Book 3)
https://books2read.com/u/bojdwV

Stand-Alone Books
One Last Wish
https://books2read.com/u/mqg7D9

Finding Love In Apartment 2C (Novella)
https://books2read.com/u/bze9aZ

Acknowledgments

Like all good things, this series must also come to an end. I cannot begin to express my gratitude to the readers who have followed along with me in the Haven Brook world and have fallen in love with these characters as much as I have. When I wrote 'Til Death Do Us Part, I thought that it was just something to make off of my bucket list and that I would move on. I never expected it to be the book that started my writing career or the first series that I would write.

I'm so honored to have met so many wonderful people along the way in this journey, and I can't believe how far I've come. This series is so dear to my heart because it was another dream come true to say that I wrote an entire series in a year and a half!

To my alpha readers—you ladies are amazing. I cannot imagine a world without you two beautiful souls to help guide me and push me through when I'm ready to give up. Azucena, I'm sorry that I've created a new addiction for you, and I promise to write every day—when I can, to make sure you have your fix when you need it! Chelsea, I'm forever grateful for the wisdom that you share with me when I send you random messages asking about sports-related stuff that I have NO CLUE ABOUT! You both help me in more ways than I would ever be able to tell you.

Tillie, I've never had someone bend over backward so selflessly, the way you do when you're busting your butt to make time for me when you have your plate overflowing with a million things at one time. I appreciate your brilliant mind and love for reading, as much as I love the friendship that's blossomed between us! I will NEVER get tired of reading your honest reactions as you read my books.

Katy, you have been so much fun to work with, and I LOVE having you as a beta reader! I'm excited to continue working together on more books and truly appreciate your help and feedback. Thank you so much for everything that you do for me, you're the best!

Richard—we are officially TEN books in, and I will never grow tired of expressing my gratitude to you. From listening to me talk about books for hours on end to helping me with all of the formatting and technical stuff, I appreciate all that you do for me. Someday, I'll make it big with my books, and we'll travel the world with our girls and find the inspiration for my next bestseller!

To the readers, bloggers, and everyone else who has supported me along the way—thank you so much! I couldn't do this without you, and I am so honored that you've chosen my books to read. I hope that I've created a world that you love and characters that will stay with you for a long time. If you've enjoyed this series, be sure to check out my other books. There might be a new book boyfriend or two waiting for you in another series.

As always, you can find me on social media or sign up for my newsletter to stay up to date with what I'm working on. I love connecting with readers and look forward to seeing you around! If you have a few minutes and wouldn't mind, please consider leaving a quick review for me on whichever platform you choose. They mean the world to me!

About the Author

Samantha lives in the southwest with her husband and two small children after abandoning her childhood dream of living in a cabin in Colorado when she found that she couldn't afford to live there and was deathly allergic to the woods. When she's not writing she's usually spouting off sarcastic remarks while drinking wine out of a coffee mug to look like a functional adult while chasing down her toddlers. She enjoys spending time with her family, watching reruns of Friends, and the 24/7 flow of coffee that can be found in her veins. Be sure to follow her on social media for updates on what she's working on.

You can find her here:

Facebook: https://www.facebook.com/AuthorSamanthaBaca

Instagram: https://instagram.com/author_samantha_baca

Goodreads: http://www.goodreads.com/authorsamanthabaca

Facebook Reader Group:
https://www.facebook.com/groups/2945710968775398/

Webpage: https://authorsamanthabaca.wordpress.com

Newsletter: http://eepurl.com/g0NcSj